DEATH
AND OTHER
OBSESSIONS

Robert Mills

Matador
9 Priory Business Park,
Wistow Road, Kibworth Beauchamp,
Leicestershire. LE8 0RX
Tel: 0116 279 2299
Email: books@troubador.co.uk
Web: www.troubador.co.uk/matador
Twitter: @matadorbooks

ISBN 978 1838592 769

British Library Cataloguing in Publication Data.
A catalogue record for this book is available from the British Library.

Printed and bound in the UK by TJ International, Padstow, Cornwall
Typeset in 11pt Minion Pro by Troubador Publishing Ltd, Leicester, UK

Matador is an imprint of Troubador Publishing Ltd

To Robin

With best wishes

"I know it looks like suicide," said Inspector Tewksbury, "but I am absolutely convinced that Colonel Bradshaw was murdered."

Joan Templeton: *The Riddle of the Silent Soldier.*

Prologue

She drained the glass and placed it carefully in the sink.

"That's better," she said out loud to the empty kitchen.

Going through to the sitting room, she rummaged in a handbag that was on the coffee table.

"Damned keys," she muttered.

She retraced her steps and almost immediately spotted her car keys on the kitchen table next to a large bunch of flowers. *Dear Martin*, she thought and brushed away a tear. Then she put on her coat, picked up the keys and flowers and went out through the back door.

Slipping into the car, she started the engine and backed out of the garage. As she approached the junction with Copse Hill the car seemed slow to stop. *I must get Alan to check the brakes,* she thought, *I knew I couldn't trust that garage.*

As she drove along the Ridgway all seemed well. She relaxed. Then she remembered that Alan and Sarah were coming for lunch the following Sunday and began to panic. She told herself to calm down. She would cook them roast lamb. Then she would have cold meat to last her the rest of the week. She'd go shopping on Friday, after meeting Anne.

As she approached the mini-roundabout at the top of Wimbledon Hill her foot automatically went to the brake pedal. It depressed easily, too easily, but the car didn't slow down. Fighting with the wheel, she somehow managed to make the right turn. Then she was on the hill descending towards the town centre. The car was gathering speed. She braked again.

Nothing happened. She stabbed at the pedal. Nothing. Her heart was racing. Her turning was up ahead now. She was going too fast. She swung the wheel. She hit the pedal again. Still nothing. *Wrong pedal*, she thought. The car accelerated. She pushed down harder. *What's wrong?* She made the turn much too fast. Out of control. A rear wheel hit the kerb. The car slewed across the road. A building approached at speed. Buckling metal screeched in agony. She was thrown forwards.

Chapter One

Detective Superintendent Barry Cheeseman sat at his desk reading the latest directive from Scotland Yard. He was struggling to concentrate on the document and had read the same section two or three times without taking it in. Thinking back, he realised that the happiest time in his career had been the period when he was a chief inspector leading a team of investigators on a day-to-day basis. Promotion had brought advantages, but he found the administrative burden that went with the job a pain in the arse at times.

He put down the document, which he was only halfway through, and called his secretary.

"Can you ask Chief Inspector Taylor to come and see me?" he said brusquely, when she answered.

"OK, Superintendent," she said and he heard the line go dead.

He went back to his reading.

Shortly afterwards there was a knock at the door and Tracy Taylor came in.

"You wanted a word?" she said.

"Grab a seat," said Cheeseman, gesturing vaguely at the chairs in front of his desk.

Taylor removed a pile of papers from one of them, sat down and ran her fingers through her hair. Cheeseman was aware of the large blue eyes that fixed him with a steady gaze and aura of French perfume that had followed her into the room. Chief inspectors hadn't worn perfume in his day and he wasn't at all sure it was a good thing.

"I wanted to remind you we've got a new DS starting with us today; his name's Patel," he continued. "He's one of these university graduates they've fast-tracked into CID. You and I came up through the ranks so we knew the ropes when we became sergeants. As for this new breed, well, I'm sure you know what I mean."

The expression on Taylor's face suggested that she didn't know what he meant, or more likely that she took a different view. He decided to press on.

"Normally I wouldn't have assigned an officer like him to your team but someone at Homicide and Major Crime Command insisted. Seems they see him as a potential high-flyer. On top of all that he doesn't know the area, so I think he'll be a bit out of his depth. I'd like you to keep a close eye on him; is that all right?"

Taylor nodded.

"No problem," she said. "I'll pair him up with an experienced constable."

"Good idea," said Cheeseman. "Who did you have in mind?"

"Owen."

The Welshman, he thought. He didn't have anything against the Welsh in general but he did have some doubts about DC Paul Owen. Still he'd probably be good as a babysitter.

"Fine," he said. "Don't give Patel too much responsibility, until you see what he's capable of."

"OK."

Cheeseman detected a note of irritation in the chief inspector's voice. She was another example of the way in which appointments were made with minimal input from local senior officers. As in the case of Patel's promotion, there had been a more-than-adequate local candidate for the job but he had been passed over. In fairness though, she was good at her job and the men seemed to accept her leadership, well, most of them anyway. And he had to be careful. The Borough Commander thought she was the best thing since sliced bread. He leaned forwards in his chair and dropped his voice. "It's not because he's Indian I'm saying all this, you understand."

"No of course not, Barry," said Taylor with a half smile. "Didn't think that for a moment."

Which wasn't exactly the response he'd been hoping for.

*

It was the middle of March and the grey sky and bitter wind made it hard to believe that spring was only a few weeks way. Sanjay Patel sighed as he emerged from Wimbledon Station, turned up the collar on his coat and set off in the direction of the police station. He could feel a tight knot in the pit of his stomach. As he approached the entrance to the station he hesitated for a moment before climbing the steps and opening one of the glazed doors. Once inside he approached the desk where a uniformed sergeant was peering intently at the screen of his mobile phone.

"I'm Detective Sergeant Patel," he said. "I'm supposed to report to Superintendent Cheeseman."

"Good morning, sir," said the sergeant. "It's down that corridor, third door on the left."

Patel didn't move.

"Anything else, sir?" said the sergeant.

"Is there a toilet I could use?"

"End of the corridor on the right."

"Thanks," said Patel and headed in the direction indicated.

When he came to wash his hands the water came out of the tap in a rush, soaking the front of his trousers. He dried himself off with paper towels but an obvious wet patch remained. *It looks like I've wet myself*, he thought; *just what I needed this morning, not.*

He emerged from the toilet and approached the door marked 'Superintendent B. J. Cheeseman, Head of CID'. He knocked. He heard a muffled "Come in," and opened the door. He found himself in a small office in which a secretary sat behind a desk typing on a computer keyboard.

"Can I help you?" she said, looking up from her work.

"I'm Sergeant Patel," he said.

"Oh yes, he's expecting you." She picked up the phone and spoke into the receiver. "The new sergeant's here. OK." She turned to Patel. "Go right in," she said.

Cheeseman's office was quite a large room and a window behind his desk looked out onto Queens Road. On one of the walls were a number of grim-faced portraits of senior officers. Patel wondered if his picture would ever join them. If he were photographed for this purpose, he decided he would smile while the picture was being taken. Opposite was a bookcase with a cupboard below the shelves. On the lowest of these, several weighty tomes were arranged in a haphazard manner. The scratched upper surfaces of the remainder were empty, yet somehow longing to be filled.

Cheeseman was partly bald and his remaining hair, sticking out at an angle, gave him a clown-like appearance. Indeed, it was said around the station that he had been given his nickname, 'the Cheeseburger', because of his resemblance to Ronald McDonald. He had a ginger and brown moustache which was in constant need of trimming. The shoulders of his dark suit jacket were, as usual, covered in a thin layer of dandruff and his tie was carelessly tied with a small knot. Patel noted his mildly plethoric complexion suggesting the possibility of high blood pressure and early coronary artery disease.

"So, you're the new DS," said Cheeseman. "Welcome to Merton CID. Come in and sit down."

Patel smiled and took a seat. He crossed his legs, hoping that this would make the wet patch on the front of his trousers less obvious.

"Thank you, sir," he said.

"I've got your CV here somewhere," said the superintendent. He rummaged in a disorderly pile of papers on his desk. "Ah yes, here it is. Let me see, you were a medical student. What made you join the police force?"

"I decided I didn't want to be a doctor," said Patel. "To be honest I'd always wanted to be a detective."

"I see," said Cheeseman, in a manner that suggested he wasn't entirely satisfied with this reply. "So, where are you from?"

"London; my parents were living in Mitcham when I was born actually."

Cheeseman smiled.

"Oh really," he said. "And your parents?"

"They're from Ludhiana. It's in India."

This answer seemed to satisfy Cheeseman and he sat back in his chair.

"OK," he said. "Have you managed to find somewhere to live?"

"We're renting a flat at the moment."

Cheeseman inspected Patel's CV again.

"Ah yes, you're married I see," he said. "How does your wife feel about living in South London?"

"She's fine with it. Her parents live in Beckenham."

"Good. You'll be working with my colleague Chief Inspector Taylor," said Cheeseman. "She'll show you the ropes, break you in gently. She's in a meeting at the moment so why don't you go through to the CID office and make yourself at home?"

"Right," said Patel, "thank you, sir."

*

The CID office was a large room in which there were a dozen or so desks, each with a computer on it. There were in trays piled with files, some neatly arranged and others in haphazard heaps.

Coffee mugs vied for position with pens, staplers and rolls of sticky tape.

Almost immediately Patel spotted a small man with a receding hairline sitting at one of the desks. He was wearing a beige sweater and an open-necked shirt and there was a leather jacket draped over the back of his chair.

"Can I help you?" he said in a lilting Welsh accent.

"I'm the new detective sergeant, my name's Sanjay Patel."

The man smiled, got up and came towards him, offering Patel his hand. The handshake was firm but a little tentative.

"Welcome aboard," he said. "My name's Paul Owen. I'm a detective constable."

"Pleased to meet you," said Patel. "Have you worked here long?"

"A couple of years," said Owen. "I was in Wandsworth before, in uniform. I came here when I joined the CID."

They stood facing each other and it seemed to Patel that his new colleague found the situation as uncomfortable as he did. He wondered whether Owen was in line for promotion and had been passed over for the post that he now filled. Perhaps, though, he was simply ill at ease meeting new people, especially those from a different background.

"I'm supposed to speak to DCI Taylor when she's free," he said. "What's she like?"

Owen gave a half smile.

"Tracy?" he said. "She's a great boss to work for, good detective as well."

"Great," said Patel.

He looked around the room.

"Does everyone have a desk?" he said.

"Yes," said Owen. "Yours is over there."

He pointed to a desk beside the large window that overlooked Queens Road.

The door of the CID office opened and a stocky man wearing jeans and a black down jacket walked in. His limp brown hair was cut short in a manner that added to the impression of someone who didn't care about his appearance.

"You got that report finished?" he said to Owen.

"Nearly," he replied.

"What's taking so long? I need it now, OK?"

"It'll only take a couple of minutes, guv," said Owen.

The newcomer stopped dead in his tracks.

"You interviewing suspects in here?" he asked, pointing at Patel.

"No, sir," said Owen. "This is DS Patel, he's joining the team."

Patel studied the newcomer's face to see if he was joking but he maintained his deadpan expression.

"Oh yeah," he said. "Tracy said something about it. I'll be in my office."

With that he went through a door with 'DI C. M. Brewer' on it and closed it behind him.

"That's Colin Brewer," said Owen when he was out of earshot. "Don't mind him, he can be a total arsehole at times but he's a good bloke underneath." He checked his watch. "I'd better get this report done, do you mind?"

"Of course not," said Patel.

Owen returned to his computer and Patel sat down at the desk Paul Owen had indicated and took out his mobile phone. There was a text message from Amber that said, *Hope it's going well, love A.* He dashed off a reply and then checked his emails and had a look at the Facebook page for Merton Police.

He was wondering what to do next when he heard the door open and looked up to see a slim woman of about forty-five wearing a tailored suit with a skirt and high-heeled shoes. Her thick dark hair was cut short and her fine-featured face was dominated by a pair of large blue eyes. Patel noted a slight enlargement of her thyroid gland when she swallowed but could detect no signs of thyroid over-activity.

"I'm Tracy Taylor," she said, smiling. "You must be DS Patel."

Sanjay jumped to his feet.

"Yes, I'm Patel," he said. "Pleased to meet you."

"Welcome to the Merton Major Investigation Team," said Taylor. "Bit of a mouthful, isn't it? We need to have a quick chat so grab a seat." Patel sat down and the chief inspector drew up a chair opposite him and crossed her legs. "Have you spoken to Superintendent Cheeseman yet?" she asked.

"Yes, when I first arrived," said Patel.

"Good," she said. "I'm going to ask Paul Owen here to show you the ropes. All right, Paul?"

"No problem, boss," said Owen.

"Where were you before?" asked Taylor.

"Hackney," said Patel.

Taylor smiled.

"Oh yeah? I used to work in Newham," she said. "I imagine you'll find we work in much the same way here. Anyway, to start you off I'm going to ask you two to liaise with our colleagues in traffic. There was an RTA yesterday morning at the junction between Wimbledon Hill and Alexandra Road. The driver was an older lady. Fortunately no one else was involved. There's a suggestion the car she was driving was tampered with in some way, so they want our input. I want you to take a look at the scene and report back to me, OK?"

"Yes, of course," said Patel.

She turned to Paul Owen.

"You free to go now?" she said.

"I've got this done, so I'll pop it through to Colin and then I'm all yours," said Owen, as he retrieved a sheaf of paper from a printer.

"Right then, I'll leave you to it."

Taylor got up and headed for the door of her office.

CHAPTER TWO

Patel and Owen walked over Wimbledon Bridge and turned into Alexandra Road. Not far along the street on the right-hand side the window of a funeral parlour was boarded up and the pavement adjacent to it, on which some fragments of glass could be seen, had been cordoned off. A heavily built uniformed police officer was standing nearby.

As they approached him Owen said, "Morning, Sergeant Cox, what's all this about then?"

"Hello, Taffy, so they've sent you, eh?" said Cox.

"Yeah, I'm the lucky sod," said Owen. He gestured towards Patel. "This is DS Patel. Joined us today. "

"Lucky you," said the big man, grinning. "Right well, around seven o'clock yesterday morning the driver of a silver-coloured Toyota Camry saloon lost control of her car as she turned into Alexandra Road from Wimbledon Hill. The car careered across the road and crashed into the front of this funeral parlour."

He gestured towards it with his hand.

"The driver, a Miss Joan Templeton, was killed outright. Quite frankly, it was lucky no one was coming the other way or we might have had more deaths. At first we thought it was an accident but because there'd been a fatality we shipped the vehicle down to HQ and got our vehicle examiner to take a look. He found the pipes from the master cylinder to the brakes themselves had been cut."

Patel frowned.

"It seems odd to me that she lost control of the car, even if the brakes had gone," he said.

"Maybe she panicked and hit the accelerator instead of the brake," suggested Owen.

"Seems unlikely," said Cox. "Still you never know. It was raining at the time, so the roads would have been more slippery than usual. Anyway, however it happened, she ended up over here."

Patel noticed that Owen was grinning.

"'Ere, what's so funny?" said Cox.

"Well," said Owen, "she was an old bird and it's almost as if she was ram-raiding the undertakers."

Patel didn't laugh but Cox let out a loud guffaw.

"Very amusing, Taffy," he said.

"Do we know exactly how old the deceased actually was?" asked Patel.

"I'll need to check," said Cox. He consulted his notebook. "Oh yes, she was sixty-eight."

"That's not very old by modern standards," said Patel. "Was she married?"

Cox consulted his notes again.

"Apparently not," he said.

"Any witnesses?" said Owen.

"There was a bloke getting money out of the cash dispenser down there," said Cox, pointing in the direction of Wimbledon Hill. "When he'd finished he turned round to see the car turn into Alexandra Road at speed, go diagonally across the opposite lane and crash into the funeral parlour. He phoned us on his mobile."

"Was she wearing a seat belt?" asked Patel.

"No, she wasn't," said Cox.

Patel surveyed the scene. The junction between Wimbledon Hill and Alexandra Road is wide and he still couldn't fathom how the driver had been unable to avoid the crash, even without the use of her brakes.

"Anything else?" he said.

"We've already spoken to the proprietor of the funeral parlour," said Cox. "He wasn't on the premises at the time of the crash. He said that the member of staff who opens up in the morning doesn't usually get there until eight o'clock."

Patel noted that there was a nail bar next door to the undertakers. A sign on the window indicated that it didn't open until nine o'clock.

"What's above these properties?" he asked.

"It's offices," said Owen. "The entrance is beyond that beauty salon place."

"We interviewed some of the staff," said Cox. "No one was there when the crash happened. No one lives on the other side of the road either."

Patel shrugged.

"I don't think there's anything else we can usefully do here," he said.

"Do you want to see the wreck?" said Cox.

Patel looked at Owen who nodded.

"Yes please," he said.

"Right then, my vehicle's over there."

Cox led the way to a police car that was parked a little further down the road. As they were pulling away from the kerb he said: "One of the lads says the deceased wrote detective stories."

"The name Templeton doesn't mean anything to me," said Patel.

Owen shook his head.

"Me neither," he said.

"My wife will probably be able to tell me all about her," said Patel. "She's a crime fiction fan."

"Not my cup of tea," said Cox.

"I presume the next of kin has been informed already," said Patel as they passed South Wimbledon Tube station.

"Yes," said Cox, "it's her niece, a Mrs Sarah Musgrove."

They turned off the main road into an industrial estate and were soon driving through the gateway that led into the car park of the South West Traffic Unit. Cox parked the car and led them towards a large hangar-like building. One of the doors had been raised and Cox led them inside. They were greeted by the smell of petrol and damp cardboard.

The wreck of the car was standing near the wall on the left and beside it was a small man wearing glasses who was holding a clipboard.

"This is Ken Bridges," said Cox. "What he doesn't know about car wrecks isn't worth knowing. I'll leave you to it. When you're done pop into the office and I'll give you a copy of the report."

"Thanks," said Patel.

"Come over here and I'll give you the guided tour," said Bridges. "You can see the front of the vehicle has sustained considerable damage." He scratched his head. "The sad thing is this lady would have been all right if she hadn't panicked when the brakes failed."

"How do you mean?" said Owen.

"Well the thing is, there are various ways to slow a car down in these circumstances," said Bridges. "On a manual car you shift into lower gears to do it, but this one's automatic. Like all cars with automatic transmission, it's got manual gears, but rather than being marked on the gate, as in a lot of other models, they're accessed by pushing the stick towards the plus or minus sign when you're in 'drive'. I imagine the lady always used automatic and didn't know how to switch to manual."

"Can you shift into 'park' while you're driving?" asked Patel. "That would stop the car, I imagine."

Bridges shook his head.

"No, you can't," he said. "There's a thing called a brake switch that makes that impossible."

"What about the handbrake?" said Owen. "Could she have used that to stop the car?"

"Yes," said Bridges, "the handbrake operates the brakes via a cable, so it's totally separate from the brake pedal system, which is hydraulic. Mind you, you have to apply it carefully or the wheels lock up and you lose control of the vehicle."

"Was there any evidence she tried to use the handbrake?" asked Patel.

"No, there wasn't."

"Which means either that she didn't know she could use it or that she wanted to crash the vehicle."

Bridges shrugged.

"That seems to be a reasonable conclusion," he said.

"When do you think the brakes were tampered with?" asked Owen.

Bridges scratched his head.

"It wouldn't have taken very long for the braking system to fail once the car was moving," he said. "My guess is it was done that morning or the night before."

Patel turned his attention to the car itself. The front of the Toyota had been compressed like a concertina, but the passenger compartment was more or less intact. It seemed to him that the driver might have survived the crash if she had been wearing a seat belt. As it was, the cracked, bloodstained windscreen was evidence that she had been thrown against it with considerable force when the car hit the front of the funeral parlour.

The crumpled bonnet had been opened, probably with some difficulty, to expose the engine.

"The vehicle hit the shop front at an angle," said Bridges. "That may be why the airbag didn't deploy, but I can't say for sure it wasn't faulty. If it had, she might have survived, though of course airbags aren't very effective when a seat belt isn't worn properly."

Patel nodded. Bridges pointed to the interior of the engine compartment.

"This is where the brake lines were cut," he said indicating two tubes that emerged from an irregularly shaped engine component. Both had obviously been severed. "Whoever it was must have used something pretty blunt to do it, the cut ends are all chewed up."

"What do you think would have been used to cut them?" asked Patel.

"Hard to say; a hacksaw maybe, or some kind of knife."

"How easy would it be to get inside the bonnet to do this?" asked Owen.

"The bonnet release is inside the car," said Bridges, "but it's not impossible to break it open without access to the passenger compartment. There would probably be some damage which the driver might or might not notice before she got in the car. In this case there's no clear evidence of forced entry to the engine bay, though it's hard to be absolutely sure about that with the car in this state. Alternatively, you could crawl under the car and get at them from below. That would be the easiest way to do it if you knew what you were doing and didn't have the keys."

"Thanks," said Patel. "That's been really helpful."

"One more thing," said Bridges, "there was a bunch of flowers on the passenger seat."

Patel frowned.

"I can't see the relevance of that," he said. He turned to Owen. "I think it's time for us to report back to DCI Taylor."

*

They headed back to Wimbledon Police Station and went straight to the chief inspector's office. She wasn't there and they were told she wouldn't be back until mid afternoon, so they decided to go for lunch. Afterwards, they studied the report from Traffic and put together their initial thoughts on the case.

When they returned to DCI Taylor's office, they found her sitting at her desk, apparently working on her computer.

"Ah there you are lads," she said. "So, what have you found?"

"It's a bit of an odd one," said Patel. "At first it seemed like an accident, as you know. There was nothing at the scene of the crash to suggest otherwise, so we went and had a look at the wreck and there doesn't seem to be any doubt that the pipes leading from the brake master cylinder were deliberately cut. Most probably it was done the night before the accident, but it could have been early that morning. If the deceased didn't use her car the day before the accident it's even possible that it could have been done even earlier, I suppose."

"What about forensics?" said Tracy Taylor, removing her reading glasses and brushing her hair off her forehead with her hand.

Patel consulted the report that Sergeant Cox had given them.

"Unfortunately the car had been moved to Traffic HQ before the fingerprint boys got to it, which isn't ideal," he said.

The chief inspector nodded.

"They managed to get one clear print off the driver's door and one off the filler cap of the brake fluid reservoir. The chances are they belonged to Miss Templeton, but if they don't, the odds in favour of murder would increase. If she was murdered and the fingerprints don't belong to someone else, we'd have to assume that the killer wore gloves. Oh yes, and they didn't find any fibres or anything that might give us DNA."

"You might get some joy with the one on the brake fluid reservoir," said Taylor. "Mind you, you may well find it belongs to the mechanic who last serviced her car."

"Right," said Patel. "Death was probably due to a blow to the head when she hit the windscreen. I imagine she had injuries to her chest from the impact of the steering wheel as well. The post-mortem will confirm the details."

"I don't suppose there's any chance that vandals did it?" said Taylor. "The brake lines I mean."

"They'd have had to crawl under the car to get at them," said Owen, "so I think it's very unlikely. It's too much trouble to go to without a significant motive."

Taylor sat back in her seat and fixed Patel with her large blue eyes.

"What's your gut feeling, Sergeant?" she said. "Do you think it's murder or suicide?"

"To be honest, I'm really not sure," said Patel weakly. "Quite frankly it's an unusual method to choose for either."

Taylor frowned.

"I see what you mean," she said. "Anyway, there'll have to be an investigation. While there's still doubt about whether it's murder or not I'd like you two to handle it, OK?"

Patel nodded.

"Of course," he said.

Taylor shrugged.

"I mean, if you turn up concrete evidence that it's murder then we'll need a bigger team," she said, "but at the moment I'm not convinced that's the case."

"No problem."

Taylor picked up a large envelope that was lying on her desk.

"These are the deceased's personal effects from the car," she said. "I'd like you to go through them and see what you can find."

Patel and Owen went through to the CID office and scattered the contents of the envelope on Patel's desk. There was a small handbag containing a purse, two sets of keys, a mobile phone, a ballpoint pen, a cotton handkerchief with the initials 'J. E. T.' embroidered in the corner, a diary and a bottle of perfume. One of the sets of keys clearly belonged to the Toyota, so the others were probably house keys. Patel opened the diary. On the 'Personal Notes' page, below the name of the owner, there was an address: 14 Beachcroft Road, London SW20.

Patel turned to the part of the diary covering the weeks prior to the death of its owner. There were few entries: an appointment with a hairdresser, one with a dentist and another with a doctor in Harley Street. The final entry had been made a couple of weeks before Miss Templeton's death and read simply: 'Martin's funeral 2.30'. The purse contained three credit cards in the name of the deceased, a debit card, forty pounds in notes and some loose change. Patel turned his attention to the mobile phone. It was an old model with a keypad and he had some difficulty switching it on. He checked to see if there was a record of calls made and received by the owner. Having failed to do so, he handed the phone to Paul Owen.

"Let's have a look," said Owen. "Oh yes, I used to have one like this. You press this button in the middle to get into the menu section; then you select this icon that looks like a telephone with arrows going in opposite directions on it and you get a list of recent calls in and out. Umm, looks like she didn't make or receive many calls. These are good, because if the number's in your phone book, the name of the person comes up on the list. She made two calls to someone called 'Sarah', one to a 'David' and two to someone called 'Edith'. There's another to 'The London Clinic' and one to a number that's not in her phone book. There's three incoming calls from 'Sarah', one from this 'Edith' and another from a number with no name."

"Make a note of the callers and numbers," said Patel. "They may not be relevant, but they just might turn out to be important. It's a pity she didn't have a smartphone."

Owen raised his eyebrows.

"That's true," he said.

Patel took out his phone and opened his *A to Z* app.

"Let's see what route she would have taken to get to Alexandra Road," he said.

He zoomed in on the relevant section of the map and scrolled sideways and then downwards.

"Most likely she drove up Copse Hill and then along the Ridgeway," he said. "She'd have had to turn right at the roundabout at the top of Wimbledon Hill; presumably the brakes were still working at that stage, but had failed by the time she got to the bottom."

"Maybe it took a while for enough brake fluid to leak out to make them fail," suggested Owen.

Patel nodded.

"That sounds a reasonable explanation," he said.

"What next?"

Patel looked at his watch.

"It's bit late to do anything more today," he said. "Tomorrow morning we'll get over to Beachcroft Road and have a look at where she lived." He cleared his throat. "Fancy a quick drink?"

"All right," said Owen, "where do you suggest?"

"Where do you lot normally go?"

"Depends, I prefer the Alexandra myself."

"Right, let's go there."

The interior of the bar was pleasantly warm and they peeled off their coats as soon as they were inside. Patel was relieved that there was no background music and that the television mounted on one of the walls was switched off. He turned to his companion.

"What would you like?" he asked.

"Bitter for me, sir," said Owen.

Patel approached the bar and was confronted by a bewildering array of taps. The barman was youthful in appearance and had a bushy beard and glasses.

"What can I get you?" he asked.

"Er, a lager and a pint of bitter," said Patel.

"This one all right?" said the barman indicating one of the taps.

"Er, yes," said Patel, hoping he'd made the right choice.

18

The barman set to work and Patel looked around. Two bearded men were standing a short way from him. One of them was almost completely bald while the other had long hair tied in a ponytail. The bald man launched into a lengthy monologue while the other nodded between sips from his drink.

The drinks arrived and Patel paid and carried them over to where Owen was sitting. He had selected a high table with benches on both sides of it and soon Patel found himself perched on one of them sipping his drink.

At first there was an uneasy silence, then Owen said: "It wouldn't be easy to break into the car to bugger the braking system. OK, it's an easy job for an experienced car thief, but I can't see the average member of the general public managing it. Cars like that usually have alarms; surely it would have gone off if someone tried to tamper with it?"

Patel nodded.

"I checked the door locks carefully to see if there was any evidence that someone had tried to force them and there wasn't," he said. "As the bloke said, it's more likely that someone would have done it from below if they didn't have the key. If Miss Templeton did it herself, she'd have used her keys to get access to the engine compartment. Of course, a murderer might have been able to get hold of the car key, or a copy of it at any rate, but rather than going to all that trouble he'd simply slide under the car."

"I know we can't be sure whether it was murder or suicide," said Owen, "but you must have an opinion one way or the other."

"As I said to DCI Taylor, I really don't know at the moment. It did occur to me that she might have accelerated deliberately to make sure she hit the undertaker's at speed."

"Maybe," said Owen.

They drank in silence for several moments, then Patel said: "You married?"

"Yes, last year," said Owen. "You married yourself?"

"Yes."

"Children?"

"Not yet."

Owen finished his drink.

"If you'll excuse me, sir, I have to be going," he said. "Gemma'll have the dinner on the go by now."

"Yes, right, see you tomorrow," said Patel.

When Owen had gone, Patel looked around the bar. It was early and there weren't many customers. The atmosphere was congenial but somehow he felt out of place. He left his drink unfinished and headed for the door.

CHAPTER THREE

When Sanjay arrived home his wife Amber was in the kitchen stirring the contents of a saucepan. Her long blonde hair was tied back in a ponytail and she was wearing jeans and a T-shirt with 'Queen Mary University London' emblazoned across the front.

"How was your day?" she asked, pecking him on the cheek.

"OK, it was pretty good actually."

"There you see, there was nothing to be worried about, was there?" she said smiling. "I told you it'd be fine, didn't I?"

"I know and you're right – as usual."

Amber checked the contents of another saucepan on the hob.

"This is nearly done," she said. "Why don't you relax and I'll give you a shout when it's ready."

He went through to the living room and examined her section of the bookcase. As he had expected, he found several novels by Joan Templeton. He selected one at random and inspected the cover. The title was *Dead Men's Shoes* and the cover featured a picture of a man's body lying on a floor wearing socks but no shoes. He turned the book over and read: 'In one of his most baffling cases, Inspector Tewksbury investigates a series of murders in which there is one common factor: none of the victims are wearing shoes when their bodies are discovered. However, there is no obvious link between the victims, which begs the question: are they random killings by a madman or is there a more tangible motive for the murders?'

He opened the cover of the book and found a page entitled 'About the Author'. He read: 'Joan Templeton was born in Haywards Heath in 1945 and educated at Saint Leonard's School and at Cambridge University, where she read English. Having completed a BEd., she taught English at various schools in South London. She published her first novel, *The Killer Within*, in 1975. Following its success she became a full-time writer. She has never married and still lives in South London. She won a Gold Dagger Award from the Crime Writer's Association for her novel *Conflicting Evidence*. Her other books include *The Murder of Elliot Poe*, *A Question of Balance* and *The Body in the Cave*. She has also published two collections of short stories.'

Sanjay was not in the habit of reading crime fiction. In his, admittedly limited, experience, writers of this genre usually displayed a lack of knowledge of police procedures and constructed what he saw as implausible plots. In their early days together he had teased Amber about her fascination with murder mysteries but he had long ago stopped doing this. She enjoyed the books, which for her were a form of escapism, and she never criticised him for reading science fiction.

He glanced at the other Joan Templeton novels one by one. They all featured the character known as Inspector Tewkesbury, a detective described as having a 'supreme mastery of deduction and an almost uncanny knack for determining the truth.' The Metropolitan Police could do with such a man in its ranks, but Sanjay suspected that this paragon of investigational logic and intuition probably did not exist in real life.

Amber came through to say that dinner would be ready in five minutes.

"Can you lay the table?" she asked.

He set about this task and soon they were enjoying beef stew with carrots and boiled potatoes, followed by bananas and ice cream. Afterwards Sanjay made coffee while Amber enjoyed a well-earned rest. He brought the mugs through to the sitting room and they sat in silence for a while.

Then Sanjay said: "I'm investigating the death of one of your favourite authors at the moment."

Amber sat up straight in her chair.

"Who is it?" she asked.

"Joan Templeton."

Amber gasped.

"Oh that's awful," she said, "how did she die?"

"It was a car crash."

"Oh well at least she wasn't murdered."

"That's not quite clear at the moment," said Sanjay. "Someone had cut the pipes leading from the brake master cylinder on her car."

"Wow, do you know who did it?"

"No and we can't rule out the possibility she did it herself."

"But why? It doesn't make sense," said Amber, wide-eyed.

"I don't know at the moment."

She drained her coffee mug and put it back on the tray.

"I went to hear her talk at the Hay Festival once," she said. "It was during my last year at university and a group of us decided to go."

"I don't remember you doing that."

"It was during the period we weren't speaking," said Amber. "You know, after we had that row. I went with Jen and Wendy. We camped in a field and it rained almost the whole three days. Still, we had a good time in spite of everything."

"What was she like?" he asked.

"Not very tall; she had mousy brown hair and spectacles," said Amber. "She wore a full skirt and a blouse. She looked like a schoolteacher, which of course she was before she became a full-time writer. At first she seemed rather reticent, but once she got going she was really insightful and witty as well. I enjoyed her session more than any of the others we went to. She was promoting a book called *Conflicting Evidence* at the time and I managed to get a signed copy. I was thrilled; I've still got it somewhere."

"Thanks for that," said Sanjay. "We've only just started the investigation so we need all the help we can get."

"My favourite book of hers is the last one she brought out, *Deadly Reckoning*," said Amber. "There's a really clever bit, well, I think it's clever. The murderer has had dinner with the victim before killing him and realises his fingerprints will be all over the plates, cutlery and glasses he's used, so he puts all dinner things in the dishwasher and puts it on before he leaves the scene."

"What about fingerprints on the table and other areas he's touched while he's been there?" said Sanjay.

"Oh, he cleans them all, well, those areas he can remember touching anyway," said Amber. "Of course he forgets that he touched a wine bottle when he topped up his glass during the meal. That's how they catch him."

Sanjay smiled broadly.

"Very ingenious," he said.

"You may well scoff," said Amber, "but I think something like that could really happen."

Sanjay realised he was now on dangerous ground and decided to change the subject.

"Anyway, how was your day?" he said.

"We're going to court next week so there's a lot of preparation to do," she said. "Pretty routine and boring compared to what you've been up to. Actually I've brought some work home with me. I'll get stuck into it now if you don't mind."

"Go ahead."

CHAPTER FOUR

They parked the car in front of the house. Beachcroft Road is a cul-de-sac and the houses along it are semi-detached and have bay windows. While they are not overly large, their location and proximity to train and bus services ensures that they are not cheap to buy. Number 14 was in a good state of repair and the original windows had been replaced with modern double-glazed units. Patel tried the keys one by one until the front door opened.

The hall was narrow and there was a flight of stairs in front of them to the left. To the right of the staircase the hall narrowed further and led to a door that was ajar. The walls had been painted white, which gave what might otherwise have been a rather gloomy space a bright and airy feel, enhanced by the light-coloured wooden floor. There was a smell of air freshener and furniture polish.

On the right an open door revealed a dining room with a window, adorned with festoon blinds, which looked out onto the street. Further on, a second door led into a sitting room from which there was access to the garden via French windows. Both these rooms also had white walls and were tastefully furnished with modern furniture. At the rear of the property there was an unexpectedly large kitchen fitted out with modern units that had high-gloss black fronts. On the left side of the room was a small table with two chairs. Everywhere was neat and tidy, with little evidence of human habitation.

However, there was a half-empty bottle of sherry on one of the work surfaces and a wine glass with a residue of golden liquid in it stood in the sink.

Patel assigned Owen to check the dining room and kitchen while he concentrated on the sitting room. The fireplace had been removed and the chimney breast filled in. At the level where a mantelpiece might have been, a large flat-screen television was mounted on the wall. In front of this there was a leather reclining chair and footstool, while to the right was a beige settee. On the other side of the chair was a small occasional table with a couple of magazines on it. One was called *Women's Health* and the other was the *Times Literary Supplement.*

On both sides of the chimney breast there were shelving units from floor to ceiling crammed with books. Patel inspected them carefully. It was clear that their owner had eclectic tastes in literature. There were a number of books on crime, forensic science and police procedure, which the writer had presumably used to gather information for her stories. However, novels and collections of short stories heavily outnumbered works of non-fiction. These were drawn from a variety of genres and included books in French and Italian.

As he was working his way along one of the shelves, he came upon a repair manual for the Toyota Camry. It seemed somewhat out of place. Surely this elderly spinster who could afford to live in a house like this one didn't need to repair or service her own car? On the other hand, maybe it was one of her hobbies. It was an item that could have a bearing on the case, so he popped it into an evidence bag. As there was nothing else that seemed to be relevant he rejoined Constable Owen. "Did you find anything?" he asked.

"Well, I found this," he said, handing Patel a hacksaw in an evidence bag. "It was in the cupboard under the sink."

"I hope you wore gloves when you bagged it up."

"Of course," said Owen, frowning.

"If that was the one that was used to cut the brake lines, with a bit of luck there'll be fingerprints on it," said Patel. "Anything else?"

"There were half a dozen bottles of sherry in one of the store cupboards."

"Maybe Miss Templeton had a drink problem." Patel scratched his head. "Mind you, I expect a lot of older ladies like a sherry now and then. Is that all?"

"Yes, the place is so tidy I don't suppose she did much cooking. I've never seen such a clean hob."

"All right then, let's go upstairs."

"This decor's a bit clinical," said Owen on the way up.

"Personally I like it," said Patel. "It's really fresh and it makes the house seem bigger."

The narrow landing with its white-painted banisters gave access to three bedrooms and a bathroom. The largest of the bedrooms was at the front of the property and there was evidence of recent occupation. The dressing table, which was under the window, had a collection of jars, bottles and other female paraphernalia on its top. A cotton dressing gown lay over the back of an upholstered chair and there was a pair of high-heeled shoes beneath it. The larger of the other two bedrooms appeared to be a little-used guest room, while the third was small and fitted out as a study.

This room was, in contrast to the others, untidy and cluttered. Much of the space within it was taken up by a large desk, on which there was a computer and a printer. The rest of its surface was covered in piles of papers and there was an open notebook close to the keyboard. Patel examined the pages that were on display. At the top of the one on the left the words 'chapter 19, page 147' had been written and then crossed out. Below that was 'chapter 21, page 160', followed by 'chapter 24, page 186'. On the facing page the word 'Dropbox' was underlined and below it was a list that Patel took to be the titles of books. Each one was accompanied by a date and all but one had been ticked.

At that moment Owen joined him.

"There's nothing in the spare bedroom that seems relevant," he said. "The cabinet in the bathroom is stuffed with pills and medicines, so I imagine she wasn't in good health."

"What sort of pills?" said Patel.

"Painkillers, stomach pills, cough medicine, that sort of thing."

"I'd better take a look."

Patel led the way to the bathroom. He opened the cabinet and several boxes fell out.

"I had difficulty getting it all back in," said Owen apologetically.

Patel sifted through the boxes, bottles and strips of pills. As well as over-the-counter medicines and prescribed drugs there were a number of herbal remedies and homeopathic preparations. His eye alighted on a packet containing strips of small white tablets.

"Interesting," he said.

"What is it?" said Owen.

"It's called tramadol," said Patel. "It's a moderately strong painkiller, an opioid. It makes some people agitated."

"Could it make someone suicidal?" said Owen, showing genuine interest for the first time.

"I don't know about that," said Patel. "I'll need to look up the side effects. Also, we need to have a word with her GP."

"Right, I'll organise it," said Owen. "Anything interesting in the study?"

"I don't think so, but we'll need to go through all the papers and her computer in detail at some stage," said Patel. "Did you check the cupboard under the stairs?"

"No I didn't; I could do it now if you like."

Patel sent him downstairs and then returned to examining the desk in the study. A thick pile of paper caught his eye. The top page had the words 'Templeton_8451_prelims_B-format Template' in the top left-hand corner. In the middle of the page it read: 'The Riddle of the Silent Soldier by Joan Templeton'. After flicking through a few of the pages he concluded that this was an unpublished manuscript. He wondered if it was ready for publication or as yet unfinished. Close by he found what appeared to be a covering letter from her publishers, a company called Romulus Books. The contents indicated that the enclosed manuscript was a proof that required checking by the author. Perhaps someone else could do the proofreading, in which case it might still get published.

The desk had a single drawer. He slipped it open and examined the contents. Inside there was a stapler, a hole-punch and a collection of elastic bands. In one corner he spotted a small bundle of letters tied up with string. He untied them and examined their contents. The most recent was dated 1st November 1998. All of them were written in the same spidery hand and were signed simply 'Michael'. He popped them into an evidence bag.

Deciding that that there was nothing of obvious importance on the desk, he went downstairs to where Owen was waiting for him.

"What's next, Sarge?" he asked.

"I think we've done all we can here for the time being," said Patel. "We'll head back to the station and write a report on what we've found so far."

*

Soon after five o'clock, Patel boarded a tram at Wimbledon Station. There were no free seats so he stood in the area between the doors sandwiched between a girl with elaborately braided hair and a man in a tracksuit and trainers. As the carriage swayed he wondered if the unpublished manuscript had any bearing on the case. It was possible that it might at least give some indication of the deceased's state of mind at the time of her death. Such information would very likely be more easily obtained from people who were close to her and before he had left for the night he had asked Paul Owen to contact Joan Templeton's next of kin and arrange a meeting with her. The idea of reading the manuscript did not fill him with enthusiasm and he couldn't imagine that Paul Owen would volunteer to do it. In any case it might prove to be a time-consuming waste of effort.

After dinner Sanjay and Amber settled on the sofa and watched the evening news.

Amber sipped her coffee.

"Joan Templeton hasn't brought out a new book for about five years now," she said. "It's a real shame, I've read all the old ones."

"Actually she was working on a new book when she died," said Sanjay.

Amber's face brightened.

"How exciting," she said, "when's it going to be published?"

Sanjay shrugged.

"I don't know if it will be now she's dead," he said. "What I found in her house was the uncorrected proofs of a new novel. The thing is, I don't know if there's anything in it that would shed any light on her death. It's a long shot, but I was wondering if you would be willing to read it for me?"

Amber's eyes widened.

"You want me to read a Joan Templeton novel that no one else has ever seen," she said. "Of course I'd be delighted to do it. Have you got it with you?"

"No, it's still at the house," he said. "I plan to go back and get it when I've spoken to her next of kin. Bringing it home is a bit irregular but I know you'll look after it and I'll put it back on the victim's desk when you've finished it."

"It won't take me long," she said rubbing her hands. "Her books are always an easy read."

"OK, well I'll get you the manuscript as soon as I can."

Chapter Five

When Sanjay entered the CID office Paul Owen was sitting in front of his computer apparently engrossed in a search of some kind.

"What time are we seeing Mrs Musgrove?" he asked.

"I said we'd be round about ten thirty," said Owen. "She lives in Kingston so we'll need to leave soon."

"When's the PM?"

"This afternoon at around three."

"OK, anything else to report?"

"Not really," said Owen. "Oh, I've arranged for us to see her GP tomorrow morning."

As he checked his emails, Patel wondered if he should ask DCI Taylor if it was OK to let Amber read the unpublished manuscript. Most probably it wouldn't contain anything relevant to the investigation, in which case he would replace it in the house and say nothing about it. But what if there was a clue or a suggestion for a new line of enquiry? He could say he'd read it himself and keep Amber out of it. That might be best. Alternatively he could change his mind and leave the manuscript untouched but then he would be left wondering if he'd overlooked something important. Also, Amber would be disappointed. She was obviously looking forward to reading the story. If Taylor refused permission he would have an excuse for not allowing Amber to have the manuscript, but he would still feel guilty about letting her down. By nature he was someone who played by the rules but on this occasion he decided to bend them a little.

When he looked over to where Owen was sitting he saw that he was reading a book. Going over to his desk, he saw that it was called *Police Sergeant Exam: A Step-by-Step Guide to Prepare for Your Promotion Exam*. He knew it well.

"Got exams coming up?" he said.

"Yeah," said Owen. "I hope I pass this time."

"Sorry to disturb you," but I think it's time we headed over to Kingston."

*

Sarah Musgrove lived in the ground-floor flat of a late Victorian house in a quiet residential road close to Kingston's shopping centre. A brick path led up to the front door. On its left was a row of wheelie bins, their backs against an unkempt hedge. On its right a large motorbike stood on a paved area in front of a bay window. Patel and Owen climbed the steps to the front door and rang the bell.

A plump young woman wearing a loose-fitting V-neck sweater, under which an old grey sweatshirt was visible, opened the door. Her hair had a natural curl which, it seemed, stubbornly resisted her attempts to organise it into a coherent style. Her glasses had thick lenses and frames that were held together by sticky tape.

"Mrs Musgrove?" said Patel, showing his warrant card.

"Yes, you'd better come in," she said without enthusiasm.

Mrs Musgrove led them along the entrance hall, which had a faded tiled floor. There was a narrow table against one wall on which an assortment of envelopes was scattered. Most of them looked like junk mail.

They were ushered through a door on the right. This opened into the sitting room, a small room with a high ceiling and an ornate cornice. The furniture was old and might well have been second-hand. On the large mantelpiece stood a wedding photograph featuring a younger-looking Sarah Musgrove and a man with limp brown hair and a synthetic smile. Beside it was a rather formal-looking photograph of Joan Templeton taken some years earlier, possibly for the jacket of a book. The grate of the open fire was empty but a brass fork and shovel hung from a stand in the hearth, as if waiting patiently for the fire to be made up.

There was a chill in the air and the room had a slight smell of damp. Patel noted that he was surprisingly comfortable with his outdoor coat buttoned up. He and Owen sat on the settee while Mrs Musgrove settled in an armchair with a hastily discarded blanket on one of its arms. Owen removed a notebook and pen from his coat and opened it at the first blank page. Patel began by confirming that she was Joan Templeton's niece.

"That's right," she said. "My mother was Joan's older sister. Mum died a couple of years ago."

"Did Miss Templeton have any other family?" he asked.

"Not really," said Mrs Musgrove. "There's a second cousin who lives in Canada but I've never met him and I don't think Aunty was in regular touch with him. Basically, I'm the only family she had."

"I see," said Patel. "Did you see her regularly?"

"I tried to pop in and see her every other week. She told me that there was no need and that I fussed too much but I sort of felt responsible for her after Mum died."

Mrs Musgrove wiped away a tear with her hand and Owen passed her a box of tissues that was on the coffee table between them. She removed one of them and clutched it in her right hand.

"What was her frame of mind during the period leading up to her death?" asked Patel.

Mrs Musgrove sighed and fiddled with the edge of the blanket.

"She was very down," she said. "It's hardly surprising; she had cancer you see."

Patel glanced at Owen who raised his eyebrows fractionally in response.

"I didn't know that," said Patel. "Was she very ill?"

"I wouldn't say so, but she told me that she had pain in her tummy from time to time and that the doctors had told her it would get worse."

"Was she receiving any sort of treatment?" asked Patel.

"Not as far as I know."

This seemed odd to Patel but perhaps the tumour was incurable and the only treatment option was palliation when the symptoms warranted it.

"Had she been given any idea of her prognosis?" he said.

"I don't think so, but she said the doctors weren't being completely honest with her," said Mrs Musgrove, tucking her paper handkerchief into her sleeve. "They were trying to protect her from the truth but she knew she was living on borrowed time. That's why she was so keen to finish her book."

"Oh yes," said Patel. "We found the manuscript. Is it likely to be published now she's passed away?"

Mrs Musgrove frowned.

"I'm not sure," she said. "Her editor or someone at the publishers could probably do the final proofreading, so it might still get into print."

"Who is her editor?" asked Owen.

"Her name's Edith Skinner."

"Had she worked with Miss Templeton for long?" asked Patel.

"Ooh, about fifteen years I think," she said, looking up at the ceiling. "Aunty hadn't been writing much for a while before she started this new book, so they hadn't been in touch for a year or two. She was relieved when Edith agreed to work on *The Riddle of the Silent Soldier*. She didn't want to have to get used to someone new."

"Where does Edith Skinner live?" said Owen, pen poised to take down her address.

"Somewhere in Malden I think," said Mrs Musgrove. "I know her home wasn't too far from Aunty's."

"Was your aunt in the habit of drinking alcohol?" said Patel.

Sarah laughed mirthlessly.

"What, Aunty?" she said. "No, she hardly touched a drop. She'd have a glass of sherry at Christmas or if there was something to celebrate but otherwise she was pretty much teetotal."

Patel frowned. He couldn't decide whether the witness was trying to mislead him or whether she really believed what she was telling him was the truth. He decided to press her further.

"There was a half-empty bottle of sherry in the kitchen when we looked round the house," he said, "and we found some unopened bottles in one of the cabinets. That suggests to me that she drank regularly."

Sarah Musgrove fidgeted in her chair and shrugged.

"I imagine she got them at Christmas time," she said. "We, my husband and I that is, had a glass with her when we went round to see her on Boxing Day. She invited us for lunch. We all had a small glass of sherry before the meal. We took along a bottle of wine, but she hardly had any and we didn't finish it because Alan was driving. She told us to take what was left with us because she wouldn't drink it herself."

"That doesn't explain why she had another half-dozen bottles stashed away," said Owen.

Mrs Musgrove reddened.

"I expect she got them because they were on special offer," she said. "Aunty loved a bargain. She was always buying stacks of stuff she didn't really need because it was cheap. I used to tell her it was stupid, but she said she'd get through it eventually and in the meantime she wouldn't have to go shopping so often."

"There's another thing," said Patel, "she wasn't wearing a seat belt. Does that surprise you?"

Mrs Musgrove shook her head.

"Not at all," she said. "She never wore one, she said they were uncomfortable and she was afraid she wouldn't be able to get out of the car if there was an emergency. I told her it was silly and she'd be safer wearing one, but she wouldn't listen. It sounds awful to say it at a time like this, but she was a terrible driver. I tried to avoid going with her in the car if I possibly could. She really scared me sometimes."

"I see," said Patel. "Where do you think she was going on the morning she was killed?"

Mrs Musgrove did not reply immediately and looked pensive.

"I expect she was going to Waitrose to get some groceries," she said at last. "She usually did her shopping early in the morning so that she'd be free for the rest of the day."

Patel was conscious that his next question might cause distress but decided it had to be asked.

"Do you think your aunt was capable of killing herself, in the present circumstances?"

Mrs Musgrove nodded.

"Yes I do," she said. "She was terrified of dying in pain. I think it was because of what happened to Mum when she was dying of cancer. Towards the end the painkillers didn't seem to work any more."

"Was she interested in car maintenance?" said Owen.

Mrs Musgrove gasped and turned to face him.

"What? No, why would she be?" she said. "The car always went to the dealer for servicing."

"We found a repair manual for her car in her sitting room," said Patel. "Do you have any idea why she bought it?"

"Not really." She hesitated then added: "Maybe it was research for something she was writing."

"That could well be the case," said Patel. "Did your aunt have any enemies?"

Sarah Musgrove blinked furiously.

"No, of course not; why would she?" she said.

Patel smiled.

"I'm sorry, I have to ask these questions," he said. "I know it's difficult for you."

Sarah Musgrove retrieved her tissue and blew her nose.

"I'm sorry, this has been a terrible shock for me," she said.

"I do understand." Patel paused while Mrs Musgrove collected herself, then he said, "The crash occurred around 7am, so she must have been up early that morning."

"That wouldn't be unusual, she was always an early riser."

"Can you think of anywhere else she might have been going that morning, other than the shops I mean?" said Owen.

Mrs Musgrove frowned.

"Not really," she said, "Aunty didn't have many friends and she didn't go out a lot. She was a solitary sort of person."

"Is there anyone she might have confided in?" said Patel. "Someone else she was close to?"

"I think she was in touch with a couple of her friends from university who live in South London."

"Who would that be?" said Owen.

"Well, there's Pearl Bailey," said Mrs Musgrove.

"Is that the writer?" said Owen.

"Yes, that's right," she said. "She lives in Wimbledon, but I don't think they met very often. The other one is called Rosemary Rogers. She's in Earlsfield."

"I see," said Patel. "There was an entry in her diary which said 'Martin's funeral 2.30'. Do you know who Martin was?"

"I've no idea. She didn't say anything about it to me."

"Thank you very much for your time," said Patel. "It's possible we'll need to speak to you again, depending on what else we turn up during the investigation."

Sarah Musgrove looked at them wide-eyed.

"Do you really think she killed herself?" she said.

"It's clear that she had good reason to do so," said Patel, "but it's odd that she chose a car accident, assuming she was the one who disabled the brakes on the car. We've only just started the investigation so it's too early to draw any firm conclusions."

When they were walking down the street to where the car was parked, Owen said, "I don't think she could have been going to Waitrose."

"Why?" said Patel.

"Well, it doesn't open until eight o'clock, see, and it's just down the road from where she crashed. I know because my wife, Gemma, worked there for a while."

Patel wondered where she had been going. It might be important but it could just as easily be irrelevant. A thought occurred to him.

"How did you know Pearl Bailey was a writer?" he said.

"Gemma likes her stuff," said Owen, blushing a little. "I haven't read anything of hers myself."

"What kind of books are they?"

"Romantic fiction, I think."

Patel thought for a moment.

"Perhaps it would be worth having a word with her at some stage," he said. He looked at his watch. "Come on, we don't want to be late for our appointment with the pathologist."

Chapter Six

Doctor Alison Jarvis was in her office dictating a report when Owen and Patel arrived. She was wearing a cream blouse with a knee-length pencil skirt and her red hair was pinned up in an elegant style. She had surgeon's hands, Patel thought, strong but delicate with long, clever fingers.

"Who's this, DC Owen?" she said, putting her dictating machine down on the desk and turning to face them.

"It's Detective Sergeant Patel," said Owen. "He's joined us this week."

"Pleased to meet you," she said, looking him up and down. "Come and take a seat, I'll finish this later."

Patel gave a half-smile. The forensic pathologists he had come across previously were older men with what seemed to him to be a morbid interest in dead bodies. Professor Gamble, whose lectures he had attended at medical school, had a dry sense of humour but, as he had discovered when the professor was the guest speaker at a Medical Society dinner, he was distinctly lacking in small talk. He had to admit that Dr Jarvis was a breath of fresh air. He cleared his throat.

"We were wondering what you'd found," he said.

"This one's pretty straightforward," said the doctor. "She sustained a number of injuries at the time of the accident. There was a head injury caused by being thrown forward into the windscreen and she had an extensive chest injury due to hitting the steering wheel on the way. Was she wearing a seat belt, by the way?"

"No, apparently she normally left it undone," said Patel.

Dr Jarvis shook her head.

"It's amazing there are still people who don't wear them," she said. "The evidence that they prevent serious injury is overwhelming. Anyway, a fractured rib had punctured her lung and there was quite a lot of bleeding inside her chest. However, it was probably the head injury that actually killed her."

"We've been told that Miss Templeton was suffering from terminal cancer," said Patel. "Can you confirm that?"

Dr Jarvis frowned and scratched her head.

"No, I can't," she said. "All her organs were healthy. Actually, she was in better shape than a lot of people of her age, or at least the ones that come my way. How did you get the idea she had cancer?"

"Her next of kin told us that Miss Templeton was suffering from intermittent abdominal pain, supposedly due to some kind of tumour," said Patel.

"I've examined the abdominal cavity and I can assure you there's nothing like that there. I'll take another look, but I'll be surprised if I find anything."

"Do you have any idea why she would have told her niece that if it wasn't true?" said Patel, realising as he spoke that it was probably not a question best answered by a pathologist.

Dr Jarvis shrugged.

"It's hard to say," she said. "Perhaps she was looking for sympathy."

Good answer, he thought.

"That's certainly possible," he said. "The lady lived alone and didn't have any other family."

"We'd also like to know if she had alcohol in her bloodstream," said Owen.

"I've sent the usual samples so you should have an answer on that by Monday."

"Thank you, Dr Jarvis," said Patel with a smile.

"Don't you want to see the body?" said Dr Jarvis, with a note of disappointment in her voice.

"I don't really think that's necessary," said Owen. "You've summarised the findings and I think we get the picture."

"That would be very helpful," said Patel.

"Come this way then."

The post-mortem room with its tiled walls bore some resemblance to a public lavatory. However, instead of urinals and washbasins there were porcelain tables on one of which lay the body of Joan Templeton. The skin of her scalp had been turned forwards over her face to allow the skull to be opened and the brain was exposed. The chest had also been opened and Patel recognised that the right lung had collapsed and that there was some residual blood in the dependent part of the chest cavity. Dr Jarvis went over the injuries, pointing to areas damaged by trauma and commenting on how they had occurred. Patel followed everything she said but he suspected that Owen was a bit out of his depth. He also noted that his colleague was looking rather pale and sweaty.

When the guided tour was over they left the room and discarded their gowns, and masks. Owen breathed a sigh of relief, to Patel's mild amusement. He smiled at Dr Jarvis.

"We'll get back to you if we have any queries," he said. Turning to Owen he added: "What time are we seeing Joan Templeton's GP? We need to get to the bottom of this phony cancer story."

"Nine thirty tomorrow morning," said Owen.

"I'd also like you to phone her solicitor and see if you can get a copy of her will. Meanwhile, I'm going to get the keys to the house and have another look at her study."

*

Sanjay parked his car on the drive of Joan Templeton's house and let himself in through the front door. Although he knew that Owen would have made a thorough search during their

41

first visit, he went through to the kitchen and checked that there was no additional hidden stash of alcohol. Having confirmed that this was not the case, he went upstairs and sat down at the writer's desk. He removed pages from the top of the manuscript until he came to the first chapter and began to read.

The body of Colonel Bradshaw lay on its left side facing away from the door. Through the letterbox Carol Edwards could see that there was blood on the right side of his head and on the floor nearby. There was a firearm of some sort lying on the floor beside the body. She let out a gasp and steadied herself against the door. When she had regained some degree of composure, she took out her mobile phone and called the police.

The uniformed officer who was first on the scene forced the door open and inspected the body.

"You know who he was?" he asked.

"Yes, his name's Colonel Bradshaw," she said.

"He's a friend of yours, is he?"

"No, I do cleaning for him. Is he dead?"

"He's dead all right," said the constable. "Looks like suicide to me, but we'll have to get CID to take a look. I'll need to take down your particulars. What's your name, madam?"

"Carol Edwards."

"Can you tell me the full name of the deceased?"

"I always called him 'Colonel Bradshaw', I never knew his first name."

Patel replaced the page and sat back in the chair. It seemed that the book involved an apparent suicide, though this death seemed to be considerably more straightforward than the one he was investigating. A military man was likely to choose to blow his brains out with a service revolver if he planned to kill himself. Since this was page one, the author presumably introduced some additional evidence that would show that this was not what happened, evidence that was only obvious to the brilliant super-sleuth, Inspector Tewksbury.

At this stage of the investigation he couldn't rule out the possibility that Joan Templeton had killed herself. If so she had chosen a more unreliable method than that used by the character she had created. It seemed more likely to him that someone else had cut the brake lines. The same objection applied in that case, assuming that the perpetrator had intended to kill the writer. There was no guarantee that the driver of the disabled car would die in any resulting accident.

He gathered up the papers and loaded them into a bag he had brought for the purpose. Amber could read the rest of the story and report back on her findings.

He turned his attention to the other contents of the desk. The jumble of papers included an advance information sheet for *The Riddle of the Silent Soldier*, a letter from Merton Council about the council tax, a notification of her tax code for that year and a credit card bill. Patel noted with passing interest that the balance on the bill was modest, suggesting that Joan Templeton probably didn't have any reason to worry about money or at any rate that she preferred not to use the card. There was also a large notebook that contained outlines for a number of plots for novels and short stories. They were written in a small, neat hand and included many crossings-out and notes in the margin.

It seemed to him that this woman had lived a solitary life in the confined but well-ordered world she had created for herself. Perhaps she had lived her life, vicariously, through her characters. Whatever the reality of her existence may have been, it appeared that something or someone had disrupted the smooth running of her routine and this had somehow led to her death.

CHAPTER SEVEN

"Have you got an appointment?" asked the receptionist, eying the two policemen suspiciously.

"Yes," said Patel, showing her his warrant card. "Sergeant Owen phoned and made one yesterday."

"Oh, I see you're the police," she said in a more emollient tone. "Very well then, take a seat and the doctor will be with you shortly."

The waiting room of the Meadowbank Health Centre was not overly large but the chairs looked new and there was a collection of magazines on two low tables in front of them. There was also a machine that allowed patients to measure their own blood pressure. This intrigued Owen and he took off his jacket, rolled up his right sleeve and thrust his arm into it. The machine spat out a small piece of paper with numbers on it.

"The trouble is I don't know what my blood pressure should be," he said as he studied the result, "so I don't know if it's normal or not."

"Let's have a look," said Patel. He glanced at the results. "It's within the normal range."

"That's a relief," said Owen. "Wait a minute, how do you know?"

Patel was not keen to reveal his past to his colleagues, though he supposed in the end it was bound to leak out. In any case, Owen was his partner and it seemed churlish to keep him in the dark.

"I learned about blood pressure at medical school," he said. "I dropped out at the end of the fourth year."

Owen looked surprised but said nothing. At that moment they were summoned to the doctor's consulting room.

Dr Lydgate was a woman of about forty with shoulder-length fair hair. She was wearing a blue polo shirt with the words 'Meadowbank Health Centre' on the front of it just below the practice logo. She smiled genially and asked them to take a seat.

"I gather you want to talk about Joan Templeton," she said. "What a terrible business, her dying in a crash like that."

"Am I right in thinking that she was your patient?" asked Patel.

"She was registered with me but she used to see other members of the practice if I wasn't available," said the doctor. "She was a very regular attender, so that happened quite frequently."

"Why did she come to the surgery so often?"

"She regularly thought she had significant symptoms and when she did she almost always consulted us about them." She picked up a thick pile of cards that was lying on her desk and flicked through them. "Sore throat, blurred vision, dizziness, blocked nose, abdominal pain, headaches, back pain, she'd had most of the symptoms that our patients complain of at one time or another."

"Her niece told us that Miss Templeton had said to her she had cancer," said Patel. "Do you know why she would have done that?"

"She had a morbid fear of developing malignant disease," said Dr Lydgate. "She attributed most of her symptoms to a tumour of some sort in whichever part of the body she was complaining about at the time. It was difficult to persuade her that she was in fact in good health. In the trade we call people like her 'heart-sink patients' because of how we feel when we see that one of them is next to be seen. The problem is that, while more than nine times out of ten there's nothing physically wrong with them, just occasionally they do actually get sick and then it's easy to overlook the fact."

"Yes I see," said Patel. "Had she been investigated for all these symptoms?"

"Oh yes," said the doctor. "As well as having tests here at the surgery, she'd seen a number of hospital specialists as well. She usually saw them privately; it seemed that money was no object and she couldn't bear the thought of having to wait to be seen."

"There was an appointment with a doctor in Harley Street in her diary for the week before she died. What was the reason for that visit?"

"Let me check." She flicked through the bundle of record cards. "Oh yes, one of my colleagues referred her to a physician because of her abdominal pain. He didn't find anything on physical examination and sent her for some tests. We haven't had another letter back from him yet so I don't know if they were normal or not."

"Can you tell me his name?"

"Yes, it was Dr Mervin Hackwood. We send him a lot of outpatients, both NHS and private. We find he gives a good opinion."

"And when did you last see Miss Templeton yourself?"

"Umm, oh yes, it was three months back," said the doctor. "She'd found a lump in her neck. Well, she thought she had. I examined her and couldn't find anything abnormal. I think what she was feeling was muscle spasm. It's pretty common."

"Indeed," said Patel. "Would you say that Miss Templeton suffered from depression?"

"Not really, she was more the anxious type."

"Did the colleague who saw her most recently think she was depressed?"

"I'll see what he wrote." She consulted the record card on the top of the pile. "No, nothing about depression, just abdominal pain and constipation," she said.

"Might he have thought she was depressed but not recorded it on the record card?"

"I suppose so," said the doctor doubtfully. "I could ask him. He might not remember, of course. We all see so many patients every day that you can't retain every detail about them."

"I'd be grateful if you could and let me know by calling this number," said Patel, handing her his card.

As they were getting up to go the doctor said, "I imagine she would have had a post-mortem." Patel nodded. "Did they find anything that we'd missed?"

"No, Doctor, I can reassure on that point," he said. "Miss Templeton died of her injuries and appeared to be in good health."

"Well, that's something," she said, placing the pen she'd been fiddling with on her desk. "It's always good to get feedback."

Owen already had his hand on the door of the consulting room when Patel turned back to face the doctor.

"There is one other thing," he said. "We found some tramadol in Miss Templeton's bathroom cabinet. I was wondering what she was taking it for."

The doctor grimaced and returned to the record cards.

"Oh yes," she said. "Miss Templeton had backache six months ago. I prescribed it for her then."

"Really?" said Patel. "NICE recommends non-steroidal anti-inflammatory analgesics as the first line of treatment for back pain, unless they're contraindicated for some reason. Was that the case here?"

The doctor blushed and blinked furiously.

"She had a history of asthma," she said. "I therefore considered it inappropriate to prescribe that type of medication. I must say I don't think it's appropriate for a policeman to question the decisions of an experienced medical practitioner. What makes you think you know better than me?"

"Well, I've got a degree in pharmacology," said Patel. "As part of it I did a project on the use and abuse of analgesics, as a matter of fact."

Dr Lydgate went pale and didn't speak. Patel smiled.

"I think that's all for now," he said. "Thank you for your time."

When they had left the consulting room Owen said: "I thought you said you were a medical student."

"I was," said Patel. "As part of the course I did a BSc in pharmacology. It meant I was a year behind the group I started with. To be honest, I regretted signing up for it."

CHAPTER EIGHT

When they got back to Wimbledon Police Station they found a copy of Joan Templeton's will on Patel's desk, which had been faxed through from her solicitor. They settled down to study the contents. The largest item in her estate was her house, the value of which had been estimated to be around £900,000. She had two savings accounts, each containing around £80,000. There were a few shares and a life assurance policy. When everything was added up, the value of Joan Templeton's estate came to approximately £1.5 million. There was a sole beneficiary: her niece, Sarah Musgrove. In addition there were the copyrights to the novels, most of which also went to Mrs Musgrove. The exception was the rights to *Dead Men's Shoes*, which went to an animal charity. Patel presumed that the value of these bequests depended on future sales of Joan Templeton's books and were therefore difficult to estimate. *With a bit of luck they just might provide a steady income for the beneficiaries*, he thought.

"It's not mega-bucks but it's a tidy sum," said Owen.

"The question is, does it constitute a motive for murder?" said Patel.

Owen shrugged.

"I can't see Sarah Musgrove being able to bugger her brakes," he said. "She seemed like the helpless type to me."

"It's also hard to imagine Miss Templeton doing it herself," said Patel. "I think we need to find out more about Sarah Musgrove's husband."

"I say," said Owen, "do you think that Mrs Musgrove told us that story about her aunt having cancer to make us think she killed herself?"

Patel considered this for a moment.

"It's a possibility," he said. "I still think it's an odd way of going about killing someone. It's simply too hit and miss. I think we should pay the Musgroves another visit in the early evening when we're likely to catch Mr Musgrove at home."

"Do you want me to phone and arrange a time?" said Owen.

"No," said Patel. "I think it's better if we arrive unannounced."

"OK," said Owen. "What do you want me to do this afternoon?"

"I'd like you to phone Joan Templeton's publishers and find out who was handling her account. The company's called Romulus Books. I want to know if there have been any problems with the new book; late delivery of the manuscript, unusual behaviour by their client, that sort of thing. Ask them if anyone in the office knew her well. I'd like to get a clearer picture of what Miss Templeton was really like. After that I want you to get contact details for her editor, Edith Skinner. I'd like to talk to her on Monday, if possible. It would be helpful to have another opinion on Miss Templeton's state of mind in the run-up to her death and it seems likely that this lady knew her quite well."

Owen went over to his desk and logged onto his computer. Patel took out his mobile phone and called Amber.

"I'm going to be late tonight," he said when she answered. "There are some witnesses I want to interview before the weekend. You go ahead and eat without me."

"All right, I'll do that," she said. "I'm getting on well with that manuscript, by the way. I'll tell you all about it when I see you."

"Great, I'll look forward to hearing what you make of it."

*

The traffic was heavy and it was after six thirty by the time they arrived at the Musgrove residence. Sarah Musgrove answered the door and was obviously surprised to see them.

"There are a few more questions I'd like to ask you," said Patel, by way of explanation.

"You'd better come through to the lounge," she said.

Her husband was a thin man with a narrow face and a mean little mouth. He wore an open-necked blue shirt and a pair of trousers that looked as if they belonged to a suit. He was sitting in an armchair reading the evening paper, but put it down when the two policemen entered.

"It's the police, Alan," said Mrs Musgrove.

"Do you want me to leave you alone with Sarah?" said Alan Musgrove.

"I'd like you to stay, sir," said Patel. "I have one or two questions for you as well." He turned to Sarah, who was now perching on an arm of her husband's chair. "Some new evidence has come to light since we last spoke to you. The results of the post-mortem show that your aunt died as a result of the injuries she received in the crash and that she was in good health when she died. In particular, there was no evidence of cancer. I am therefore puzzled by the fact that you told us that Miss Templeton was terminally ill. Can you explain this discrepancy?"

Sarah Musgrove went pale and didn't seem able to speak at first. Then she said: "How awful, she killed herself because she thought she was dying of cancer when in fact she was OK. Why did the doctors tell her she was very ill if she wasn't?"

"We spoke to your aunt's GP this morning," said Patel. "She led us to believe that her doctors spent a great deal of time trying to reassure her that she was well."

"I don't understand; why would she tell me that she was seriously ill if she'd been told she was OK?"

Patel shrugged.

"That's the very question I was hoping you could help us answer," he said.

Alan Musgrove intervened. "We knew Joan was a hypochondriac," he said. "I imagine she told Sarah that her doctor had said she had cancer because she knew that otherwise we wouldn't believe her."

"That's not quite fair," said his wife.

"Come on, Sarah, you know what she was like," he said. "I'm afraid she was a bit like the boy who cried wolf at times."

Patel nodded and gave a hint of a smile.

"That makes sense," he said. "However, you are assuming that she killed herself and we are not yet convinced that that is the case."

"You surely don't think she was murdered?" said Musgrove, sitting forward in his chair.

"I'm afraid that remains a possibility, sir," said Patel. "However, it's too early in the investigation to reach any conclusions."

"Can I ask you what sort of work you do?" said Owen.

"I work for a London-based company that specialises in tunnel ventilation systems."

"I see," said Owen. "Does that mean you have a background in engineering?"

"Yes, I have a bachelor's degree in mechanical engineering."

"I presume you know about the workings of motor cars then."

"I'm not a car mechanic, but I understand how the things work," said Musgrove. "Where exactly is all this leading?"

"I was wondering if that means you could disable the brakes on a car," said Owen.

"I expect I could, but it would depend on what sort of car it was." Alan Musgrove frowned. "I'm getting the distinct impression that you are suggesting that I killed Joan," he said. "Even if I were able to tamper with her car, I wouldn't have done it, so you can forget that idea."

"As I've indicated," said Patel, "we can't rule out the possibility of murder. So far the only people we've been able to identify who would benefit from her death are you two."

"I suppose you mean Sarah's inheritance," said Musgrove. "I can assure you that we would rather have Joan alive and well than have the money."

"What a terrible thing to suggest," said Sarah, tears starting to trickle down her cheeks. "Alan wouldn't hurt Aunty, he was very fond of her."

"Nonetheless, I must ask you where you were on Monday night, sir," said Patel, fixing the witness with a steady stare.

"He was at home with me, of course," said Sarah.

"What time did you get home from work?" said Owen.

"It would have been about this time," said Musgrove.

"No, darling, you were late that night," said his wife. "You had a meeting that went on longer than usual."

Musgrove flashed an angry look at her.

"Yes, but I was still back here by seven, don't you remember?" he said.

"Oh yes, of course," she said rather unconvincingly.

"What route do you use to get home, Mr Musgrove?" asked Patel.

"I walk over London Bridge and take the Tube to Waterloo," he said. "Then I get a direct train to Kingston."

"After you got home that evening, did you go out again?" asked Patel.

"No I did not."

"Did either of you know that Miss Templeton was leaving her money to Mrs Musgrove?"

"We had absolutely no idea she was going to do it," said Alan Musgrove. "She didn't like talking about money."

Patel turned to Sarah.

"I do understand that this is hard for you but I'm sure that if your aunt was murdered you'd want us to find out who did it," he said. "We have to consider all possibilities and gather as much evidence as we can."

Sarah Musgrove returned his gaze but he could see that her lower lip was trembling.

"I don't know why you think she was murdered," she said. "I told you how depressed she was. Frankly I'm not surprised she took her own life. I was afraid something of the sort might happen. I'd told her to see someone about her depression but she said she wasn't depressed, just ill."

Patel frowned.

"You must admit that crashing a car is an odd way to kill yourself," he said.

"Yes, I suppose so," said Sarah, "but Aunty had a vivid imagination. That's how she came up with all those stories for her books. She'd have researched how to interfere with her car like she did when she was planning her novels. That's probably why she had a repair manual for the Camry."

"I thought you said it was research for a book," said Patel.

"That was my first thought when you came round before," she said. "Then it dawned on me: she bought it to help her plan her own suicide."

"Actually, I asked her to get it," said Alan Musgrove. "She used to get me to check her car from time to time."

"Oh yes, I'd forgotten," said Sarah, blushing.

Patel got up to leave.

"Thank you for your time," he said. "We'll be in touch if we need any more information."

Alan Musgrove rose and followed them into the hall.

"Next time I hope you'll have the decency to phone before you come round," he said as he showed them out. Patel said nothing.

"They're very keen to make us think it was suicide," said Owen once they were alone.

"Yes and his alibi depends on his wife and if he did do it she's probably in it up to her neck. How did you get on with the editor and the publisher?"

"It took me a while to get contact details for Edith Skinner. Anyway, I managed to reach her on the phone and I've arranged for us to talk to her on Monday. She said she'd prefer to come to the station. I got the phone number for the publisher and they told me the person who was taking care of the production of Joan Templeton's book is called Rose Austin. I got her extension number but she wasn't at her desk when I was put through and I ran out of time so I didn't call again."

"Never mind, we can do that on Monday as well."

*

When Sanjay got home Amber was watching TV.

"Your dinner's in the oven," she said. "Can you sort yourself out?"

"Of course, I'll have it in here on a tray."

While he was eating his portion of shepherd's pie, Amber's programme finished and she switched off the television.

"I'm nearly halfway through that manuscript," she said. "I'm really enjoying it. Shall I tell you about it?"

"Yes please."

"OK," she said, making herself comfortable in her seat. "A retired army officer is found dead with a pistol lying beside him on the right side of his body. At first it looks as if he shot himself and dropped the gun as he fell. However, Inspector Tewkesbury spots a set of left-handed golf clubs in the hall of the colonel's house and realises that the victim was left-handed. That means that the pistol should have been on the left side of the body, not the right."

"There's only one flaw in that argument," said Sanjay. "Some right-handed people play golf left-handed. Phil Mickelson is probably the best example."

Amber shook her head and glared at him.

"I might have guessed you'd pick holes in the story," she said. "And it's no surprise you used your nerdy knowledge of sports trivia to do it. I'm not even going to ask who Phil Mickelson is. Do you want me to carry on?"

"Sorry, darling."

"All right," she said. "Well, at first Tewkesbury can't discover a motive for the murder, but when he digs deeper into the colonel's past he finds that he has a lot of skeletons in his cupboard. Now he's got a list of suspects. Personally I think it was his ex-batman."

"Thanks for doing that," said Sanjay. "I really do appreciate it. Still, I'm rather afraid it's not going to help me solve my case."

"Did you really think it would?" said Amber.

"No, but I had to know what was in it," he said. "Just in case I was missing something."

"How did it go today?"

"We've made some progress," he said. "Miss Templeton's next of kin is convinced it was suicide and she may be right."

"You're not convinced?"

"Not entirely." He paused then added, "One other thing: have you read anything by Pearl Bailey?"

"Pearl Bailey," said Amber thoughtfully. "Oh yes, I did read a book by her once. I'm pretty sure I haven't got it now I think I borrowed it from a friend."

"What was it like?"

Amber smiled.

"It was called *Drucilla Wyngarde*," she said. "The only thing I can remember about it is the opening line: 'Drucilla dismounted, receiving maximum points for artistic impression. "That was great, Algy," she said, "can we do it again?"' It was hard not to read on after that."

"Sounds like soft porn to me," said Sanjay.

"Not really," said Amber. "It was funny rather than smutty. Basically, she's a romantic novelist."

"Apparently she was a friend of Joan Templeton's."

Amber looked surprised.

"Really?" she said "I'd have thought they'd have very little in common."

"From what you say, they certainly wrote very different stuff," said Patel. "It's just possible we'll need to interview her at some stage."

CHAPTER NINE

Edith Skinner was a plump, middle-aged woman. She had crammed herself into a black trouser suit with a cream collar, presumably with some difficulty. Her hair had been dragooned into loose curls, a style that did not entirely suit her, Patel thought. She deposited her large handbag on the table in the interview room and eyed the two policemen opposite her with a look that suggested a mixture of curiosity and disdain.

"I'm very grateful to you for coming in this morning," said Patel. "We're trying to build up a picture of what Miss Templeton was like so that we can try to understand how she came to die as she did."

"I am very happy to provide any information that I can," said Mrs Skinner.

"First of all, how long had you known Joan Templeton?"

"I first began editing her writing about fifteen years ago," she said. "I've been doing this kind of work for more than twenty years and I've edited manuscripts for a number of well-known authors during that time."

"What exactly does an editor do?" asked Patel.

"The problem with authors, and I know this because I am a published author myself, is that they are too close to their own work," said Mrs Skinner, seeming to swell with pride as she spoke. "They often can't see the inconsistencies in their storyline or the fact that a scenario they've created just isn't credible. Their characters are usually very real to them, but sometimes not to a third party. An editor comes to a piece of writing as a fresh pair of eyes and is able to point out these deficiencies. Then, of course, we have to point out errors of grammar and punctuation. Occasionally, we also make suggestions for major changes in the plot itself or the structure of a novel, though that's something that some authors find difficult to handle. To be a good editor you have to be brutally honest but deliver your hammer blows with sensitivity. You must support your author but never flatter them."

"Does this mean that you had a close relationship with Miss Templeton?" said Patel.

"We had a close professional relationship but I don't think that either of us would consider the other to be a friend," said Mrs Skinner firmly.

"When you were working on a book with her, did you meet regularly?"

"Most of our communication was done by email. During the course of any individual project, we'd probably only meet two or three times."

"When did you last see her in person?"

Mrs Skinner frowned.

"It must have been about a month ago," she said. "One of Joan's little foibles was that she liked to buy me lunch after we'd finished working on a book together. It was quite unnecessary; I was adequately paid to do the job and I didn't need any additional thanks or reward for my efforts, but she insisted."

"How did she seem when you met her on that occasion?"

"I'd say that she was her normal self," said Mrs Skinner. "She was particularly pleased to have finished this latest book, because it was a while since she'd completed anything. I think she had started to wonder if she'd finally run out of ideas."

"Oh really?" said Patel. "Would you say she seemed depressed?"

"No, she was quite cheerful actually."

"Did she say anything about being ill?"

Mrs Skinner raised her eyebrows.

"She knew better than to broach the subject of her health with me," she said. "I had no sympathy with her obsessive preoccupation with the state of her bodily functions. I had to endure it in the early days of our association but, when I felt that we knew each other well enough, I made it clear that I didn't want to hear any more about her belly ache or her dizziness or her disgusting preoccupation with her nasal secretions. My late husband was something of a hypochondriac as well, but compared to Joan his morbid introspection was trivial."

"Would you say she was the sort of person who might take her own life?"

"I am really not qualified to answer that question," said Mrs Skinner. "If you want my opinion I'd say it is highly unlikely that she would have been able to go through with something like that. The idea might have come to her but she wouldn't have the courage to actually do it."

Patel was about to conclude the interview when another thought came to him.

"Did you ever go to her house?" he asked.

"Yes, we usually met there," she said. "I prefer not to invite clients to my home so I normally go to them or we meet in a coffee shop or some such place."

"Did she offer you alcohol when you went there?"

Mrs Skinner folded her arms and eyed Patel haughtily.

"I can assure you, Sergeant, that I never imbibed anything stronger than a cup of tea when I was at Joan's house," she said.

"Do you know of anyone else she was in regular touch with?"

"There was her agent, of course, but no doubt you've spoken to her already."

"We haven't as it happens," said Patel. "Do you know his or her name?"

"It's Susan Sharpe," said Mrs Skinner. "She works for an agency called Parker Nesbitt. They have offices somewhere in central London I think. I imagine you'll be able to find them online without too much difficulty."

"Thank you, we'll do that," said Patel. "You've been most helpful. I don't think we need to take up any more of your time."

*

"I'm glad we spoke to that lady," said Patel when they were back in the CID office. "She gives a rather different picture of Miss Joan Templeton. It's a shame their last meeting wasn't closer to the date of her death. I can't help feeling that the niece and her husband have been leading us up the garden path."

"If they had nothing to hide," said Owen, "you'd have thought that they wouldn't have suggested it was suicide. After all, working out what happened is our job."

"Yes, it's looking more and more like murder but there's a lack of solid evidence," said Patel. "Have we got the results of her blood alcohol yet?"

"Hang on, I'll check the post."

Owen left the room and returned moments later holding a piece of paper. "The blood alcohol was a hundred milligrams per litre. Dr Jarvis says here that there was alcohol in her stomach contents and urine as well. She also says that the levels were similar in the blood and urine and that the whole picture suggests that she had been drinking just before she got into her car."

"The blood level is over the legal limit but not astronomical," said Patel thoughtfully. "Still, it's got to be considered a contributory factor to her death."

"Perhaps the killer tampered with the brakes early on the morning of the crash, rather than the night before," said Owen. "He might even have encouraged her to have a drink or two and then popped out and buggered the car."

Patel nodded.

"She would certainly have allowed Alan Musgrove into the house if he'd come round early on the morning of the accident," he said. "I suppose it's also possible that he could have persuaded her to have a drink with him. He might even have spiked the sherry with something else. Did they check her blood sample for sedatives?"

"Yes, but they didn't find any."

"OK, so that's one possibility we can cross off the list." Patel shook his head. "It's hard to believe that she would have agreed to take a drink in her nephew's presence though," he said. "Drinking at breakfast time is the sort of thing you'd expect from an alcoholic."

"The niece said she hardly ever drank, but she had all that sherry in the kitchen," said Owen. "I reckon she was a secret drinker."

"That's pretty typical of alcoholism," said Patel. "It also seems to be a more plausible explanation for the blood alcohol level."

"Thinking about it," said Owen, "I find it hard to believe that he could have tampered with her car while she was in the house."

"I take your point," said Patel. "Maybe there was something wrong with the car and she asked him to take a look."

"Possibly," said Owen. "If that's what happened he must have decided to kill her on the spur of the moment."

"Maybe he'd been looking for an opportunity and grabbed this one when it came along."

Owen nodded enthusiastically.

"Yes, and maybe Sarah Musgrove knew nothing about it," he said. "You know what, I reckon it's more likely that the brakes were buggered the night before the crash. The killer would have had to get up very early to be round there before she left the house that morning. And another thing, Alan Musgrove could have made up the story about working late to cover up the fact that he'd been to Beachcroft Road on the way home."

"Yes, we need to find out exactly where he works," said Patel, running his fingers through his hair. "What I still don't understand is why she got into the car early on the morning of her death, despite the fact that she'd been drinking. It seems out of character."

"Maybe she always had a sherry at breakfast time."

"Maybe. What about the fingerprints?"

"The results aren't through yet."

Patel swung round in his chair to face his desk.

"All right, I want you to pull together all the evidence we've got so far and get it to Chief Inspector Taylor so that she has a chance to look over it before we meet with her this afternoon," he said. "In the meantime I'm going to phone the publisher."

Patel dialled the number of Romulus Books and asked to be put through to Rose Austin's extension. The phone rang but at first no one answered. Then, just as Sanjay was about to ring off, someone picked up the receiver.

"Rosie Austin here, how can I help you?" said a youthful voice.

"This is Sergeant Patel from Merton CID here," he said. "I understand that you've been working on the latest book by Joan Templeton."

"Yes, that's right, though everything's in limbo at the moment because she passed away."

"Had you worked with her on other books?"

"Gosh no, I've only been with the company for two years," said Rose. "Her last book came out ages ago."

"Did you meet her at all?"

"Oh no, I hardly ever meet our clients," she said. "We do all the work by email and letter."

"What was she like to work with?"

"Well, quite frankly, she was a bit of a nightmare. She wasn't good at answering emails; I don't know whether she didn't look at her inbox very often or if it was because she just didn't get round to replying. This book has taken much longer to get to this stage than is the case for most of our other writers."

"Did you get any impression of what she was like as a person?"

"I'd say she was rather obsessional," she said. "We've had an unusually long series of exchanges at the copy-editing stage and we're already on the third set of proofs."

"This may be a hard question to answer," said Patel. "Did you think she seemed depressed?"

"I honestly couldn't say," said Rose. "I mean, it's not like I really knew her. Why don't you talk to her agent?"

"We are planning to speak to her in the near future," said Patel. "Thanks for your time. Just as a matter of interest, will *The Riddle of the Silent Soldier* be published?"

"Oh yes, we've invested too much in it to just let it drop. We'll finish the proofreading in house and get it out there as soon as we can. It seems awful to say it, but her being dead may actually boost the sales."

CHAPTER TEN

Chief Inspector Taylor studied the pile of reports while eating a sandwich and drinking from a large paper cup of coffee. Glancing at her watch she noted that she only had another five minutes before Patel and Owen were due to arrive to discuss the case. There was no way that she could read all the evidence they had collected before they arrived, so they would just have to fill her in on the rest. She noted with approval that they arrived on time.

"I'd like you to summarise the evidence you've gathered so far, so that I can get an overview of the case," she said.

Patel went through everything in detail, trying not to leave out anything important. When he had finished, Taylor leaned forward in her chair.

"Now you've got more information, do you think it's murder or not?" she said.

"On balance, I think that's the more likely explanation for the facts as we know them," said Patel. "I think we should launch a full murder enquiry."

Tracy Taylor looked pensive.

"I can see that the Musgroves had a motive for killing her, but do we know whether or not they knew that the money was coming to Sarah? Some people are very secretive about their wills."

"I put that question to Mr and Mrs Musgrove," said Patel. "The husband said that Miss Templeton didn't like discussing money."

"It's an important point," said Taylor. "It's hard to believe anyone would plan a murder on the off chance that they might get a legacy, even when that person is likely to be a beneficiary, as in this case. I can also see that Alan Musgrove's alibi is distinctly dubious but you need to confirm if he really did work late that night or not."

"We were planning to do that."

"Where was this car parked and how easy would it have been for someone to get at?" she asked.

Patel and Owen looked at each other.

"I imagine it stood on the street in front of the house," said Owen.

"You're not sure?"

"I don't think there was anywhere else she could have left it," said Owen. "It's permit-parking on that street and as a home owner she would have been entitled to one."

"But you don't know she had one."

"No."

"Well, you'd better find out, hadn't you?" said Taylor.

"Yes, boss."

Taylor sat back in her chair and chewed on a pen she was holding in her left hand.

"From what you've told me it seems that passers-by would have been able to see the car while the killer was working on it," she said. "That's assuming it was parked on the street as you suggest."

"Yes, I suppose so," said Owen.

"Surely someone who was planning to do the old girl in wouldn't have wanted to be seen while they were tampering with the car?"

"Alan Musgrove is the obvious suspect for that very reason," said Patel. "He was a regular visitor to the house and the neighbours might well know him by sight. If they asked him what he was doing he could say that his aunt had asked him to check the car for her."

"That works for the neighbours," said Taylor, "but what about a stranger? The last thing a murderer wants is someone who can identify him or her."

"It's quite likely that the brake lines were cut from below," said Patel. "In that case the murderer's face would have been hidden from view under the car while he or she was doing it."

Taylor nodded.

"All right, you've obviously thought it through very carefully so I'll authorise a full investigation," she said. "When's the inquest?"

"This afternoon," said Owen.

"You'll need to attend but it's unlikely it'll turn up anything useful," said Taylor. "OK, I'll be the CIO of course and we'll need a bigger team. We've got Colin Brewer, Mike Pringle and Shelly Drake for starters. Brian Todd should be able to join you the day after tomorrow and we'll get more bodies as and when they become available. I'll request the setting up of an incident room and we'll have a meeting of the full team tomorrow morning. OK, off you go then."

*

As expected the inquest was opened and adjourned, having heard evidence from Patel, Dr Jarvis and Sarah Musgrove. Mrs Musgrove had not deviated from the story she had told previously, but she did omit her speculations about her aunt having committed suicide.

When it was all over, Alison Jarvis turned to Patel and smiled.

"Sounds like you've still got a lot of work to do on this case," she said. Patel nodded. "For what it's worth I don't buy the suicide story," she continued. "There are many easier ways to do yourself in."

"It's also an odd way to commit murder," said Patel. "The trouble is I can't see how it could have been an accident."

"I have to agree with you there," said Dr Jarvis.

As they walked out together a young woman in jeans confronted them.

"Mary Ogundipe, *South London Echo*," she said, flashing an identity card. "I'd like to ask you some questions about the death of Joan Templeton."

"I don't have any comment to make at the moment," said Patel, trying to slip past her. "We'll be making a statement to the press in due course."

The reporter blocked his way.

"This lady was kind of like a local celebrity," she said. "I think my readers are entitled to know what you're doing to catch her killer."

"You'll have to excuse me," said Dr Jarvis and headed off in the direction of her car.

"We haven't established that she was murdered as yet," said Patel. "I'm not prepared to speculate on the basis of inadequate information."

"Oh come on," said the reporter. "Your seniors don't put an officer from the Major Investigation Team on a case if there isn't reason to think that a serious crime's been committed."

"I'm sorry, I've nothing more to say." He slipped past the woman and headed down the street.

"I'll be writing an article for my paper," the reporter called after him. "And it won't just be about the inquest."

Chapter Eleven

The following morning Chief Inspector Taylor held a detailed briefing for the officers who had been assigned to the case in the newly established incident room, which was equipped with computers and flip charts and had a large pinboard taking up most of one wall. The team sat around a large table while the DCI stood at its head. She was wearing a trouser suit with a short jacket that showed off her neat figure to good effect. She began by asking Patel to outline all the evidence suggesting that Joan Templeton had been murdered in order to bring the new team members up to speed. Patel remained seated as he spoke and tried to sound calm and knowledgeable, though he felt anything but.

"There remains the possibility that it was suicide rather than murder," he said in conclusion. "Think about it: we know she had a reason to be depressed, even though her health problems were imaginary rather than real, and she had a repair manual for her car in her house. Her niece's husband says he asked her to buy it but that doesn't mean she didn't use it to work out how to disable the brakes on her car. Maybe she reached a point where everything got on top of her, so she cut the brake lines and deliberately crashed it early the next morning."

"That's an interesting idea," said Brewer, with a half smile. "However, suicides usually leave a note and my understanding is you haven't found one."

"Actually only about a third of people committing suicide leave a note," said Patel. "Also it's just possible there's one in the house that we've overlooked."

"Seems unlikely," said Brewer, smirking. "In any case, if you were going to kill yourself, would you really go to all this trouble rather than taking some pills or connecting your exhaust to a hose and sticking it through the window of your car?"

"I agree with you," said Taylor, "but we can't afford to dismiss any possibilities at this stage. I want Pringle and Drake to go back to the victim's house and make sure we haven't missed a suicide note or any other clues that might suggest suicide, or anything else for that matter. Patel and Owen have been all over it already but you may spot something they've missed. In particular, I want you to try and find a spare set of keys for the Camry. If they're not there, it could mean that the killer somehow got hold of them so that he or she could get access to the car without arousing suspicion. That shouldn't take you long, so after that I want you to talk to any neighbours who are at home and find out if any of them saw someone working on that car during the relevant time period. Also ask them what they know about the deceased.

"Brewer and Owen can go to Alan Musgrove's place of work. The company's called Ventilation Solutions; I've got the address here. Talk to his workmates and in particular find out if the meeting he says he was at on the afternoon before she died really took place. When you're done meet me back here for more orders. This morning I have an appointment to see Dr Mervin Hackwood, the doctor who was treating Miss Templeton just before she died. Patel can come with me. All right, let's get on with it."

*

Patel had arranged for them to interview Dr Hackwood at a local private hospital. He was a slightly built man in his forties with short hair and blue eyes. He wore a dark grey suit teamed with a white shirt and a purple tie. He gave a forced smile as Taylor and Patel entered his consulting room and invited them to take a seat in one of the leather chairs that were arranged facing his large mahogany desk.

"I gather you want to talk about Joan Templeton," he said. "I was so sorry to hear that she'd been killed but I didn't really expect her death to be a police matter."

"There is clear evidence that her car had been tampered with, either by the lady herself or someone else," said Taylor. "Sergeant Patel here is going to ask you some questions about her state of health when you last saw her."

The doctor nodded and consulted a folder that was lying on his desk.

"She was referred by her general practitioner because of recurrent abdominal pain for which he could find no cause," he said. "I examined her and sent her for some relevant investigations. When she returned for a follow-up appointment the week before last, I was able to tell her that all the results were normal."

"How did she react to that news?" asked Patel.

"With disbelief," said the doctor. "She was absolutely convinced that there was something seriously wrong with her. I tried to reassure her as best I could but I don't think she was convinced."

"Do you think she was depressed?"

"That's not how I would describe her state of mind," said Dr Hackwood. "I thought she was suffering from anxiety rather than depression." The doctor paused before adding: "I should say that I'm not a psychiatrist, but the reality is that a lot of my time is spent dealing with patients whose problems are psychological rather than physical."

"Yes I see," said Patel. "Did you suggest any treatment?"

Hackwood consulted the folder again.

"I thought about asking her doctor to prescribe a benzodiazepine, but decided against it," he said. "Some patients become dependent on that type of medication and I thought that there was a strong chance of that happening in Miss Templeton's case. I offered her a review consultation in three months' time so that she didn't feel abandoned and suggested that she kept a food diary to see if her symptoms were triggered by anything in particular."

"Did you think she was suicidal?"

Hackwood raised his eyebrows.

"No I didn't," he said. "There are some patients who have a psychological need for what is sometimes called 'the sick role'. It probably arises from a deep-seated need to elicit sympathy from family and friends. I think that Joan Templeton would have been lost without her symptoms."

"Don't you think they were really a cry for help?" said Patel. "Some people with psychiatric disease present with physical symptoms."

"That's undoubtedly true," said Dr Hackwood. "Are you suggesting I should have sent her to see a psychiatrist?"

"Possibly," said Patel.

The doctor looked down his nose at the detective.

"I had the very strong impression that she would have refused to agree to a suggestion of that sort," he said.

Tracy Taylor gave the doctor one of her radiant smiles.

"Thank you very much, Doctor," she said. "I'm sorry to have taken up so much of your time."

When they were back in the car she said: "I know all about your background but we're investigating a probable murder, not trying to second-guess her doctors. You're a detective now, not a shrink."

"Sorry, Chief Inspector," said Patel. "It won't happen again."

CHAPTER TWELVE

Patel sat at a computer in the incident room staring blankly at the screen. He was still smarting from the chief inspector's rebuke. He hadn't intended to annoy the consultant physician, only to engage in a debate about a topic that interested him. Still, she was right; he was a detective now, not a medical student with a naturally enquiring mind. The door opened and he looked up to see Brewer and Owen enter.

"How did you get on?" he asked.

"Where's DCI Taylor?" said Brewer, avoiding eye contact with Patel.

"She's in her office reading the pathologist's report on the post-mortem."

"You seen it?"

"Yes."

"Anything useful in it?"

Patel shrugged.

"Not really," he said. "It doesn't add anything to what she told us herself."

At that moment Tracy Taylor came into the room and perched on the edge of the table.

"What did Musgrove's workmates have to say?" she asked.

"The people we spoke to confirmed he was at a meeting on the afternoon before Miss Templeton died, like he said," said Brewer. "Mind you, it was over by five o'clock. I think it's unlikely he would have had time to get over to Beachcroft Road, bugger the brakes and still get home before seven as he claims he did, but that needs to be checked. It wouldn't surprise me if he lied about the time he got home. The problem is going to be finding a witness who can confirm when he arrived."

"Did you ask what time he normally finished work?" said Patel.

"We did," said Owen. "One of his colleagues said that it was supposed to be five o'clock but it wasn't unusual for him to be still in the office until six."

Taylor frowned.

"So he finished work at the normal time that afternoon," she said. "As I recall he said he was home around seven when you interviewed him and that his wife corrected him. It could mean that they'd agreed a story beforehand and she fluffed her lines or that he hadn't had a chance to tell her what to say. I'd like some of you to talk to the Musgroves' neighbours and find out if one of them saw him come home. There's another thing that's bothering me: how difficult is it to disable the braking system on a car? Could anyone do it, or would you need specialist knowledge?"

"A mate of mine's a mechanic," said Owen. "I could ask him. He works in a Toyota garage too, so he'd know about this type of car."

"Good idea," said Taylor. "Maybe you and Patel could pop round and see him. Where does he work?"

"In that Toyota garage by the Kingston bypass."

*

Owen's friend Reg was a powerfully built man in his early forties with an aura of stale sweat and engine oil. Owen introduced him to Patel and, having established that this was not a social call, he got a colleague to take over the job he was doing. They retired to the mechanics' tearoom and Owen explained the details of the crash and the way in which it had been caused.

74

"I get the picture," said Reg. "It wouldn't be a difficult thing to do, but you'd need to know a bit about modern braking systems. They all use hydraulics to activate the brakes when you press the pedal, so if there's a leak in the system, they fail. But, nowadays you've got a master cylinder with two pistons and two separate lines feeding the front and rear brakes. If there's a leak in one of them, the master cylinder continues to function as a single piston system. That means that you've got to cut both brake lines to stop them working. If you just do one of them, the front or rear brakes will continue to function. In those circumstances you'd just have to push harder on the pedal. The master cylinder is fed from a reservoir and when the fluid gets low a sensor triggers a warning light in the car, so the driver knows there's a problem."

"Where is the master cylinder located?" asked Patel. "Is it easy to get at?"

"It's under the bonnet," said Reg. "The exact location depends on the model. What kind of car did you say it was?"

"A Camry," said Owen. "It's probably about two years old."

"OK then it's not quite so simple," said Reg. "They've got what we call a 'brake booster system' using the vacuum in the engine's manifold. What that means is that when you press the brake pedal the brake booster increases the force applied to the fluid in the master cylinder."

"But you can still disable the brakes by cutting the lines?" said Patel, trying to prevent a note of irritation creeping into his voice.

"Oh yeah."

A thought occurred to Patel and he turned to Owen.

"Where was Miss Templeton's car serviced?" he asked.

"I don't know," said Owen.

"We're the local Toyota main dealer," said Reg. "I could check and see if we did the servicing on the vehicle if you like. Have you got the registration number?"

"Yes please," said Patel. "Have you got the number, Paul?"

Owen consulted his notebook and scribbled on a piece of paper.

Reg went out and returned ten minutes later with a folder in his hand.

"We supplied the car to the lady and did the servicing on it," he said. "She brought it in whenever a service was due, so we've got a complete record for the vehicle. It was last in two months ago."

"Were there any problems with the car at that time?" asked Patel.

Reg flipped open the folder.

"No," he said. "It was just a routine service."

"Would you have checked the brakes then?"

Reg consulted the folder again.

"Yeah, they were checked and found to be in working order."

On the way back to the police station Patel said: "It seems to me that the murderer has got to be either someone who knows a lot about cars or was prepared to find out about the subject. That makes Alan Musgrove an even more likely suspect in my book."

"It seems to me it's unlikely that the killer's a woman," said Owen. "It's all a bit too technical for the female brain."

"Oh I don't know so much," said Patel. "You get women mechanics nowadays. Still, I don't think Sarah Musgrove falls into that category."

"What's our next move then?"

Patel checked the time.

"It's a bit late to start on anything else today," he said. "I'll see you in the morning, all right?"

CHAPTER THIRTEEN

When Chief Inspector Taylor arrived for the morning briefing she noted that Colin Brewer was absent.

"Where's Inspector Brewer?" she said.

"He's got a dental appointment," said Mike Pringle, a fresh-faced young DC who had recently joined the team. "He said he'll be with us about ten."

"I see," said Taylor. "Paul, you went to Musgrove's place of work with him, didn't you? Perhaps you can fill the others in on what you found out."

Owen told them that Musgrove had attended a departmental meeting on the afternoon before Miss Templeton's death. He had stayed on afterwards to write up the minutes, or at least that was what he had told a departing colleague.

"Apparently he always does that," he said. "Everyone says Alan Musgrove is a hard worker and a good colleague. He's been with the firm for about five years. One bloke said Musgrove had said something about being short of money. It seems none of them have had a pay rise for quite a while."

"If they're in debt they might have seen killing Miss Templeton as a way out of their problems," said Taylor. "We'd better look into their finances in more detail. Pringle, you make a start on that this morning."

"Right, boss," said Pringle.

"It would help if we could establish that they knew about the will," Taylor continued. "They deny it but that doesn't prove they were in the dark about the legacy. Quite frankly, if the inheritance came as a surprise to them, there's no motive."

"We could ask her lawyer," said Patel.

Taylor turned to face him.

"You can do that this morning," she said. "Of course, as they're her only next of kin they might reasonably have expected something, but the real question is: did they know how much the old girl was worth?"

"The house was obviously worth a bit," said Owen. "Mind you, she might have had a mortgage."

Taylor nodded.

"We'll need to check on that," she said. "Anyway, Mike and Shelly, how did you get on in Beachcroft Road?"

"We didn't find a suicide note or a set of car keys," said Pringle.

"Did you discover anything by talking to the neighbours?"

"A lot of them were out," said Drake, a heavily built young woman whose hair was cut very short. "The lady who lives next door said Joan Templeton pretty much kept herself to herself. She passed the time of day with her occasionally but that was it. She didn't even know that she was a writer."

"An old bloke down the street said he saw her out walking in the afternoons sometimes," said Pringle. "He knew she lived nearby, but he never spoke to her."

"All right," said Taylor, "you two can get back down there and try and talk to some more neighbours. Are there any local shops?"

"Only a newsagent and that's not very close to the house," said Drake.

"Still worth checking out," said Taylor. "Shelly, you can go in there and talk to the staff to find out if they knew her. If she was a regular customer she might have chatted to them when she went in." Drake pulled a face. "Owen can go to Kingston and talk to the Musgroves' neighbours; try and find out more about

78

them and ask if they know anything about them having money trouble. Also ask if any of them saw Alan Musgrove come home on the evening before the murder. DC Brian Todd is joining the team later this morning so I'm going to fill him in on what we know so far. After that I'll send him down to Kingston to help Paul. If Inspector Brewer chooses to favour us with his presence later on, I'll send him as well. What about the victim's agent?"

"I have an appointment with her this afternoon," said Patel.

*

Patel checked the contact details for Joan Templeton's solicitors. The firm of Byers and Knox had an address in the centre of Croydon. He dialled the number and was put through to a Mrs Bulstrode by the receptionist.

"I understand you handle the affairs of the late Joan Templeton," he said when she answered.

"That's right," said the lawyer in a cut-glass accent. "I've acted for her since I first became a partner here."

"You very kindly sent us a copy of her will and the provisions are straightforward but I was wondering whether anyone, other than Miss Templeton, had a copy?"

"We have one in the office, of course," she replied, "and it says here that we were asked to send one to her executor."

"Who's that?"

"Her niece, a Mrs Sarah Musgrove."

Patel could feel the hairs standing up on the back of his neck.

"You're certain of that?" he said.

"Absolutely."

"I'd really like to get a signed statement from you. Would it be OK if I came to your office this morning?"

"I suppose so," said the lawyer. "I could fit you in around eleven if that's convenient."

"I'll be there."

Patel put down the phone and sat back in his chair. It was now clear that Alan Musgrove had lied to him, unless his wife hadn't told him about the will. Somehow that seemed unlikely. Alan Musgrove would have to be confronted with this new evidence in the near future. He would have to come up with a very good reason for his failure to disclose this information if he was to avoid becoming their number-one suspect.

*

The lawyer's office was sandwiched between a fast-food outlet and a shop selling second-hand gadgets. Patel arrived on time but was kept waiting for twenty minutes. The lawyer was full of apologies when he was eventually shown into her office. She was a woman in her fifties with thick grey hair and old-fashioned glasses that gave her a rather severe appearance.

After she had signed the statement she hesitated before passing it to Patel.

"Why all this interest in my client's will?" she said. "It all seems pretty straightforward to me."

"We are conducting an investigation into the circumstances of Miss Templeton's death," said Patel.

The lawyer frowned.

"My understanding is that she died in a car crash."

"I'm not at liberty to go into details," said Patel. "However, there are some aspects of the circumstances that need to be investigated."

"I see," said the lawyer. "Do you think she committed suicide?"

"Why do you ask that?"

"Miss Templeton took out a large life assurance policy six months ago," she said. "I advised her which company to approach, so I know they won't pay out if she took her own life."

"Do you know why she did that?" said Patel.

"She'd got it into her head she hadn't got long to live," said the lawyer. "The insurers required her to have a medical examination before issuing the policy. To her apparent surprise the report said she was in good health and so the company agreed to insure her."

"According to the terms of the will, Mrs Musgrove will be the beneficiary of the payout, won't she?"

"That's correct. She told me she wanted the policy to make sure her niece was well provided for."

*

Back in the office Patel sat at his desk thinking about what he'd just learned. It seemed very odd that the Musgroves had suggested that Miss Templeton had committed suicide when that would lead to them losing part of their inheritance. It could mean that they weren't as interested in the victim's money as he had thought. On the other hand, perhaps they had decided that the provisions of the will would yield a big enough return and their suicide theory really was a ploy to cover up the murder.

At that moment Colin Brewer came bursting into the office. His face fell when he saw Patel.

"I hope Pringle told Tracy I had to go to the dentist," he said.

"Yes he did," said Patel.

"I woke up with bad toothache," said Brewer, touching his right cheek. "They had to take it out."

"Are you OK to work?"

"Oh yes, I've had some painkillers and antibiotics."

"I've just been talking to Miss Templeton's solicitor," said Patel. "The Musgroves knew about the contents of the will."

Brewer's face brightened.

"Did they?" he said. "That's a turn-up for the book. Sounds like we'll be making an arrest sooner rather than later."

Patel's initial enthusiasm had diminished as he thought about the inconsistencies in the picture that was emerging. He wasn't sure what to make of it all.

"Don't you think it's odd they lied about it though?" he said. "They must have known we'd speak to her lawyers. It seems such an elementary mistake."

Brewer shrugged.

"They didn't think it through," he said. "You caught them on the hop."

"Oh what a tangled web we weave," muttered Patel.

"You what?" said Brewer.

"Oh what a tangled web we weave when first we practise to deceive."

Chapter Fourteen

The offices of Parker Nesbitt, literary agents, occupied the ground floor of a Victorian house in a largely residential street on the edge of Camden Town. Patel was met at the door by a young woman in jeans who introduced herself as Faith and led him to a door on the right side of the hallway. She knocked and waited for an answer. Soon they were in what would have probably been the back parlour of the house when it was originally built. In the centre of the room was a desk on which stood a computer. To its left was an in tray piled high with bundles of paper. There were bookshelves on two of the walls displaying a varied selection of books neatly arranged according to size rather than content. A woman in her thirties came forward to greet him.

"I'm Susan Sharpe, do have a seat," she said.

Patel chose one of the armchairs that were arranged in a semicircle in front of the desk and Susan Sharpe subsided into another. She was tall and very thin with dark curly hair, cut short, and large-framed glasses.

"I understand you want to ask me about Joan Templeton," she said. "I'm not sure I'm going to be much help. The thing is, I only started working with her three years ago and during that time she's only produced one book, *The Riddle of the Silent Soldier*, so I've actually had very little to do with her."

"Oh I see," said Patel. "Who was her agent before you took her on?"

"My predecessor, Anne Gregory," said Sharpe. "She acted for her from her first novel onwards."

"Where is she now?" asked Patel.

"She lives down in Thames Ditton," said the agent. "She retired early to look after her husband who wasn't well. He's since passed away. She pops in from time to time to see how we're getting on and if she can help out, so I know for sure she's still there."

"I may need to talk to Mrs Gregory," said Patel. "Do you have an address for her?"

Susan Sharpe eased herself out of her chair and went across to the desk. She leaned forward so that she could see the screen of her computer and operated the mouse. Then she wrote on a piece of paper and returned to her seat.

"There you are," she said, handing it to Patel.

"What did you make of the lady when you did come into contact with her?" he asked.

Susan Sharpe adjusted her spectacles.

"She was rather quiet and unforthcoming," she said. "Some writers are like that; after all, they generally have a solitary existence so it's not really surprising that they aren't very sociable."

Patel nodded.

"When was the last time you saw her?" he said.

Sharpe pursed her lips.

"It was four or five weeks ago," she said. "We went over the details of the contract with her publishers for the new book."

"How did she seem to you then?"

"Pretty much her normal self, I'd say," said Sharpe. "The contract was pretty straightforward, so she didn't stay long."

"Would you say she was depressed?"

Susan Sharpe shook her head.

"No, not really," she said. "She was always rather taciturn, but I wouldn't say that she was any less chatty than normal. She even smiled once or twice, if I remember rightly." She paused and looked at Patel quizzically. "Given the fact that you're a detective, I have to assume that you are treating Joan Templeton's death as suspicious. The line of your questioning makes me think that you suspect suicide. Am I right?"

"That's one possibility," said Patel.

Susan Sharpe raised her eyebrows.

"So you think it could be murder?" she said.

"We don't have enough evidence to establish the background to her death."

"I read in the paper that she died in a car crash," said Sharpe with a half smile. "If she was murdered, it would be a scenario even more bizarre than some of the things she wrote in her books."

Patel grinned.

"It sounds as if you weren't a fan of her writing," he said.

Susan Sharpe shrugged.

"I can't say her work was really to my taste," she said, "but she was a commercially successful author, so my opinion about its literary merit is neither here nor there."

"It can't be easy to sell stuff that you don't much like to publishers."

"Most of the authors on my list were taken on by the agency after I joined them," said Sharpe. "I'm passionate about their work and I do my best to get it into print. The simple truth about Joan Templeton's books was that they didn't need selling. Her publishers were delighted to get another Inspector Tewkesbury story from her because they knew it would fly off the shelves. Whatever you or I think about her work, she has a very loyal readership who will devour the new book as they have all her others."

"I am aware of that," said Patel. "My wife's a big fan as it happens."

"What about you?" said Susan Sharpe with a wry smile. "Do you read detective stories in your spare time?"

"I have enough involvement with crime during the week," said Patel. "Come the weekend, I'm looking for a different kind of escapism."

Susan Sharpe smiled broadly.

"I will say this for her," she said. "She maintained the standard of her writing better than a lot of authors. *The Riddle of the Silent Soldier* is as good, or at least no worse, than her other books. There are some original elements in the plot and she keeps her readers guessing until the end; well, at least I didn't work out who'd done it. There are some authors who get themselves a reputation based on their first few books and then produce stuff that, if a first-time author had written it, would end up on the slush pile. It still gets published because of their name and people buy it for the same reason. Still, ours is not to reason why."

"One other thing," said Patel. "The lady's niece said she was friendly with another writer, Pearl Bailey. Do you know her by any chance?"

"I do," said Ms Sharpe. "She's another of my clients. And before you ask, I'm not a fan of her work either. Actually, if I had to choose between them I'd rather read something by Joan Templeton."

"Was she a client of your predecessor as well?"

"Yes she was."

Patel got to his feet.

"I mustn't take up any more of your time," he said. "Thank you for your help."

*

As he was walking back to his car, Patel reflected on the picture of the victim that had emerged so far. It was clear that she was a solitary, rather neurotic individual but they had failed to uncover anything that could be considered a clear-cut motive for suicide. A number of witnesses they had spoken to had not seen the victim close to the time of her death, but there was nothing to suggest that anything significant had changed in the writer's life during the period immediately before her demise.

The evidence seemed to exclude the possibility of accidental death, which left murder as the only other possibility. The trouble was that she could easily have survived if she had known what to do to slow the car and kept a level head. The killer must have been counting on her ignorance of the functioning of the brakes and gears on her car. He, or she, must also have had reason to believe that she would panic when she tried to brake and got no response. This in turn implied that the killer knew the victim very well indeed and the only people who appeared to fall into that category were Sarah and Alan Musgrove.

It occurred to him that Alan Musgrove might have bought the manual for the Camry and placed it in the house after disabling the car's braking system to make the police think that Miss Templeton had planned her own death, despite his assertion that he had asked her to buy it. He wasn't sure if the book had been checked for fingerprints and resolved to look into this when he got back to the station. Alan Musgrove's fingerprints would almost certainly be on it so this line of enquiry might get him nowhere. But what if there was another set of fingerprints that didn't belong to Musgrove or Miss Templeton?

Sarah Musgrove had suggested that the car manual had been purchased by her aunt as part of her research for a book. He made a mental note to ask Amber if a Toyota Camry featured in *The Riddle of the Silent Soldier*. If this proved not to be the case, there remained the possibility that the author had started on another story. A cursory inspection of her computer had not revealed any evidence of this, but a more thorough inspection was warranted.

In any case, at the time of his second interview with Sarah Musgrove she had changed her story and suggested that her aunt had acquired the manual so that she could plan her own death. She had presented both these explanations as being speculative so the change of story might not be significant. After all, she had had time to think about the reason for the purchase of the manual after the two policemen had left. It was odd that she had made these suggestions despite the fact that her husband said he had asked Miss Templeton to buy the manual, but perhaps he hadn't told her about his request.

On his way back to the station Patel did an Internet search on his mobile phone to find out the opening time for the Wimbledon branch of Waitrose. The answer was 8am, so Paul Owen was right. Miss Templeton would not have left around six thirty to go shopping there, but she might have been going to a store with twenty-four-hour opening. A further search revealed that the nearest one was in New Malden, in completely the opposite direction to the route she had taken. So where was she going? Of course Sarah Musgrove couldn't have known where her aunt had been headed, so her answer had been pure speculation. Still, it left another loose end that would have to be followed up.

There would be a need to re-interview both Sarah Musgrove and her husband, probably under caution, but Patel suspected that Tracy Taylor would want to wait until the results of the forensic tests were available.

*

When Patel returned home that evening, he found Amber in the sitting room leafing through a magazine. "I finished reading that manuscript today," she said. "I really enjoyed it."

"I don't suppose the story featured a Toyota Camry," he said.

"No, the colonel had an old Jaguar and Inspector Tewkesbury always drives his beloved Alvis," said Amber. "Why do you ask?"

"It's to do with the case," said Sanjay. "I thought it was a long shot and it turns out I was right."

"You won't be surprised to hear that the colonel didn't commit suicide," said Amber. "I was wrong about the batman though. The killer turned out to be a nephew who was short of money."

"Now that is interesting," said Sanjay. "The prime suspect in my case is the husband of the victim's niece. If it turns out that he did it, it's almost as if Joan Templeton was prophesying the manner of her own death."

Amber laughed.

"That's a bit far-fetched, isn't it?" she said.

Sanjay sighed.

"You're right," he said, "I'm letting my imagination get the better of me."

Amber's eyes widened.

"Oh yes, I nearly forgot," she said, "there's a piece in the local paper about the case. You might want to read it."

Sanjay read the article and then threw the paper down in disgust.

"Bloody journalists," he said. "If they can't get the facts they need for a story they make stuff up."

"At least she described you as a 'senior detective'," said Amber.

"That's all very well, but I'd rather she'd just written a short piece about the inquest and left my name out of it. DCI Taylor will get the idea that I've been giving interviews without discussing it with her."

"Surely not?"

"Oh I think so," said Sanjay ruefully. "She'll come down on me like a ton of bricks if she thinks I'm in the wrong."

"She sounds like a pretty scary woman," said Amber.

Sanjay shook his head.

"She's OK really," he said. "It's just that I feel she's checking up on me all the time and trying to find fault."

"Well, you are new," said Amber. "She'll back off when she sees how capable you are."

Chapter Fifteen

"How did you get on in Kingston yesterday?" said Chief Inspector Taylor.

"We didn't manage to find anyone who saw Alan Musgrove arrive home that evening," said Brewer. "Mind you, we didn't manage to speak to all the neighbours. Oh yeah, and the ones that were in didn't know anything about the Musgroves' financial affairs."

"I think talking to the others should be a priority today," said Taylor. She turned to Patel. "Did you get anything useful from the agent?"

"Not really," said Patel.

"Surprise, surprise," said Brewer.

"She didn't think Miss Templeton was depressed the last time she saw her," said Patel, ignoring the inspector's mocking look. "The trouble is she hadn't been acting for her very long. The agent who knew her well has retired. I think we ought to speak to her as well."

"What's the point?" said Brewer. "We've got a suspect with motive and opportunity."

Taylor looked as if she was about to explode.

"Really, Colin," she said, "we can't put all our eggs in one basket at this stage of the investigation. What if Musgrove didn't do it? We haven't got any evidence that places him at the victim's house the day before she died. Granted, he and his wife have tried to mislead us but there could be other reasons for that.

You and the rest of the team can continue on that part of the investigation but I want Patel and Owen to pursue other lines of enquiry, all right?"

Brewer was red-faced but the impression was of rage rather than embarrassment.

"Sorry, boss," he said, "I'm just giving you my point of view. You're the SIO and it's up to you what we actually do."

Taylor seemed mollified.

"All right," she said. "You get on and talk to more of the Musgroves' neighbours. Did you request the Musgroves' bank records, Mike?"

"Yeah, should be here sometime today," said Pringle.

"Good. Do we have the outstanding forensic results as yet?"

"Some of them are back," said Owen. "The fingerprints they got from the door handle of the car belonged to Miss Templeton. However, the one from the brake fluid reservoir belonged to someone else."

"That's interesting," said Taylor. "We still haven't got Alan Musgrove's prints so we need to get them when we next speak to him. Mind you, the one on the brake fluid reservoir will probably turn out to have been left by whoever last serviced her car. What about that hacksaw?"

"We should get the results for that tomorrow."

"OK," said Taylor, "there's a limit to what we can do until we get the rest of the forensics back, but I'm hoping we'll be able to wrap this one up pretty quickly if they find something incriminating. All right, get on with it."

When they were on their own, Paul Owen said, "That's a turn-up for the book, Sarah Musgrove knowing about the will. I wonder why she didn't tell us she had a copy?"

"Actually it was Alan Musgrove who denied it, but she could have corrected him," said Patel.

"Oh yeah, that's right," said Owen.

"As I said during the briefing, we need to talk to Joan Templeton's former agent," said Patel. "She's called Anne Gregory. Give her a bell and see if we can visit her some time today."

Owen dialled the number while Patel looked up 'Thames Ditton' on Google maps.

When Owen replaced the receiver he said, "The lady says she'll be available this afternoon. We can arrive any time after two."

"Shall we drive down?" asked Patel.

"Probably better to take the train," said Owen.

*

As they weren't interviewing Mrs Gregory until after lunch, Patel decided to return the manuscript of *The Riddle of the Silent Soldier* to Miss Templeton's house. It couldn't really be considered to be evidence, but it was one of the deceased's personal effects. This would also give him the chance to examine her computer in more detail.

The house seemed colder and less inviting on this occasion. He went straight upstairs and replaced the manuscript on Joan Templeton's desk. Then he turned his attention to her computer. As might have been expected, given the neatness and tidiness of the house, her files were organised into folders and not spread across the desktop in a haphazard manner, as on his laptop at home. Each was clearly labelled. There was one for each of the novels she had published and another called 'short stories'. He decided to start by opening this one and examining its contents. Most of the files in the folders within it had not been touched for more than a year, but there was one that had been opened during the few weeks before her death. It was called *Death by Misadventure* and, unlike almost all her other stories, did not feature the omnipotent Inspector Tewkesbury. It was also unusual in that it was written in the first person, the protagonist being an elderly woman called Abigail Edgar. It was clearly unfinished, but in it Miss Edgar described how she planned to take her own life in a way that would make it appear to be murder.

A number of methods by which this could be achieved were examined and rejected, but none of them involved crashing a car on which the brakes had been disabled. In addition to the draft manuscript itself there were other documents that had clearly been saved as part of the research for the story. These included PDFs, and text from websites that had been copied and pasted into Word documents. A lot of the material had come from a website called www.enditall.com, which presented data to indicate that shooting yourself in the head or taking cyanide were statistically the most successful ways of taking your own life. However, cyanide was described as being almost impossible to obtain. This method was rejected as unworkable in the story for that very reason. The fictional Miss Edgar had concluded that a firearm to the head would be the best bet, if she could bring herself to pull the trigger, but had not decided how this could be contrived to look like murder when the narrative came to an abrupt end.

Patel couldn't help thinking back to the opening passage of *The Riddle of the Silent Soldier*. It seemed to him that a writer of Miss Templeton's experience would feel the need to make up a new scenario for the death of her latest character. Alternatively, perhaps the unfinished short story had been the inspiration for the final Inspector Tewkesbury novel. If nothing else, his discovery confirmed that the writer had been thinking about suicide during the period leading up to her death. This did not, he realised, necessarily imply that she was planning to kill herself.

A set of well-kept spreadsheets confirmed that the deceased had no reason to be worried about her financial status. In a folder marked 'correspondence', he found only letters to her bank, her solicitor and the Inland Revenue. Their contents were routine in nature. Here was a lady with a well-ordered life that had been terminated abruptly and prematurely.

Chapter Sixteen

Anne Gregory lived in a large red-brick bungalow that was approached through wrought-iron gates. The area in front had been paved but no vehicles were parked there and there was no garage. There were gables over the windows on either side of the front door and these had been painted white and featured mock-Tudor black wooden beams.

The policemen were shown into a small sitting room with French windows overlooking the small, neatly kept garden. Beyond the back fence there was a line of trees, their bare branches raised forlornly skywards. The room itself was furnished in an old-fashioned style that seemed to prize comfort over appearance. One wall was entirely taken up by shelves, all of which were crammed with books.

Mrs Gregory was a lady in her early sixties with straight grey hair who had a pair of gold-rimmed spectacles hanging on a chain around her neck. She was slim and not very tall and was wearing black trousers and a grey woollen jumper. She appeared relaxed as she sat in her armchair, eyeing the policemen expectantly.

"We're very grateful to you for seeing us at such short notice," said Patel.

"That's perfectly all right," she replied. "I've been half expecting a call from you ever since I read in the paper that Joan had been killed."

"Why was that exactly?"

Mrs Gregory smiled.

"Well, the circumstances of her death, as described in the press, were to say the least odd," she said. "I imagined there would have to be an investigation."

"Did you know Joan Templeton well?"

"Our relationship was professional rather than personal but I think it's fair to say that I knew her as well as most of her acquaintances," said Mrs Gregory. "She was a very private person and, as far as I could tell, she had few friends. I always thought that she felt at ease in my company."

"Did you meet her very often?"

"During periods after she had finished a new book we met at least once a month until all the details were settled with the publisher," she said. "In between we'd meet as and when there was something to discuss. Quite often it was to do with foreign rights for her books. She's been translated into a number of languages other than English. For some reason I cannot fathom her stories go down very well in Spain."

"There is some reason to believe that she might have killed herself," said Patel. "Do you think that's a possibility?"

"You must appreciate that I haven't seen much of her since I retired," she said. "However, based on what I know of her, I'd say that it was highly unlikely."

"We found a partly written short story on her computer about an elderly lady who wanted to kill herself and it was evident that she'd been doing research on methods of committing suicide."

"I can see how that would make you think that she was suicidal but that's because you didn't know her when she was alive," said Mrs Gregory. "Joan lived in two very distinct compartments: the real world, which for her was fairly humdrum and ordinary, and the one she had created in her imagination, which was full of murder and intrigue. She was always meticulous in her research, so I'm not surprised you found material about suicide. Over the years that we worked together, I formed the impression that she had a morbid obsession with death, particularly violent death."

"Miss Templeton believed that she had cancer, though we now know that wasn't the case," said Patel. "Couldn't that have made her consider taking her own life?"

Mrs Gregory gave a little laugh.

"If fear of illness had made her suicidal, she would have killed herself years ago," she said. "She was obsessed with her health and almost always told me about some new ailment when we met. I think I bore the brunt of it because I was willing to listen to her. She told me that other people she knew changed the subject when she started talking about health matters. I suppose I must be a good listener. In any case, I knew from experience that it was difficult to get her to concentrate on whatever we were supposed to be discussing until she'd got her latest health concern off her chest."

"Supposing she had decided to kill herself," said Patel, "do you think she could have gone through with it?"

Mrs Gregory frowned and shifted in her chair.

"I find that a hard question to answer," she said. "I imagine she could have taken some pills or something like that. I read that she was killed in a car crash and frankly I couldn't imagine her deliberately driving into something."

"Someone had disabled the brakes on her car so that she lost control of it," said Owen.

"And you think that Joan did that?" said Mrs Gregory. "I find that idea hard to accept."

"We found a repair manual for her car in her house," said Patel.

Anne Gregory nodded.

"I see," she said. "Joan was rather paranoid; she told me that she didn't trust the garage where she took her car to be serviced. She used to get her niece's husband to check it over after it had been in the garage to make sure that the work had been done properly and that she hadn't been ripped off. I imagine he asked her to get the manual. He might even have bought it for her."

So it seemed that Alan Musgrove had been telling the truth about the repair manual after all.

"Did she talk much about her niece and her husband?" said Owen.

"Not a great deal, but she did tell me that she relied on them to help her out from time to time," said Mrs Gregory. "I gained the impression that she would have been lost without them."

"Do you think she was fond of them?"

"The niece, certainly. I'm not so sure about her husband but she certainly found him useful."

Patel had only met Alan Musgrove once but had formed the impression that he was a cold fish unlikely to attract genuine affection from an elderly spinster.

"Do you know if her niece had a key to Miss Templeton's house?" he said.

"I don't, but it wouldn't surprise me," she said. "In my experience, people who live alone usually feel the need to leave a spare key with someone they can trust."

"You said she had few friends," said Patel. "Did she ever mention someone called Martin?"

"No, that name means nothing to me," said Mrs Gregory. "I presume you've already spoken to Pearl Bailey."

"We haven't actually," said Patel, "but her niece said they were friends. I believe you were her agent as well."

"Yes I was," said Mrs Gregory. "She was one of the first authors I took on when I started at Parker Nesbitt."

"Would you say she was a close friend of Miss Templeton's?"

"She was certainly a very old friend," said Mrs Gregory. "They were at university together."

Patel couldn't see the relevance of this new piece of information but filed it away in his memory in case it proved to be important.

"Do you know where she lives?" he said.

"Wimbledon; she has a house not far from the station. I do think it would be worth having a word with her."

"Thank you, Mrs Gregory," said Patel. "We are planning to speak to Ms Bailey. You've been most helpful."

Mrs Gregory smiled.

"Glad to help," she said. "Give me a ring if you think of any more questions."

Chapter Seventeen

The following morning the forensic report on the hacksaw was waiting on Patel's desk when he arrived at the office. It confirmed that the fingerprints on its handle belonged to Miss Templeton, which was hardly surprising. Disappointingly, there were no particles on the blade that might have come from the brake lines of the car. There were also results for the fingerprints on the car manual. Miss Templeton had left a set but there was another that didn't belong to her. Patel went to DCI Taylor's office and knocked.

When Taylor had digested the new information, she said: "It seems that we can dismiss the idea that the hacksaw we found in the house was used to cut the brake lines. Assuming she was murdered, that's hardly surprising. It's likely the killer would have removed whatever he or she used to do it. It would be too risky to leave it behind."

Patel didn't disagree but something else had occurred to him while Taylor was speaking.

"I suppose so," he said. "Mind you, if the killer wanted it to look like suicide, you'd have thought he or she would have used the saw from the house and replaced it afterwards. Obviously, they'd have worn gloves. There was always the risk of being seen going in or out of the house, but it could be done."

"I see what you mean," said Taylor.

"From what Mrs Gregory told us, it's clear that Alan Musgrove was very familiar with Joan Templeton's car," said Patel. "If he'd been asked to check it regularly in the past, he would have known where the brake lines were and how he could get at them. We can ask him about that when we next speak to him. The trouble is that even if the fingerprints on the brake fluid reservoir turn out to be his, they could be explained by the fact that he was almost certainly asked to look at the car by the deceased after its recent service; same with the fingerprints on the Camry manual."

"Obviously we need to get his fingerprints, but I'm afraid you're right," said Taylor.

"There is one other thing," said Patel. "It's probably not relevant now we've got this report but it might be worth checking to see if Miss Templeton's saw was blunt. You remember what the bloke who examined her car said about the blade that was used."

"I'll get someone to ask forensics about that," said Taylor. "They'll still have the saw. Right, it's time for the morning briefing."

When they entered the incident room the team was already assembled. Taylor brought them up to speed with the results from forensics and asked Patel to give an account of his interview with Anne Gregory. While he was speaking, Brewer fiddled with his mobile phone.

When Patel had finished Taylor turned to Brewer.

"How did you get on with the Musgroves' neighbours yesterday?" she said.

"We didn't find anyone who remembers seeing him arrive home that day," said Brewer. "We've spoken to all of them now, so it seems unlikely that we're going to find anyone who can confirm his story."

"Pity," said Taylor. "I suppose it's not surprising in the circumstances. Do we know how he normally travels to and from work?"

"He goes by Tube and then takes the train from Waterloo to Kingston," said Owen. "We asked him about it when we first spoke to him."

"So you did," said Taylor. She turned to DC Drake. "Shelly, check out train times for that route. Meanwhile I want Patel and Owen to speak to Pearl Bailey."

"Who's she?" said Brewer.

"She's another writer who lives in the area," said Taylor.

Brewer scoffed.

"What's the point of speaking to her?" he said.

"She was an old friend of the deceased," said Taylor. "As Patel told us, if you were listening, they had the same agent."

Brewer grunted but said nothing.

"What about the Musgroves' financial situation, Mike?" said Taylor.

"The bank said they'd send us details of their accounts but they haven't arrived yet," said Pringle. "I'll chase them up this morning."

"Good," said Taylor. "You can take a look at them and report back to me. Colin can give forensics a call. I want to know if that hacksaw was unusually blunt."

Brewer grimaced but said nothing.

*

Pearl Bailey's house was on one of the roads that meander down Wimbledon Hill from the Ridgway to Worple Road. The area in front of it was covered with tarmac and a silver-coloured Range Rover was parked near the front door. The house itself was double-fronted with a façade of yellowish brick. The heavy front door was recessed beneath a white-painted portico. On either side of it were bay windows with lace curtains preventing prying eyes from viewing the interior.

Patel and Owen parked on the road outside and rang the doorbell. A young woman wearing shorts and a T-shirt opened it.

"Is Miss Bailey in?" said Patel.

"Yes, I'll give her a shout," she said. "Who are you by the way?"

"Police. I'm Sergeant Patel and this is DC Owen."

"I see," said the girl. "You'd better come in then."

"And you are?"

"Oh, I'm Helena," said the girl, blushing slightly. "I'm the lodger."

Pearl Bailey was a tall, slim lady whose closely cropped blonde hair and minimalist make-up gave her a stylishly austere appearance. She was wearing a cream cashmere sweater and grey wool trousers teamed with a silk neck scarf. Patel was able to identify some signs of ageing but it was difficult to believe that she and Joan Templeton were contemporaries. He suspected an expensive plastic surgeon was responsible for her apparent youthfulness.

Having established who her visitors were, Pearl Bailey invited them into the sitting room, a large room that looked out onto a manicured lawn through patio doors. It was furnished with an eclectic mix of pieces, including a sofa and armchairs upholstered in a fabric with a large floral pattern, an assortment of occasional tables of different designs and a pink chaise longue. The walls were adorned with paintings in a variety of styles and Patel couldn't help noticing that many of them featured naked women. The focal point of the room was a large fireplace with a marble surround and mantelpiece.

"Do take a seat," said Pearl Bailey with a half smile. "What can I do for you?"

"We're investigating the death of Miss Joan Templeton," said Patel. "We've been led to believe that you were a friend of hers."

Pearl Bailey sighed and put a hand to her forehead. The gesture appeared contrived and it seemed to Patel that she was putting on an act for his benefit.

"I was terribly upset when I heard about her death," she said. "To answer your question, I've known Joan for many years. I wouldn't say we were close, but I think I can say that I knew her quite well. Do you mind if I smoke?"

She removed a cigarette from a silver case and loaded it into a black holder. Patel was very much aware that they were guests in the author's home but he had a strong dislike of cigarette smoke, which had been reinforced by his observations of the patients he had seen on the chest unit during his student days.

"I'd rather you didn't," he said.

Pearl Bailey blushed slightly and placed the cigarette on a large glass ashtray. She gave Patel an icy stare, which he made a point of ignoring. Out of the corner of his eye, Patel could see Paul Owen squirminging his chair.

"When did you first meet?" he said.

"We both read English at Girton," said Miss Bailey. "You could say we were thrown together by fate."

"And you both became writers."

"In the end, yes," said Miss Bailey. "I was a journalist for a while after Cambridge and Joan was a teacher."

"Have you seen much of her in the recent past?"

"We haven't met often," said the writer. "We lost touch for a number of years after university but met up again after she became an established author. I'm not a big fan of detective stories but I saw her name on the programme when I was appearing at the Edinburgh Book Festival and couldn't resist going along to hear what she had to say. Afterwards we went for a cup of coffee together and talked about old times. I've seen her a few times since then; the last time was quite recently at a friend's funeral."

"Was the friend called Martin?" asked Patel.

Miss Bailey looked surprised.

"Yes, Martin Rogers," she said. "How did you know?"

"The funeral was in her diary."

Pearl Bailey smiled.

"Typical Joan," she said, "she was always one for making a note of things. To be perfectly honest she was pretty obsessional."

This certainly fitted with what they already knew about Joan Templeton, but Patel had already formed the opinion that Pearl Bailey was not a reliable witness. He found it hard to put his finger on what it was that made him think this. During his short CID career he had had hunches like this before. They had generally been met with scepticism by his colleagues but he had been proved right more than once.

"Was Mr Rogers a close friend of Miss Templeton's?" he said.

Miss Bailey nodded.

"When we were students, yes," she said. "He looked upon her as a friend but she was completely besotted with him. She was very upset when he married Rosemary."

"Rosemary?" said Patel.

"Rosemary Smart," said Miss Bailey. "The remarkable thing is that she and Martin stayed together until his death. Quite a feat in this day and age."

"Was she a student as well?"

"Yes, a medical student," she said. "Very bright girl, too clever to be a doctor really. She went into research. She works at Imperial College."

"Do you think Miss Templeton went on loving him?" said Patel. "After Cambridge I mean."

Pearl Bailey smiled.

"I'm certain of it," she said. "You should have seen her at the funeral, she was more distressed than the widow. You'd have thought Rosemary would have said something about it but she seemed not to notice."

Patel wondered if Miss Bailey's assessment was entirely correct. Surely the widow would have been aware of Joan Templeton's outpouring of grief if it was that obvious? Perhaps she was just being polite.

"Why do you think that was?" he said.

"I imagine she thought it was just Joan being Joan."

"Meaning?"

"Joan was an emotional woman," said Miss Bailey with a dismissive wave of the hand. "She always tended to wear her heart on her sleeve."

It probably wasn't relevant to the enquiry, so Patel decided to move on.

"Did you talk to Joan Templeton at all on that occasion?" he said.

Miss Bailey nodded.

"We had a chat," she said. "I tried to calm her down but it was no use, she was in such a state."

"You may not feel able to answer this question but I have to ask it," said Patel. "Do you think that Mr Rogers' death was enough to make Miss Templeton want to kill herself?"

"Ah, I see," said Miss Bailey, "you're wondering if it was suicide. I'm an author, not a psychiatrist, so I can't give a definitive answer to that question. Still, I suppose it's a possibility."

"Where was Mr Rogers' funeral held?" asked Owen.

"The service was at St Steven's Church," she said. "He was buried at Wandsworth Cemetery."

"Did he live locally then?" said Owen.

"Earlsfield," said Miss Bailey. "Martin went into advertising after Cambridge. He did pretty well for himself, I believe."

"Can you think of anyone who might have borne Miss Templeton a grudge?" said Patel.

"No I can't," said Miss Bailey. "Joan was probably the most inoffensive person I've ever met."

"Did you ever fall out with her yourself?"

Pearl Bailey gave him a disarming smile.

"No, of course not," she said. "Why on earth would I?"

"Thank you for your time," said Patel, handing her his card. "If you should think of anything that might be relevant I'd be grateful if you'd give me a ring."

"Certainly," said Miss Bailey, "but it's highly unlikely I will."

While they were on their way back to Wimbledon, Owen said: "It seems Miss Templeton had something else to make her depressed."

"Yes," said Patel, "and I'm beginning to think that perhaps it was suicide after all. To be honest I'm wondering if we should have launched a murder enquiry."

"There has to be an investigation and this way we get more manpower," said Owen.

"I suppose you're right."

"Do you think we should have a word with Martin Rogers' widow?" said Owen.

"I'm not sure it would help at this stage," said Patel. "She's probably got enough on her plate at the moment. We'll see what DCI Taylor says."

"I mean to say we've only got Pearl Bailey's word for what happened at the funeral."

"True," said Patel. "I don't think Pearl Bailey was completely honest with us but I can't see why she would lie about that. On the other hand, I am wondering if Pearl Bailey had some reason to hate Miss Templeton."

"Like what?" said Owen.

"I don't know at the moment."

"Sounds pretty far-fetched to me. Are you suggesting she might be the killer?"

"Not at the moment but I think we need to find out more about her," said Patel defensively.

"Well, I can't see her crawling under the car and cutting the brake lines," said Owen. After a pause he added, "I think I know where Miss Templeton was going. Assuming she meant to turn into Alexandra Road, she could have been on her way to Wandsworth Cemetery."

Patel considered this for a moment.

"So you think she was going to visit Martin Rogers' grave?" he said.

"Yes," said Owen. "If you remember there was a bunch of flowers on the passenger seat of the car."

"Oh yes, of course," said Patel, "but would the cemetery have been open so early in the morning?"

"I don't know but I'll find out."

Chapter Eighteen

Colin Brewer left Superintendent Cheeseman's office with a spring in his step. DCI Taylor had called in sick and the Cheeseburger had asked him to take temporary charge of the investigation. Heading up the team in a case like this was a great opportunity for him and this one seemed to have brownie points written all over it. He went straight to his office and settled down to reread all the reports on the case. When he'd finished, he went through to the incident room where the other team members were waiting for the morning briefing.

"Right, folks," he said, "Superintendent Cheeseman has asked me to take over this enquiry for the moment."

"What about Chief Inspector Taylor?" asked Shelly Drake.

"She's not well," said Brewer, barely suppressing a grin. "I'm sure she'll be back in a day or two. Right then, you've all got copies of the reports, yeah?" They nodded. "Unfortunately forensics weren't much help so we've still got a lot of work to do. Mind you, we haven't got Alan Musgrove's fingerprints yet. That's obviously a high priority but this morning Brian and I are going to take another look at Joan Templeton's house."

"Sergeant Patel and DC Owen went there right at the beginning of the enquiry," said Drake, "and Mike and I had another look round the other day."

"I'm aware of that," said Brewer, "but I want to be sure of my ground before I interview our friend Mr Musgrove. While we're doing that, you can interview some more of the neighbours in

Beachcroft Road and surrounding streets. That includes Patel and Owen."

Shelly Drake sighed.

"We've already talked to the neighbours," she said, "and in any case there won't be many of them at home on a Monday morning. Most of them go out to work."

"Be that as it may, sweetheart, I want you to have another go at finding a credible witness who saw Musgrove in the area the evening before the old dear was killed. The point is, we're very close to nailing him, but we need something concrete to place him at the scene of the crime at the relevant time. What about those bank records?"

"Still not here," said Pringle.

"Never mind," said Brewer. "What else is there? Oh yes, you spoke to a friend of the victim's, didn't you, Patel?"

"Yes, sir."

"She tell you anything the rest of us need to know about?"

"The funeral Miss Templeton attended just before she died was of a friend from her university days," said Patel. "Apparently she was very upset about him dying."

"I suppose you're going to tell me you think it was suicide after all," said Brewer. Patel was about to answer but Brewer didn't give him the chance. "There are easier ways to kill yourself, so I'm not buying it, all right?" he said. "Yes, Owen?"

"DCI Taylor asked me to find out if the victim had a resident's parking permit for her street," he said. "I checked and she didn't."

"Where did she keep her car then?" asked Brewer.

Owen shrugged.

"No idea," he said.

"So that's one more little mystery for us to solve. Now let's get on with it."

*

Todd parked the car outside Joan Templeton's former residence and he and Brewer headed up the drive, while the others set off down the street.

"It's bloody daft that a small semi like this goes for nearly a million quid," said Brewer as they went in through the front door. "All right, let's get this over with; you start upstairs while I have a look out the back."

Once Todd had disappeared upstairs, Brewer took out his cigarettes and lighter and went out into the back garden. He lit one and inhaled deeply. The garden was long and narrow and, as an estate agent would have it, 'mostly given over to lawn'. There was an unruly hedge at the far end of the plot and Brewer decided to find out what lay behind it. To his surprise he found a concrete garage with a flat roof that opened onto a lane that ran behind the row of houses. There had been no mention of this in Owen's report. He tried the door in the side of the garage and it opened. Inside there was enough space to accommodate a car the size of a Camry and the other contents of the garage, which included a lawnmower and a collection of garden tools, were arranged around the walls to make this possible. Brewer smiled to himself. It was now clear that the killer would not have needed to work on the car on the street in front of the house in full view of anyone who happened to be passing. He, or she, could have disabled the brakes in the seclusion of this garage. It also explained why Miss Templeton hadn't bothered to apply for a resident's parking permit.

It was impossible to say if the side door had always been left unlocked but if it had, access was not a problem either. Someone who was a regular visitor to the house would have known that they would be able to get into the garage easily and that they were not likely to be spotted from the house. The person who best fitted this description was Alan Musgrove.

Next he went out again and tried the gate that led onto the back lane. It was locked, but Brewer was fairly certain that any reasonably athletic individual would have little trouble climbing over it. It seemed that sloppy police work was the trademark of the new detective sergeant. He would have great pleasure in reporting his discovery to the Cheeseburger when he next spoke to him.

He went back to the house and commenced a detailed search of the rooms downstairs. He was disappointed not to find anything else that had been overlooked. As Drake and Pringle had written in their report, there was no sign of a suicide note or a spare set of car keys, which in his eyes supported his view that the lady had been murdered.

*

When the team reassembled outside the house Pringle asked if they'd found anything new.

"Nothing in the house," said Brewer, "but we did find a garage." He paused for effect. "There's one at the bottom of her garden and by all appearances that's where the Camry was parked. I didn't see any mention of it in the previous reports."

"We didn't go into the garden," said Drake.

"I would have thought that the garage would be visible from the back bedroom window," said Brewer.

"I was the one who searched that room the first time we came here," said Owen. "The blinds were down and I didn't open them."

"Let that be a lesson to you," said Brewer, wagging his finger. "Attention to detail is the hallmark of a good detective. One other thing: I'm still wondering what happened to the spare keys. Most cars have at least one spare set."

"I suppose they could have been lost rather than stolen," said Owen.

"It's also possible that Alan Musgrove got hold of the spare set," said Todd. "After all, we know he was a regular visitor to the house."

"Just what I was thinking," said Brewer. "You lot can grab some lunch and then knock on some more doors in Beachcroft Road."

"What are you going to do, chief?" asked Pringle.

"DC Todd and I are going to pursue enquiries elsewhere," said Brewer, "but not until we've had a bite to eat."

*

It was a long, tedious afternoon and little was achieved. Back at the station Brewer surveyed his somewhat demoralised troops.

"Right," he said, "what we need is a team bonding session. We'll go for a drink at the Prince of Wales."

Patel groaned inwardly. He glanced at his watch. Brewer spotted him doing this.

"You got somewhere to go?" he said.

"No, sir," said Patel.

"Right, off we go then."

When they arrived Brewer led them up to the bar.

"What are we having then?" he said. "Patel?"

"A half of lager please, sir," he said, trying unsuccessfully to sound relaxed.

"Lager's a poof's drink," said Brewer. "You'll have a pint of bitter. Unless of course it's against your religion."

"I don't have a religion," said Patel.

"Good," said Brewer. "Now what about you, Drake, would you prefer a glass of white wine perhaps?"

"A pint of bitter's fine for me, sir," said Drake.

"Good girl," said Brewer. "Right, that's six pints of bitter, landlord or barman or whatever you are."

Drinks in hand they found a table large enough to accommodate the group and sat down. Patel watched as Brewer took a long drink from his glass.

Putting it down, the inspector said, "I know you all feel we've got nowhere today but that's the nature of police work. It's not like on the telly. It's about hard graft, not brilliant deductions based on fuck-all. Right now we've got a puzzle with missing pieces, but sooner or later it'll all come together."

"Finding that garage at the bottom of the garden was a step forward," said Todd.

"Indeed it was," said Brewer, rubbing his hands together.

Patel saw Brewer look pointedly at him and deliberately avoided making eye contact.

"Do you know when the chief inspector will be back?" said Drake.

"We don't know at the moment," said Brewer. "Don't worry, we can solve this without her."

"I miss her too," said Todd, grinning broadly. "She's a cracking bird."

Brewer laughed but Patel took a drink from his glass to conceal his embarrassment.

"Now, now, Brian, this is a senior officer we're talking about," said Brewer. "Mind you, in this case I wouldn't mind having her under me."

There was a peal of raucous laughter. Owen smiled but Patel remained stony faced.

"What's your problem, Sergeant?" said Brewer, turning to face him. "Don't you have a sense of humour?"

Patel met his gaze without flinching, but his pulse was racing.

"I didn't think it was funny, sir," he said.

"Oh really," said Brewer. "I suppose it's not sophisticated enough for a university man like yourself. So sorry to have lowered the tone of the conversation. Let's change the subject. Shall we discuss the economic situation or the crime rate in Bongo Bongo Land?"

"Actually I have to go," said Patel, putting down his drink. "My wife's expecting me home."

Brewer laughed and twisted his thumb on the top of the table.

"Off you go then," he said. "I wouldn't want you to get into trouble."

As Patel headed for the exit the group fell silent.

As he opened the door he heard Brewer say, "All right then, who wants another drink?"

Chapter Nineteen

When Colin Brewer arrived for the following morning's briefing he was pleased to note that all the team members were already there. He cleared his throat and looked at his watch.

"All right, let's get started," he said. "As you know Mr Alan Musgrove is our prime suspect for this killing but we don't have enough to arrest him just yet. If we could establish what time he arrived at Kingston Station on the evening of the murder, we'd have a pretty good idea what time he arrived home. Unless I'm much mistaken they'll have CCTV at various locations around the station. If one of the cameras caught him arriving, we'd know what time he got there. Someone who knows what Musgrove looks like had better go through the footage. Which of you has met him?"

"DC Owen and I," said Patel.

"OK, well Owen can do it then," said Brewer, "under my supervision of course. Do you know which platform his train stops at?"

There was no reply.

Then Todd said, "No, but I can find out."

"We're going to divide into two teams today," Brewer continued. "I want Brian Todd and Shelly Drake to do background research on Alan Musgrove. We've already got an outline of his previous employment history from the personnel department at his place of work, but I want more detail. I'd also like you to find out a bit more about Sarah Musgrove. The neighbours say she's not going out to work at the moment. It's possible that she lost her job and that's what's made them short of cash. It may lead nowhere, but it might help us to understand just how severe their financial problems are.

"With regard to the CCTV, we'll need to get a search warrant under Section 9 of PACE. Brian can do that when we've finished here. I want you, Pringle, to get onto the transport police and arrange for us to go through what they have for the relevant period while I'm speaking to the Cheeseburger."

"What is the relevant time period?" said Pringle.

"He says he got home between six thirty and seven that evening," said Owen.

"Right," said Brewer. "We've got to allow for the time he took to walk home from the station, so let's say from six onwards. Remind me what route he uses to get home."

"He says he goes to Waterloo and gets a direct train from there," said Patel.

"OK, Drake can find out which platform the Waterloo trains arrive at while Brian gets the warrant," said Brewer. "When you've done that you can look at other routes he might take, just in case he's not telling the truth."

"The only other station he could start from is Victoria," said Patel, "but he'd have to change at Clapham Junction."

"You got that, Drake?" said Brewer.

Shelly nodded.

"When we get to Kingston I want Pringle to check how long it would have taken for him to walk home from the station. All right, let's get on with it."

"Are we going to re-interview Alan Musgrove in the near future, chief?" asked Todd.

"We are, but we're going to wait until we've got more evidence," said Brewer. "We'll be in a stronger position to nail him if we've been able to prove that he got home later than he said he did."

"What about me, sir?" said Patel.

Brewer looked out of the window. Rain was still falling, lashed by a cold east wind.

"There are still some householders in Beachcroft Road and the neighbouring streets who haven't given us statements," he said. "You can see if any of them are in."

*

When they arrived at Kingston Station a constable from the British Transport Police was there to meet them.

"We've got CCTV at various locations in the station," he said. "There's one up there covering the barriers for a start."

Brewer looked up at the camera.

"That's no bloody good," he said. "Our suspect was leaving the station; a picture of the back of his head's no use."

"We've got them on the platforms as well," said the officer, blushing. "Come on, I'll show you."

It was soon evident that the cameras at the exits from the platforms were the ones most likely to capture images of passengers arriving at the station.

"Right," said Brewer, "we're going to concentrate on platform two where the Waterloo trains come in, starting from six, like I said."

"Until when?" said Owen.

"Hard to say at the moment," said Brewer. "If he did go to Beachcroft Road and bugger the brakes that evening he might have got home quite late."

It was a long, tedious morning and by lunchtime Owen was heartily fed up with watching commuters scuttling along the platform and going up the stairs to the station exit. Brewer sent Pringle out for coffee and sandwiches and suggested they take a break. When they'd finished eating Brewer excused himself and went to the toilet.

"This could turn out to be a complete waste of time," said Owen, when Brewer was out of the room. Pringle nodded.

Brewer came back in and sat down beside them.

"All right, how's it going?" he said.

"I've worked through the period he would have arrived at the station, if he got home at the time he said he did, and drawn a blank," said Owen. "Mind you, that could be because the cameras didn't pick him up."

"A positive sighting is the only useful piece of evidence," said Brewer. "If he wasn't picked up by the camera it doesn't prove anything one way or the other."

"Maybe he took another route home that night," said Pringle.

"Come on, let's get on with it," growled Brewer.

Half an hour later Owen exclaimed: "I think I've found him."

Brewer and Pringle came over and he replayed the sequence for their benefit. The camera had only captured him briefly and the image filled only about a quarter of the screen.

"It's a shame that other passenger walks in front of him when he gets closer to the camera," said Brewer. "What time was this recorded?"

"Seven forty-five," said Owen.

"Remind me how long it takes to walk to his place from the station," said Brewer.

"About fifteen minutes," said Pringle.

"That means he would have been home around eight o'clock and not before seven like he told us," said Owen.

"Looks like we've got him," said Brewer, rubbing his hands.

"Maybe," said Owen, "at the very least Mr Alan Musgrove has a lot of explaining to do."

Brewer grinned broadly.

"He has," he said. "We'll pay him a little visit tomorrow."

CHAPTER TWENTY

Brewer and Todd were shown into Musgrove's office and asked to take a seat.

"What can I do for you?" asked Musgrove. "We're rather busy at the moment, so I hope it won't take long."

"We have a few more questions for you, Mr Musgrove," said Brewer, adopting a superficially cordial tone. "You told my colleagues that you were home by seven o'clock on the evening before Miss Templeton died, is that correct?"

"It would have been about then; I can't tell you the exact time."

Musgrove appeared relaxed. Brewer felt a surge of excitement as he prepared to ask his next question.

"How is it then that you were identified on CCTV arriving at Kingston Station around seven forty-five?" he said.

"You must be mistaken," said Musgrove evenly. "I imagine you spotted someone who looked similar to me. I was already home by then, so it couldn't have been me. My wife can confirm I'm telling the truth."

"I've no doubt you've told your wife what to say," said Brewer. "The pictures tell another story."

Musgrove went red in the face and sat forwards in his chair.

"This is preposterous," he said. "I take great exception to what you're implying. In any case, if I had visited my wife's aunt that day I wouldn't have gone home by train. I'd have walked down to Coombe Lane and picked up a bus."

Brewer had considered this possibility.

"If you'd done that you could have got a train from Raynes Park," he said. "You could even have walked to Raynes Park Station if you fancied a stroll."

"That's miles out of my way," said Musgrove. "Why would I do that?"

"You did it in order to make it appear that you were coming home from work and not from your aunt's house."

"Are you calling me a liar?"

"Yes, sir, I am," said Brewer. "I think you went to your aunt's house that day, let yourself into her garage and disabled the brakes on her car."

Musgrove scoffed.

"You clearly know nothing about Miss Templeton's habits," he said. "She always kept that garage locked when the car was in it. Since I don't have a key for the garage I couldn't have got in."

"You could have asked her for the key," suggested Brewer.

"I'd have had to give a reason for wanting to look at the car."

"You could have made one up easily enough."

For the first time Musgrove appeared to be rattled.

"Well, I didn't," he said.

"I only have your word for that," said Brewer. "The problem is that you and your wife have told us a pack of lies from the beginning. You said you didn't know what was in Miss Templeton's will but the lady's lawyer informed us that you had a copy of it. You said you were home before seven that day, but in fact you didn't get there until eight. It is very clear to me that you have something to hide."

"I think it's time to terminate this interview," said Musgrove. "If you have anything further to ask me, you can do it in the presence of my solicitor."

"I do have more questions and quite frankly I'd advise you to get a lawyer," said Brewer. "In my view you're going to need one."

Musgrove was fuming.

"I find this line of questioning totally unacceptable," he said. "I think I should warn you I'm considering making a formal complaint."

"Go ahead," said Brewer suppressing a grin. "In my experience it's the guilty who squeal loudest. We are leaving now but you can be assured you haven't heard the last of this. Before we go, Constable Todd here is going to take your fingerprints."

Musgrove submitted to this procedure without complaint, which surprised Brewer a little but didn't shake his confidence that Musgrove was his man.

When Todd had finished Musgrove said: "This won't help you. I wasn't at Joan's house that evening so I can't have left any prints then. In any case, it's highly likely you'll find some because I've visited the house on many previous occasions. This is an appalling waste of police time."

"If you've told us the truth you have nothing to worry about," said Brewer. "Constable Todd and I are simply doing our jobs."

*

When they had left the building, Brian Todd said: "What's next, Colin?"

"We're going back to the station. I want to take another look at the CCTV images. I want to make sure we can make this stick. Meanwhile I want you to get these fingerprints fast-tracked. With a bit of luck they'll find a match with the one on the brake fluid reservoir."

"The trouble is Musgrove will say he made it when he was checking the car after its last service," said Todd.

Brewer realised he should have thought of that himself.

"Was that recent?" he said.

"Two months ago," said Todd. "A witness said Miss Templeton always got her nephew to check the car after a service."

"Shame," said Brewer. "Still, it's a piece of physical evidence and there's precious little of that."

They drove on for a while then Todd said: "I've been meaning to say to you, Wandsworth Cemetery opens at 8am."

Brewer frowned.

"And?" he said.

"DCI Taylor asked me to find out about it. She thinks the victim was going there to visit someone's grave."

"Well, that's all very interesting but it ain't going to help us catch her killer."

CHAPTER TWENTY-ONE

Superintendent Cheeseman reread the letter and sat back in his chair thinking. It was typed on the headed notepaper belonging to a city firm of solicitors and had been delivered by hand that morning. In it Alan Musgrove's lawyer requested access to the CCTV images allegedly showing their client arriving at Kingston Station so that they could have them examined by an independent expert. He asked for copies of all the reports on the Templeton case that had been filed to date and worked his way through them. Then he examined the CCTV images. When he'd finished he buzzed his secretary.

"Can you ask Inspector Brewer to come in and see me right away?" he said.

Brewer was briefing his team when the call came through.

"Can it wait a bit?" he asked. "I'm in the middle of something right now."

"He made it clear he wants to see you now," said the secretary.

"OK, I'll be there in a minute."

"I'll come straight to the point, Colin," said Cheeseman, when Brewer was seated in front of his desk. "We've had a letter from a lawyer acting for Alan Musgrove requesting a copy of the CCTV images that we say show him at Kingston Station."

"My view is that we should refuse," said Brewer. "I'm planning to interview him again under caution and I want him to feel under pressure."

"Under the 1998 Data Protection Act he's entitled to have

access to a copy," said Cheeseman. "Strictly speaking he should apply to the rail company to get it. We could delay things by insisting that he applies to them direct, but I can't really see what purpose that would serve. The thing is, Musgrove's face fills barely 10% of the images so they're no use as evidence if this ever goes to court. I think we'll achieve more by letting him see what we've got at this stage."

"If you say so, sir," said Brewer, "but I have to say I think we should let him sweat a bit longer. I take your point about it not being useful in court but it's all we've got. Unfortunately, none of the neighbours were able to confirm what time he got home that evening."

Cheeseman sniffed. He had already concluded from reading the files that the case against Musgrove was, to say the least, flimsy. He was only too aware that Brewer was like a dog with a bone when he had decided a suspect was guilty. The inspector reminded him of himself in his younger days but experience had given him a more considered approach to evidence. Sometimes his duty as a senior officer was to rein Brewer in, and this appeared to be one of those occasions.

"I saw that in the report," he said. "I've gone through all the evidence today and I have a few questions for you. I understand that Miss Templeton may have believed she was dying of cancer; at least according to her niece that's what she thought. She left the house before six in the morning having drunk a significant amount of alcohol and drove her car into a shop window."

"It was a funeral parlour actually, sir."

"Whatever," said Cheeseman testily. "It's not a common method of suicide, but we have to remember that we are dealing with someone who probably wasn't in her right mind in this case. The fact that she was drunk at such an early hour suggests she had a drink problem. She was a regular visitor to the doctors, wasn't she?"

"Yes, sir."

"You'd have thought that one of them would have twigged she was an alcoholic," said Cheeseman. "On the other hand, maybe she didn't have a drink before going to the surgery or she sucked breath mints. Anyway, the point is that she was clearly in a distressed state and problems always seem worse during the hours of darkness. It's perfectly possible that her life had become intolerable.

"Then there's the car repair manual. She could well afford to have someone else service and repair her car, so why would she go to the trouble of buying a manual for it?"

Brewer tried to intervene to answer this point but Cheeseman ploughed on.

"Fortunately young Patel had the good sense to bring the manual in here in case it was needed as evidence, so I was able to look through it this morning. I'm no mechanic, but from the diagrams I am pretty confident that I could disable the brakes on a Camry. We know she'd been looking at websites about committing suicide; maybe she was working out how to do it, as her niece suggested. I know she said she thought that it was research for a story when she was first interviewed, but that was pure speculation. In any case, for her it was just like doing research for the plot of one of her books. All she had to do was go down to the garage with a hacksaw, or some other tool, and cut through the brake lines. Even a woman with a blood alcohol level as high as hers could do that. She might even have done it before she started on the sherry. Remember, the only fingerprints on the hacksaw were hers. By the time she reached the bottom of Wimbledon Hill, the brakes on her car were completely useless and there was no chance she could stop crashing when she took that turn too fast. When she turned into Alexandra Road she deliberately accelerated to ensure that the crash would be fatal."

"I understand what you're saying," said Brewer, scratching his head, "but there was nothing on the blade of the hacksaw indicating it was used on the brake lines."

"So she used something else."

"OK, but on top of that there was no suicide note and I don't think that the old girl would have killed herself in that way, assuming she had wanted to, which personally I think is doubtful."

"What makes you say that?"

"Well for a start, most people who've been interviewed didn't think she was suicidal, including her doctors," said Brewer. "The last book she wrote was reasonably successful and she'd just finished a new one. I'd say she had plenty to live for. Also, there are many easier and more certain ways of killing yourself and I think that she would have chosen one of them."

Cheeseman shook his head.

"A lot of what you say is not supported by direct evidence," he said. "These artistic types walk a fine line between sanity and madness. You think that Joan Templeton thought like you and I, but I don't think that's the case. Anyway, sometimes people who appear to the outside world to have 'everything to live for' are in reality as miserable as sin."

"Fair enough, but don't forget the fact that the Musgroves have been lying to us from day one," said Brewer. "As well as the phony cancer thing, they claimed they didn't know about the contents of the will, despite the fact that Mrs Musgrove is her aunt's executor and had been provided with a copy of it. It's also a bit suspicious that she and the husband disagreed about when he got home on the night before she died when Patel and Owen interviewed them. And in any case the CCTV suggests he got home later than he said. This morning we got the report on Musgrove's fingerprints. One of the sets on the Camry manual was his."

"Didn't he say he asked her to get it to assist him when he was checking her car? Those fingerprints prove nothing. And another thing, what about the fingerprint on the brake fluid reservoir?"

"That one doesn't belong to him but it was the brake lines that were tampered with, not the reservoir."

"That's true," said Cheeseman. "If I remember rightly they

didn't get a print off the brake lines."

Brewer exhaled slowly.

"They didn't," he said, "but if he had any sense he'd have worn gloves."

Cheeseman nodded.

"True," he said, "and, like I said, you'd have expected his fingerprints to be on the manual."

Brewer sat forward in his seat.

"I know it doesn't prove he did it," he said. "We need more evidence but I really think we're on the right lines."

"All right, I was just playing devil's advocate really," said Cheeseman sitting back in his chair. "I still think letting Musgrove see the CCTV will worry him more than sitting on it. I suggest you arrange to show it to him when you next interview him. I'd fix it for tomorrow or the next day. He's already had a day or two to worry about exactly what we've got on him."

"You're the boss."

Cheeseman tapped his desk with his index finger.

"In the meantime I want you to see what else you can dig up," he said. "We really need a witness who saw him at Joan Templeton's house on the evening in question. So far the evidence we've got is mostly circumstantial. I know we've got the will, but that only tells us he had a motive. Oh and by the way, Tracy will be back tomorrow."

Cheeseman expected Brewer to leave, as he considered the interview to be over, but he showed no sign of moving.

"Was there something else, Colin?" he asked.

"When I took over this case I read all the reports that had been filed," said Brewer. "I then decided to visit the victim's house, although it had been searched a couple of times before. I was glad I did, because I found that there was a garage at the end of the garden that had been overlooked. To me that indicates negligence on the part of DS Patel."

At this point Cheeseman cut in.

"I read all this in your report." He removed his glasses and sighed. "I'm not entirely happy about having Patel on the Major Investigation Team but we've got to give him a chance. This was an oversight, granted, but I don't think it's going to affect the outcome of the investigation, all right?" He paused then added, "I will be having a word with him though."

*

Cheeseman sat back in his seat and supported his chin on his left hand. "You settling in all right?" he said.

"Yes thank you, sir," said Patel.

The summons to the superintendent's office was unexpected and somewhat worrying. He couldn't for the life of him work out what it might be about.

"It's a big step up, DC to DS," said Cheeseman. "It always takes a while to feel you're on top of it."

"Yes, sir."

Cheeseman cleared his throat.

"There is one aspect of the present enquiry that I feel I should draw to your attention," he said. "When Inspector Brewer had a look round the victim's house he found that there was a garage at the end of the garden. We have reason to believe her car was parked there, not on the street, as I believe you had suggested. Apart from anything else the old girl didn't have a resident's parking permit for Beachcroft Road."

Patel could feel himself blushing.

"It's not a serious oversight in the great scheme of things but it does indicate a lack of attention to detail," said Cheeseman sternly. "My motto has always been, 'Learn from your mistakes.' I suggest you make it yours as well."

"Yes, sir."

CHAPTER TWENTY-TWO

When Colin Brewer arrived the next morning there was a message asking him to report to DCI Taylor's office.

"Ah, there you are," she said as he opened the door and came in. "I've been reading through the reports that have been filed while I've been off and I see you've made some progress."

Her tone of voice was pleasant but her acid smile made him feel uneasy.

"I think I can say with some confidence that the noose is closing around Alan Musgrove's neck," said Brewer.

"Very dramatic," said Taylor. "Almost poetic. However, I should probably remind you that hanging was abolished in 1964."

"More's the pity," said Brewer.

"I didn't ask you in here for a discussion on capital punishment," said Taylor, removing her reading glasses and putting them down on her desk with more force than was strictly necessary. "What I want to know is what you're planning to do next."

"I've arranged for Alan Musgrove to come in this morning to look at the CCTV footage from Kingston Station and to answer some further questions," said Brewer.

"I'm surprised that wasn't done while I was off," said Taylor.

"Superintendent Cheeseman thought we should let him stew in his own juice for a day or two," said Brewer defiantly. *Put that in your pipe and smoke it*, he thought, but he was disappointed to note that Taylor appeared unruffled by this revelation.

"What about other lines of enquiry?" she said. "Have you made any progress?"

"We've been concentrating our efforts on Musgrove," said Brewer. "Patel and Owen interviewed the other writer, the Bailey woman, but she didn't tell them anything important."

Tracy Taylor sighed.

"All right," she said. "Get on with your interview and report back to me afterwards."

Brewer got up to leave.

"Yes, ma'am," he said.

Round one to me, he thought as he left the room.

*

Colin Brewer had selected Brian Todd to sit in with him during his interview with Alan Musgrove. The suspect arrived with his solicitor, a middle-aged man with thinning hair and heavy horn-rimmed spectacles. Once Musgrove had been read his rights and the audio-recorders had been switched on, Brewer began the questioning.

"I'd like to start by asking you about your movements on the afternoon and evening of the twelfth of March," he said. "When did you finish work on that particular day?"

"I've already answered that question," said Musgrove. "We've come here today to view the CCTV images that you claim show me arriving at Kingston Station."

"We will indeed be showing you the CCTV footage," said Brewer. "However, our purpose today is also to interview you under caution about the murder of your wife's aunt, Joan Templeton."

"She died in a car accident," said Musgrove. "You've dreamed up this crazy notion that she was murdered but you don't have a shred of evidence to support it."

"That is not the case," said Brewer, suppressing the anger that he could feel building within him, with some difficulty.

"Someone had cut the brake lines on her car so that by the time she reached the bottom of Wimbledon Hill her brakes were useless."

At this point the solicitor intervened.

"My client is understandably bemused by your suggestion that he was responsible for the damage inflicted to Miss Templeton's car," he said. "We do nonetheless accept that someone must have been responsible for it. I have advised Mr Musgrove to answer all your questions fully and frankly."

"Oh very well," said Musgrove. "I left my office around half past five on the day in question. I can't be more precise than that."

"And what time did you arrive home?"

"As I told you when we last spoke, it was between six thirty and seven o'clock."

"Does it normally take you over an hour to get home?"

"It can do, but if you're lucky with the connections, you can do it in fifty minutes," said Musgrove. "The twelfth of March wasn't one of those days."

"I see," said Brewer. "What time do you normally leave work then?"

"Five o'clock unless there's something to keep me in the office later."

Brewer consulted the file that was lying on the table in front of him.

"You told DS Patel you had a meeting that ran late that day," he said.

"That's right."

"We spoke to your colleagues and they said the meeting finished at five, not five thirty."

"It did finish at five but there was something arising from the meeting that I had to sort out before I left."

The suspect seemed very sure of his ground. What was needed was a question that would unsettle him.

"Fair enough," said Brewer. "Can you explain to me why you and your wife told Sergeant Patel that you didn't know what was in Miss Templeton's will?"

For the first time Musgrove looked uneasy.

"Neither of us had looked at the will," he said. "Joan's solicitor sent us a copy, but my wife put it away without reading it. She said it was morbid to look at it while her aunt was still alive."

Brewer scoffed.

"You really expect me to believe that?" he said.

"It's the truth."

"Oh come on, didn't you take a little peak yourself, just to see where the two of you stood?"

"No I didn't."

"All right, I think it's time that we showed you the CCTV pictures," said Brewer. "Brian, can you start the film for us?"

Todd opened a laptop computer that was lying on the table in the interview room and booted it up. Soon the screen was filled with commuters heading towards the exits of Kingston Station. When the face that had been identified as Alan Musgrove's came into view, Todd paused the video. Musgrove peered at the image for a few moments and then laughed.

"That's not me," he said. "This guy's wearing a light-coloured raincoat. I don't own anything remotely like it."

Brewer rewound the footage and paused it when Musgrove's face appeared again. He looked at the image and at Musgrove himself. When he had viewed the pictures before setting up this interview he had been confident that it was the same man, but now he was not so sure. He'd look foolish if it was proved that the image wasn't Musgrove.

"As I indicated in my letter," said the solicitor, "we want a copy of this so that we can have it examined by an expert in the use of facial recognition software. I take it you don't object?"

"We have prepared a copy for you," said Brewer. "We are also having the images examined by an expert, but we don't as yet have his report."

"I'm not very familiar with the use of facial recognition software," said the solicitor. "However, it seems to me that this is a case of mistaken identity. My client and his wife have suffered significant stress as a result of your unfounded allegations. When this is all over, we shall have to consider whether or not to seek compensation."

"I think you're jumping the gun, sir," said Brewer. "We are continuing with our investigations and are hopeful that we will soon have additional evidence to incriminate Mr Musgrove."

"As and when you are in possession of such evidence, we will meet again," said the lawyer tartly. "In the meantime, I hope you can give me an undertaking that you will not continue to harass Mr and Mrs Musgrove."

"If we need further clarification from either Mr or Mrs Musgrove, we won't hesitate to interview them again," said Brewer with an icy smile. "In the meantime, we will concentrate on our other lines of enquiry."

Musgrove and his solicitor rose from their chairs and were about to leave when Brewer said: "Do you have a smartphone, Mr Musgrove?"

The lawyer raised his right hand. "Don't answer that," he said.

Brewer shrugged.

"We have a disagreement about where Mr Musgrove was on the evening prior to Miss Templeton's death which could easily be resolved by examination of data from his phone," he said. "I'm simply trying to clear all this up in a timely manner."

"I've no doubt you're aware, or at least I hope you're aware that you would need a court order to obtain that information," said the lawyer. "That is unless you're going to arrest my client."

"I do not propose to arrest Mr Musgrove at this time," said Brewer. "However, if he surrenders the phone voluntarily it would be permissible for us to examine its contents."

"I have to advise him not to do that," said the solicitor. "Now if you have no further questions, I wish you both good morning."

*

When they were alone in the interview room, Brewer said: "We've missed a trick, Brian. We should have searched the house for that coat as soon as we identified Musgrove on the CCTV. Now he's seen the images, he'll most likely get rid of it."

Brewer was mildly irritated to note that Todd was looking worried.

"It might be someone else in the pictures," he said. "The bloke doesn't exactly get close to the camera."

"I know, but I've got a gut feeling that Musgrove's our man," said Brewer. "We need to recheck the journey times from Musgrove's office to his home and to Miss Templeton's place. I want you to get onto that now."

"I'll take care of it," said Todd. "I've been thinking. Maybe it isn't Musgrove at Kingston Station. Like he said when we spoke to him before, if he had gone to his aunt's place he would have gone home by bus."

Brewer considered this.

"A very fair point, Brian, me old mate," he said. "I want you to find out where the buses that go along Coombe Lane stop in Kingston. The trouble is, wherever it is there probably won't be any CCTV."

"Probably not," said Todd. "It's a shame he wouldn't let us have his phone."

"I think it's suspicious," said Brewer. "If it proves he went to Beachcroft Road he's in deep shit. If it didn't, it would undermine the case against him. I reckon if he had nothing to hide he'd have handed it over."

"I see what you mean," said Todd, scratching his head. "Mind you he might just be one of these human rights fanatics. There's been a lot in the press about infringement of privacy by police officers looking at mobile phone data."

"Only the guilty have anything to fear," said Brewer. "In any case, the papers have always had it in for us lot."

Chapter Twenty-Three

The phone call came at an inopportune moment for Chief Inspector Tracy Taylor. She was in bed in a tangle of arms and legs with a man when the ringtone of her mobile phone shattered her concentration and forced her to roll over and retrieve it from her bedside table.

"Chief Inspector Taylor here," she said, trying unsuccessfully to prevent a note of annoyance creeping into her voice.

"Sorry to disturb you, ma'am," said Patel's voice. "One of the witnesses we've previously interviewed in connection with the death of Joan Templeton has been found dead at her home. It looks like murder."

"Which one?" asked Taylor, easing herself up on her elbow and brushing a stray piece of hair out of her eyes.

"Pearl Bailey," said Patel. "I thought you'd want to know about it right away."

"Yes, thank you for letting me know," said Taylor reaching for the pen and pad she always kept beside her bed. "I'll come and look at the crime scene; where is it exactly?"

When she had a clear idea of where she needed to go, she ended the call and replaced the phone on the bedside table. Turning to her partner she said: "I'm sorry, sweetheart, we'll have to finish this later."

He smiled and kissed her bare shoulder.

"All right, but hurry back," he said.

Tracy dressed quickly and went through to the sitting room where she'd left her car keys. The blinds on the windows that overlooked the Thames were up and she could see lights reflected from the river's dark surface. She had taken out a crippling mortgage to be able to afford the flat but she had never regretted it. Watching assorted boats making steady progress up and down the river was the perfect way to unwind after a stressful day at work. She lingered for a moment and then hurried down to the car park.

As she drove south she thought about Roger. When she was a teenager growing up on a council estate in Romford she had never imagined that she would find herself contemplating a long-term relationship with a merchant banker. But here she was doing just that. Her marriage to a fellow serving officer had been a mistake; she could see that now. He had been fun to be with at first but once they had tied the knot he became moody and controlling.

In any case she needed to escape from the day job when she wasn't working, to be exposed to something completely different. Roger offered just that but she had other concerns. When you lived with someone you found out things about them you didn't appreciate when they only stayed over once in a while. And that was the dilemma for her; would Roger, her sensitive and sometimes surprisingly adventurous lover, turn into a crashing bore once they were under the same roof?

As she approached Pearl Bailey's house she could see several police vehicles parked outside. She slowed the car and parked behind one of them. The house was ablaze with lights and behind some of the windows the shadows of figures could be seen moving about. On the tarmacadam area in front of the house a Range Rover was parked. A uniformed constable saluted DCI Taylor as she approached the front door. She nodded an acknowledgement and went inside.

On the right of the spacious entrance hall a door stood open and through it she could see scene of crime officers in their white overalls going about their allotted tasks in a large sitting room. By the fireplace with its massive marble mantelpiece lay the body of a woman. Her head was bent to the left at an unnatural angle and the short blonde hair on the right side of her head was matted with blood. The silk blouse and well-fitting black trousers that she was wearing looked expensive. Glancing up, Tracy saw a bloodstain on the corner of the mantelpiece.

Close to the body stood the tall, lean figure of Sergeant Patel dressed in white overalls with the hood turned back. She noted with approval his well-shaped aquiline nose, large brown eyes and sensuous mouth. Tracy was a connoisseur of man-flesh and had been favourably impressed by the new recruit from the first time she had seen him.

Beside him stood Dr Alison Jarvis, similarly dressed, with her hood pulled up over her abundant red hair. Patel was speaking and the pathologist was gazing up at him, apparently hanging on his every word.

When he spotted her in the doorway he walked in her direction.

"I asked Dr Jarvis to stay on," he said. "I thought you'd like to hear what she has to say yourself."

"Appreciate it," said Taylor and walked over to where the body was lying. "So, Alison, what can you tell us at this stage?"

Alison Jarvis cleared her throat.

"My preliminary opinion is that she died from an impact on the right side of the head," she said, "but I can't entirely rule out other possibilities at this stage."

"Could she have simply tripped and banged into the mantelpiece?" asked Taylor.

Jarvis shook her head.

"Unlikely," she said. "She could have sustained a head injury in that way but it's less likely it would have been severe enough to cause early death." She knelt beside the body and pointed at the left temple with her gloved hand. "Also, there's some evidence of bruising here. My guess is that someone hit her with a blunt instrument and she fell towards the mantelpiece."

"That suggests to me the killer was a man," said Taylor.

"Possibly," said Jarvis, "but I don't think we can say for certain it wasn't a woman. It really depends on the weapon used. I may get a clearer picture when I have her head open."

"Time of death?" said Taylor.

"No more than three or four hours ago," said Dr Jarvis.

Taylor looked at her watch.

"OK, so it's one thirty now," she said. "What time did the call come in?"

"About eleven forty-five," said Patel.

Taylor turned to Alison Jarvis.

"You said a blunt instrument," she said. "What sort of thing did you have in mind?"

"Something fairly bulky," said Dr Jarvis. "The bruising is quite extensive."

Taylor spotted a broken photograph frame with the picture of a young woman in it on the hearth.

"Who's this?" she asked.

Patel inspected it.

"That's Miss Bailey's lodger, Helena," he said. "She was the one who found the body."

"Where is she now?"

"In the dining room," said Patel pointing to a door at the farther end of the room on the left. "She's in a bit of a state."

"I'll be off now," said Dr Jarvis, closing her bag.

"OK," said Taylor, "I'll see you at the PM."

While Dr Jarvis was on her way out Taylor examined the area around the body more closely. There was a pool of congealed blood on the hearth adjacent to the right side of the victim's head. Then she spotted pieces of a broken glass that didn't belong to the picture frame on the hearth and squatted down to get a closer look.

"Looks like a brandy glass," she said.

"There's a bottle of brandy on the small table beside the mantelpiece," said Patel.

Taylor stood up and scanned the sitting room. On a low table next to two armchairs stood another brandy glass containing a small amount of golden liquor.

"Looks like she was entertaining," she said. "Do we know who the guest was?"

"According to Helena, Miss Bailey said a friend was coming to dinner," said Patel. "She didn't say who it was."

Taylor turned to the nearest SOCO and pointed to the glass with brandy in it.

"You get any prints off that glass?" she said.

"Yeah, quite a good one," he replied.

Otherwise the room was in good order with no signs of a struggle. There was a gas fire masquerading as coal glowing cheerfully in the fireplace and an impressive display of flowers on a console table on the far side of the room.

"If the dinner guest was also the killer we should have plenty of prints and DNA," said Taylor.

"Not as many as you might think," said Patel.

"How come?"

Patel led her back into the hall and into the kitchen. She immediately spotted an open dishwasher packed with clean dishes and glasses.

"Don't tell me all the stuff from dinner's in there," she said.

"I'm afraid so," said Patel.

Looking around the kitchen she spotted two empty wine bottles on a work surface. "What about them?" she asked.

"They've managed to get prints from those," he said. "We'll just have to hope that the dinner guest helped him or herself to wine."

"Right, I'd better have a word with the lodger," said Taylor. "Have you had a look around upstairs?"

"Not yet."

"Right, off you go then."

Taylor went through to the dining room. The table was covered with a tablecloth and a young woman with thick fair hair sat on one of the chairs beside it. Her eyes were red and her cheeks stained with tears. Taylor sat down opposite her.

"I'm Detective Chief Inspector Taylor," she said. "I know you've had a terrible shock but I need to ask you some questions."

The girl nodded.

"How long have you been living here?" asked Taylor.

"Just over a year," she said.

"How did you come to be lodging with Miss Bailey?"

"I'm in my second year at uni," said Helena, brushing away a tear. "I was in a hall of residence during my first term but I hated it. Pearl's a friend of the family and she heard about it and offered me a room here."

"That was kind of her," said Taylor. "Where are you studying?"

"At King's College, in the Strand."

Taylor frowned.

"Isn't that difficult to get to from here?" she said.

"It's fine actually," said Helena. "I get the Tube."

"OK," said Taylor. "Where had you been this evening?"

"Out with friends."

"What time did you leave the house?"

"About six."

Taylor scribbled in her notebook.

"What time did you get back?" she said.

"It was just after eleven thirty I think," said Helena.

"That's early for a Saturday night," said Taylor. "Where had you been?"

"Just for a drink with a few friends," said Helena. "We didn't stay out late because we've all got masses of work to do."

Taylor folded her arms.

"When you got back here did you notice anything unusual?" she said.

"Not until I went into the sitting room and found Pearl lying there."

She buried her head in her hands and began to sob. Taylor placed a reassuring hand on her shoulder.

"I know this must be very difficult for you," she said. "We can talk some more when you're feeling better. Just one more thing, do you have any idea who might have come for dinner this evening?"

Helena sat up and shook her head.

"Honestly, I haven't got a clue," she said. "Can I go to my room now?"

"Yes of course," said Taylor.

She watched as the girl disappeared through the door leading to the hall. Shortly afterwards it opened and Patel came in.

"Find anything interesting?" she asked.

"There are four bedrooms upstairs," said Patel. "Two of them are obviously not used much. The big one at the front clearly belonged to Pearl Bailey. The small one at the back has a desk in it and there are various textbooks on the shelves. There's a single bed, but, well, I don't think it's been slept in recently."

"What makes you think that?" said Taylor.

"The bed's too neatly made up."

"Maybe Helena's a bit obsessional," said Taylor with a wry smile.

A SOCO came into the dining room.

"How did you get on in here?" asked the chief inspector.

"We couldn't get anything off those chairs but we've got some fibres off the armchairs in the lounge," he said. "There were a few prints on that table but they're a bit smudged. We've still got a couple of hours' work left to cover the rest of the place."

"Right, you'd better get on with it," said Taylor. "I'll organise a team of officers to talk to the neighbours first thing in the morning but right now I'm off home."

DCI Taylor climbed back into her car and set off home. As she exited the Tibbet's Corner roundabout and headed north towards Putney, she realised that she was exceeding the speed limit.

CHAPTER TWENTY-FOUR

The SOCOs had finished in the study so Patel crossed the hall and went inside. It was a larger, grander room than the bedroom in which Joan Templeton had written her books. At its centre was a large, elegant desk with a computer on it. Otherwise its surface was clear, save for a notepad and pen and a framed photograph of Pearl Bailey with Helena. They were sitting at a table in the open air, each raising a glass of sparkling wine. Pearl's face was a picture of happiness but Helena's smile looked a little forced.

Patel turned his attention to the large bookcase behind the desk. One of the shelves was entirely devoted to the author's own creations. He slid a fat volume out with his gloved hand and inspected it. It was called *Hermione Croker* and the front cover depicted an elegantly dressed young woman with long blonde hair. Checking the rest of the collection he found that all of them had different women's names as titles. *No Inspector Tewkesbury-type character here*, he thought.

He turned the book over and looked at the back of the jacket. He read: 'Hermione Croker appeared to have everything; the looks of an angel, a large flat in Chelsea and a good job in the city. The only missing ingredient was a man to share her charmed existence. Her search for love is in vain until handsome futures trader Bret Ingles comes into her life. But Bret has a secret.'

The story all seems to be here, thought Patel. *I wonder how she managed to produce 500 pages from that?*

He replaced the book, went across to the desk and slid open one of the drawers. Inside were a leather-bound desk diary and a new-looking smartphone. He picked up the phone and switched it on. The screen displayed a head and shoulders picture of Helena, bright-eyed and smiling. The expression on her face seemed to say 'Come and get me'. He tried to open the phone but was confronted by a keypad and the words: Touch ID or Enter Passcode. He switched it off and slipped it into an evidence bag. There was no point wasting time trying to get at the contents now. Back at the station the password would be easily bypassed and the contents made available for analysis.

He turned his attention to the diary. There was an entry for Martin Rogers' funeral and a few others indicating hair appointments and meetings with her agent but most of the pages were blank. Hopefully they would find more on the phone when its contents were downloaded.

The drawer below was full of bank statements. They indicated consistently healthy balances despite significant expenditure. There were regular deposits from her publisher, Amethyst Press, and Patel was surprised by the size of the amounts involved. However, a moment's thought led to the realisation that the house and the car parked outside hadn't come cheap.

The top drawer on the other side of the desk was devoted to tax and contained a mixture of correspondence from the Inland Revenue and a firm of accountants.

The final drawer was full of old photographs. In one packet there were black and white pictures of a group of undergraduates in gowns. Pearl Bailey was easily recognised but at first he had no idea who any of the others were. In one of them Pearl had her arm round another female student. Patel peered at it and it suddenly dawned on him that the other woman was almost certainly Joan Templeton. In a third, Pearl was pictured with Joan and two other students who were arm in arm. Could they be Martin Rogers and Rosemary Smart? he wondered. As he flicked through the pictures he found others in which these four students were together in different outfits and poses. The impression was of a group of close friends who had spent a great deal of time together during their student days. *Who was the person taking the pictures?* he wondered.

Looking at more of the photographs he noticed that in quite a few of them Pearl had her arm around Joan's shoulder or waist, while the other couple embraced each other in a similar manner. He remembered that Pearl Bailey had told him that Joan Templeton had been in love with Martin Rogers during their time at Cambridge. There was no evidence of that in the pictures in front of him but perhaps the period when she became 'besotted with him', as Pearl Bailey had put it, had occurred later in their student days. He opened another packet. This one contained pictures of Joan and Pearl together. Some of them were sufficiently erotically charged to have been considered scandalous in the less enlightened era of the 1960s.

The picture of Joan Templeton that was emerging was somewhat at odds with the one he had formed on the basis of the previous evidence he had uncovered. There was clearly more to the mousy former schoolteacher than met the eye. Of course it was possible that this was an episode from her past she had put behind her when she left Cambridge. After all, Pearl Bailey had said that they had lost touch after university, only meeting again by chance at the Edinburgh Book Festival. But he still suspected that Pearl Bailey was an unreliable witness. Even if the two writers had indulged in a sexual relationship as students it didn't explain their deaths, unless Pearl Bailey had killed Joan Templeton and someone else had killed her as an act of revenge. This scenario appeared to him too far-fetched to be credible.

The next packet contained more posed groups, several of them including another male student. He was tall with thick, wavy hair but his most arresting feature were his eyes, which stared at the camera in a manner that Patel found unsettling.

In one of them he was alone with Pearl Bailey and had his arm around her shoulder. On the back the words 'with Michael, 1965' were written in pencil. Was this the same Michael who had corresponded with Joan Templeton? There was no way of knowing. The rest of the photographs didn't seem to be relevant so he replaced them in the drawer but he scooped up the student photographs and put them in an evidence bag.

Next he turned on the computer. He was asked for a password. He tried 'pearl bailey' typed in several ways without success. He thought for a moment and then typed 'helena' and the home screen appeared. It was covered with folders, each with the name of one of Pearl Bailey's books. He clicked on 'Finder' at the bottom of the screen and opened the folder marked 'Documents'. This in turn was divided into folders with names like 'Correspondence', 'Spreadsheets' and 'Presentations'. There were also folders with names that were almost certainly the titles of books. None of the contents appeared to be relevant to the matter in hand.

Next he opened her emails. There were a great many of them in her inbox and he only examined the first few of them before deciding that the rest could wait. Her calendar was empty, possibly because it wasn't synched with her phone, he thought.

The 'Photos' folder contained more pictures of Helena. As he scrolled up through holiday photographs and selfies he came across a picture of Pearl Bailey with Anne Gregory. They were sitting in a restaurant and the picture and the date indicated that it had been taken several years earlier. There was a half-empty wine bottle on the table and an empty one stood beside it. Both women had broad smiles on their faces and were raising their glasses to the photographer. Patel presumed that they were celebrating the release of yet another bestselling book. Thinking back, he realised that there had been no similar pictures of author and agent together on Joan Templeton's computer. He recalled that Edith Skinner had told him that Joan liked to buy her lunch when the editing of one of her books was complete. Perhaps she didn't do the same with Anne Gregory. Or perhaps it was just that they didn't take photographs of these occasions. After all, there were no pictures of Joan Templeton with Edith Skinner.

Patel yawned. It didn't seem likely that there was anything else on the computer that was relevant to the case but a more thorough examination would be required in due course. He shut it down, slipped out of the chair and walked back to the living room. The SOCOs were still at work.

"I'll be off then," he said, and one of them gave him a weary nod.

His head was buzzing with possibilities as he walked to where his car was parked.

Chapter Twenty-Five

The following afternoon DCI Taylor collected Patel from Wimbledon Police Station and drove to the Westminster Public Mortuary. Once inside they were directed to the office where Dr Alison Jarvis was speaking into a small dictating machine. On seeing them she put it down and led them to the post-mortem room. They were greeted by a strong smell of body fluids and formalin.

The naked body of Pearl Bailey lay on a porcelain table. The skin of the scalp had been turned downwards and the roof of the cranium had been removed, revealing the irregular surface of the author's brain. Dr Jarvis stopped at the head of the table and donned a pair of gloves.

"She was hit on the left side of the head with a blunt object of some kind," she said. "It must have been fairly sizeable. Now that I've shaved the head you can see the bruising is more extensive than I'd originally thought. You can see it goes well up beyond the hairline. However, she died from the impact to the right side of the head."

The doctor walked round to the other side of the table and picked up a pair of forceps.

"Here on the right you can see a fracture line and the bone in this area is depressed," she said, pointing to the area just above the right ear. "The attacker was a little unlucky, assuming that he or she didn't intend to kill her. The area of the skull that took the brunt of it, just here, is unusually thin and therefore easier to fracture. The other important thing is the site of the impact. The corner of the mantelpiece hit the side of the head in an area that we call the squamous portion of the temporal bone and a fragment of bone was driven inwards." She indicated an area of bone with the forceps. "That part of the skull overlies an important blood vessel called the middle meningeal artery. A tear in this blood vessel led to massive bleeding inside the skull. This in turn led to an increase in the pressure inside the head causing compression of the brain. However, it's just possible that if she had been found earlier and treated in hospital she might have survived, because in my opinion she wouldn't have died immediately after she was hit."

"Of course, the murderer wouldn't know everything you've just told us," said Patel. "Still, you would have thought that if you'd hit someone on the head as a result of losing your temper you'd seek medical help for them rather than leaving them to die. Would it have been obvious that she wasn't dead do you think?"

"To anyone with a modicum of medical knowledge, yes it would," said Jarvis. "To an average member of the general public, maybe not."

"Was it a single blow to the head?" asked Taylor.

Dr Jarvis nodded.

"Yes I think so," she said. "It must have been delivered with a fair amount of force, otherwise the victim wouldn't have been knocked unconscious. I'm assuming that she was knocked out, because she was left to die or was thought to be dead already. After all, if she was conscious following the blow, she might have tried to reach her mobile phone to seek assistance and I imagine the killer wouldn't have wanted that. In any case, there was no evidence at the scene suggesting that she moved from where she fell."

"I found her mobile phone in a desk in the study," said Patel. "She'd have had a long way to crawl to get it."

"Was there a landline?" said Taylor.

150

"Yes, but the phone was in the hall."

Taylor nodded and frowned.

"I agree the killer would have wanted to be sure she was dead before they left, if they meant to kill her, that is," she said. "Now you've got more information, do you think a woman could have done it?"

"I don't see why not," said Jarvis. "The blow to the left side of the head only needed to be hard enough to knock her off balance. It was hitting the mantelpiece that did the real damage. If she'd been hit from the front, for example, she would have fallen backwards and the impact would have been on the thicker bone here, at the back of the head. In those circumstances she would quite likely have survived."

"What you're saying suggests to me that this wasn't necessarily a premeditated act," said Taylor.

"That's an entirely reasonable deduction," said Dr Jarvis. "After all, it's unlikely the attacker knew anything about the anatomy of the skull and cranial contents."

"I see what you mean," said Taylor. "Did you find anything else?"

"Nothing relevant," said Jarvis. "She was in pretty good shape for her age."

"Well it all seems pretty straightforward," said Taylor. "Anything you want to ask, Sanjay?"

Patel coughed nervously.

"She'd had a lot to drink on the evening she was killed," he said. "Might that have any bearing on the severity of her brain injury?"

"That's an interesting question," said Dr Jarvis approvingly. "There is evidence for a causal relationship between alcohol consumption and the severity of head injuries in RTA victims. However, there are also data to suggest that low levels of alcohol in the bloodstream may be associated with less severe brain damage."

"One other thing," said Patel. "Was she sexually active?"

"She wasn't a virgin if that's what you mean," said Dr Jarvis. "I can also say that she hadn't had penetrative sex recently."

"Thank you, Doctor," said Taylor. "That's all very helpful."

While they were walking to their car, Taylor said: "She fancies you."

"Who?" said Patel.

"Dr Jarvis."

Patel frowned. He was conscious that he felt unsettled in the company of DCI Taylor, though he wasn't entirely sure why. By contrast he felt at ease in Dr Jarvis's company. That didn't mean there was sexual chemistry between them. More likely it was because of their shared experience of medical training.

"We've worked together on these two cases and we get on well," he said. "That's all it is."

Taylor smiled.

"You may think that, but you're wrong," she said. "Trust me, I can tell."

In the car she said, "What was all that about sexual activity?"

"Well," said Patel, "we've got what seems to be a crime of passion. I just wondered if sex was involved."

"Ah I see," said the chief inspector. "You think the dinner guest was a bloke and they fell out after going to bed together."

"Not necessarily," said Patel.

"You checked the victim's bedroom. Was there anything to suggest sexual activity?"

"No there wasn't," said Patel. "I just wondered if the killer and the victim were in a relationship of some sort."

CHAPTER TWENTY-SIX

Tracy Taylor surveyed the officers seated in front of her in the incident room. Brewer was wearing a tailored jacket for once but it was rather crumpled and she thought she could detect a stain on the lapel that looked like tomato soup.

"Right," she said, "we've got another suspicious death on our hands. Those of you who have been paying attention will know the name Pearl Bailey. Sergeant Patel and DC Owen took a statement from her because she was a friend of Joan Templeton's. Well, now she's turned up dead and it seems more or less certain someone killed her."

She paused while this new information sank in.

"The question is, was she killed by the same person who nobbled Miss Templeton's brakes or was it someone else?" she continued. "We can't answer this question at the moment so I propose to divide the team into two groups. I want DI Brewer to continue exploring the theory that Joan Templeton was killed by her niece's husband for financial gain. Todd and Pringle can work with him. I will lead a second team, the rest of you, investigating the new killing."

"Surely it's too much of a coincidence," said Drake. "Isn't it more likely we've got one killer and it's not Alan Musgrove?"

Taylor smiled.

"Well I can't imagine why Alan Musgrove, or his wife for that matter, would have wanted Pearl Bailey dead," she said. "I can also see that it's a bit of a coincidence when two authors who are old friends and live in the same part of London both die in mysterious circumstances. At the same time I can't think of a motive that would link the killings or an individual who would have wanted them both dead. So, for the time being we'll treat them as separate cases. If one of you bright sparks finds a link between the deaths then we'll change tack. Always keep an open mind, that's my motto. Colin's team can get cracking but I want the rest of you to stay here."

Todd and Pringle headed for the door but Brewer came across to where Taylor was sitting.

"Can I have a word?" he said.

"In my office," said Taylor.

Brewer closed the door of the chief inspector's office and sat down opposite her.

"What did you want to talk about?" she said.

"The thing is I'm convinced he went home by bus after he nobbled the car," said Brewer. "There's loads of buses that go to Kingston from near the victim's house."

Taylor scoffed.

"Last week you were certain that it was Musgrove on the CCTV pictures from Kingston Station," she said. "What's made you change your mind?"

"Musgrove seemed convinced it wasn't him in the pictures," said Brewer uneasily.

"Maybe he was lying," said Taylor.

"Well, if he was he's bloody good at it, that's all I can say," said Brewer, flushing visibly.

"And another thing," said Taylor, "we haven't got the report from the facial recognition people yet. If they say it's Musgrove then this new theory of yours goes out the window."

"Fair point," said Brewer. "Anyway, I want to get a search warrant for the house, unless you object."

"What are you looking for?" asked Taylor.

"A light-coloured raincoat and a hacksaw, or something else that could be used to cut brake lines."

Taylor nodded.

"That seems reasonable in the circumstances," she said. "Mind you I imagine he'll have got rid of them by now. We should probably have done it earlier."

"Yeah, I know." Brewer paused, as if trying to gauge his senior officer's mood. "I also think we should put him under surveillance," he said at last.

Taylor could hardly believe what she was hearing.

"I'm sorry, Colin, it's out of the question," she said firmly. "For a start it would cost a fortune in overtime and Cheeseman would never approve it. On top of that, I can't see what it would achieve. What do you think he's going to do to incriminate himself? He knows we're investigating him, so he'll be on his best behaviour."

Brewer sighed.

"I suppose you're right, but I had to ask," he said.

Taylor almost felt sorry for him for a moment. Almost.

"Sometimes you've got to be patient in an investigation like this," she said. "I understand that you want to get a result, Colin, but we just don't have enough evidence to arrest Musgrove at the moment. You need a witness to place him at or near the scene of the crime. If you're right about him going by bus, then you need to get in touch with the bus company and find out what drivers were on that route the evening before she died. If one of them remembers your suspect getting on his bus at around the right time your case would be a lot stronger."

"We've made a start on the bus angle but there's still a lot to be done," said Brewer.

"Well then get on with it and keep me fully informed, all right?"

Taylor watched Brewer as he left the room. *You're not so cocky now, are you?* she thought. Brewer had been a thorn in her side since she had taken command of the Major Investigation Team. There had been times when she had considered asking for a transfer but she was determined not to be driven out by a sexist pig like Brewer.

*

Back in the incident room Taylor addressed the remaining team members.

"Let's make a start," she said. "We need to know the contents of Pearl Bailey's will. Judging by her house I'd say she's worth a lot more than Joan Templeton. Drake, you can get onto that."

Drake nodded.

"I think we also need to find out more about this Cambridge connection," she continued. "We know that Pearl Bailey, Joan Templeton, Martin Rogers and his wife, Rosemary, were all there at the same time and met up recently at Martin's funeral. I want Patel to interview Rosemary Rogers. Go easy on her, her husband's just died and at the moment we don't have any reason to think she's involved in either of these deaths.

"I'm also hoping we'll get something useful from that mobile phone. Owen, I want you to get the contents downloaded and have a look though it. Start with the text messages and emails. After that look at the calendar, her contacts, the apps she used, her browsing history, the works.

"I'm going to speak to Superintendent Cheeseman and see if he can give us some more manpower. I'm well aware that the results from forensics may reveal the identity of the killer but we can't count on that. We won't have them for a day or two and I want us to get a clearer picture of Pearl Bailey and the people in her life. Yes, Sanjay?"

"The other person who knew Pearl Bailey well was her former agent, Anne Gregory," said Patel. "Should I have another word with her?"

"Are you telling me she acted as an agent for both of the victims?" said Taylor.

156

"That's right," said Patel. "Also both were taken on by Susan Sharpe when Mrs Gregory retired."

"Are you suggesting one of the agents murdered them both?"

"I don't have any reason to think that at the moment," said Patel.

"We'll keep them for later then." Taylor clapped her hands. "Let's get on with it," she said.

*

Patel checked Google Maps and decided that it would be better to take the train to Earlsfield as Rosemary Rogers lived close to the station. He headed out into the street, only to be confronted by a young black woman.

"Mary Ogundipe, *South London Echo*," she said. "Can you tell me about the circumstances surrounding the murder of Pearl Bailey?"

"Not you again," said Patel. "I've nothing to say to you."

"Come on, give me a break," said the reporter, who was almost running to keep up with Patel as he strode along Queens Road. "Two local authors have died in suspicious circumstances in a matter of weeks. This is the biggest story I've ever covered."

"I can't add anything to what you know at the moment," said Patel. "We'll be issuing a statement to the press when we have something concrete to report."

"Did Pearl Bailey kill Joan Templeton?"

Patel slowed down. That thought had occurred to him as he sat in Pearl Bailey's study. He considered the idea again for a moment and quickly dismissed it. Apart from anything else, he couldn't see Pearl Bailey sliding under a car to cut the brake lines. If she had wanted to kill Joan Templeton she would have used a different method.

"No comment," he said, and quickened his pace again.

CHAPTER TWENTY-SEVEN

The Rogers residence was a substantial Edwardian terraced house situated in a quiet residential road just a short walk from Earlsfield Station. Unlike the houses on either side of it, the façade was painted white. The low wall in front of the house was surmounted by a picket fence, painted pale grey. A paved path ran up to the front door and the rest of the area in front of it was covered with multicoloured pebbles. The bay window had white half-height shutters behind it to prevent inspection of the interior by passers-by. Outside the front gate a fairly new-looking Ford Fiesta with a resident's parking permit stuck to the windscreen was parked.

When Patel rang the doorbell Rosemary Rogers opened it almost immediately. She was a heavily-built woman with an abundance of grey hair that flowed over her shoulders. This framed a face that was pleasant but certainly not beautiful. She was wearing faded jeans and a blue sweatshirt with 'Imperial College London' on it in white letters arranged around the college crest. She invited Patel to come in and sit on one of the low, wooden-framed sofas that were arranged in front of a wood-burning stove.

The ground floor of the house had been remodelled to create a large open-plan living area incorporating a kitchen and dining area at the rear. The furniture was contemporary and minimalist in style and the pictures on the walls were all abstract compositions. The entire back wall of the house was made up of bi-fold doors that opened into a small garden which was mostly paved. Around its edge a collection of shrubs were corralled by low brick walls. At the far end was a small garden shed. Everything was neat and tidy, with barely a leaf out of place.

Patel cleared his throat.

"I'm afraid I have some bad news," he said. "On Saturday night Miss Pearl Bailey was found dead at home."

Dr Rogers closed her eyes and let out a sigh.

"Oh no, that's just too awful," she said. "Do you know what she died of?"

"I'm afraid to say she was killed by a blow to the head."

"What, you mean an accident of some sort?" said Dr Rogers, sitting up straight in her seat.

"We don't think it was an accident," said Patel. "We think someone attacked her."

Dr Rogers looked bewildered.

"Was it a robbery or something like that?" she said.

"We don't think so," said Patel. "The thing is, she had a dinner guest the night she died and we need to know who it was. Was it you by any chance?"

"Me?" said Dr Rogers, putting her hand to her chest. "Oh no, I wasn't there. I can't remember the last time I went to Liz's house."

"Liz?" said Patel.

"Oh you don't know, why should you?" said Dr Rogers. "Pearl's real name is, I mean was, Elizabeth Crump. She changed it when she started writing; she didn't think she would sell many books if she used her real name."

"I see," said Patel. "I don't suppose you know who the dinner guest might have been?"

"I'm sorry," she said, "I haven't the faintest idea."

"Would I be right in thinking that the last time you saw Miss Bailey was at your husband's funeral?" said Patel.

"Yes, actually I haven't even heard from her since that day."

"We interviewed Miss Bailey in connection with the death of Joan Templeton," said Patel.

"Oh God, that was another terrible shock," said Dr Rogers.

"I can imagine," said Patel. "She told us that Joan Templeton was in love with your husband when you were all at Cambridge."

Dr Rogers' eyes widened.

"You're not serious, oh what nonsense," she said. "It was Liz she had a relationship with. I don't think she was interested in men."

"Are you telling me Pearl Bailey and Joan Templeton were both lesbians?" said Patel.

"Why yes, of course, didn't you know?" said the doctor. "Oh I know Liz wrote all those books about young women falling madly in love with gorgeous men, but she simply wasn't interested in the opposite sex herself. That's why she never married. Same for Joan."

"She also said Joan Templeton was very upset at your husband's funeral," said Patel. "She implied that she was still in love with him."

"Well it's true she got very emotional," said Dr Rogers. "That was typical of Joan. That reminds me, one of our fellow students died while we were still undergraduates and we all went to the funeral. Joan cried buckets though she'd had very little to do with the girl when she was alive."

Rosemary Rogers had corroborated Pearl Bailey's statement that Joan Templeton got emotional at funerals. However, they had given conflicting accounts of the relationships between members of their group. Patel was more inclined to believe the doctor's story, but he needed to test it further.

"But Joan Templeton wrote murder mysteries," he said. "She seemed to be preoccupied with violent death."

Dr Rogers nodded sagely.

"She was," she said. "The thing about Joan was that she was able to divide her life into compartments. She had no problem writing about people being shot or bludgeoned to death but she had a real problem confronting death in real life."

"Did you see much of her when she was alive?" asked Patel.

"Martin and I used to meet up with her occasionally, usually around Christmas or New Year. We knew she didn't have many friends and I didn't like the idea of her being alone at that time of year."

"Did you ever meet her niece, Sarah Musgrove?" said Patel.

"Only once as far as I can remember," said Dr Rogers. "I'd popped in to see her because I was in the area and the niece was there."

"What was your impression of her?"

Dr Rogers shrugged.

"She was pleasant enough," she said. "Mind you, I had the impression she was there out of a sense of duty rather than genuine affection. Perhaps I'm being unfair to her though."

Patel took out the photographs he had removed from Pearl Bailey's study.

"Would you mind having a look at these?" he said.

Dr Rogers flicked through them and her face lit up.

"Gosh, don't we all look funny?" she said.

"That is you then?"

"It's us all right." She pointed to one of the photographs. "Doesn't Martin look handsome?" she said. "I look a mess."

"Is this one Joan Templeton?" said Patel.

"Yes, that's Joan. She didn't change much over the years did she? She was born old."

Patel gave her another photograph.

"Can you tell me who this is?" he said.

"Oh my goodness, it's Michael," said the doctor, covering her mouth with her hand. "I haven't thought about him in years."

"What can you tell me about him?"

"Well, his name is Michael Groves," said Dr Rogers. "He was a medical student like me. He did his clinical at Guy's but I went to the Royal Free so we lost touch. I don't know what happened to him."

"He's not in many of the photographs," said Patel. "Was he close to anyone in your group?"

Dr Rogers hesitated for a moment.

"I can't see any harm in telling you now," she said. "Liz called him her 'little adventure'. She'd known she was gay from an early age but she decided she ought to try a man just to be certain. So she went to bed with Michael. He wasn't experienced, so I imagine it wasn't very satisfactory. At any rate after a few weeks she broke up with him. He was pretty upset at the time."

Patel remembered the letters he had found in Joan Templeton's desk. He hadn't been sure that the man in the photographs and the writer of the letters were one and the same but it now seemed to be a real possibility. He wondered if Groves had written to Pearl Bailey. No letters had been found during the search of her house but she could easily have destroyed them.

"What was he like? Michael, I mean," he said.

"Very clever, always in the top few students in our year at Cambridge," said Dr Rogers. "I'm not sure he was ideal for medicine though. How can I put this? He wasn't very good with people."

"Is there anything else you can tell me that might be relevant?"

Dr Rogers frowned and a ghost of a smile flitted across her face.

"The funny thing is, Liz was jealous of Joan," she said. "I know she made far more money from her books but what irked her was that the critics gave Joan better reviews. Some even saw literary merit in her detective stories but Liz's books were always dismissed as worthless escapism. I remember one occasion when she got very heated on the subject. She was sitting right where you are now as it happens. Martin pointed out that her readers liked her books and that was what really mattered but I could tell she wasn't convinced."

"Do you think there's any chance Pearl Bailey would have wanted Joan Templeton dead?" said Patel.

"Oh no, I don't think so," said Dr Rogers. "They were friends, well sort of. We had both of them here for dinner once and they got on just fine."

"I don't suppose you can think of anyone else who might have done it?"

Dr Rogers shook her head.

"No I can't," she said. "It's hard to imagine anyone wanting to harm Joan. She was such an inoffensive person."

"Thank you, Doctor," said Patel. "That's been very helpful. I'm sorry we had to trouble you at such a difficult time."

Rosemary Rogers wiped her eyes with her right hand.

"Martin had been unwell for quite a while, so I'd had plenty of time to get used to the idea of not having him around," she said. "Of course it's still a shock when it actually happens, but I'm coping."

CHAPTER TWENTY-EIGHT

"Umm, a pattern seems to be emerging," said Taylor. "We've got two lady authors of a certain age, both of whom fall into the 'funny she never married' category and who had a thing when they were students, who get bumped off in short order. Surely there's got to be a connection?"

"Maybe it's a lesbian love triangle," said Owen. "And the third member of the trio killed the others."

They all tried, unsuccessfully, not to glance at Shelly Drake. Drake seemed not to notice.

She said, "I read about a study the other day which found that a high proportion of women who identify as lesbians have had previous sexual experience with a man and there's reason to think some of them are really bisexual."

"Are you suggesting the third member of the triangle might be male?" said Taylor.

"Not really," said Drake. "I was just telling you what I read."

"Actually Pearl Bailey did have a male lover when she was at Cambridge," said Patel.

The others turned to look at him.

"Do you know who it was?" asked Taylor.

"It was a fellow student called Michael Groves," said Patel. "They were in the same year at Cambridge. I think it may be worth finding out more about him."

"I can't see how he's relevant after all this time," said Drake.

"The thing is," said Patel, "according to Dr Rogers he was pretty upset when she broke up with him. And, well, there's something rather odd about him in the photographs."

Drake pulled a face.

"Oh come on," she said, "you'll have to do better than that."

Patel could feel himself blushing. He was cross with himself for allowing Drake to get under his skin so easily.

"I found some letters from someone called Michael in Joan Templeton's desk," he said. "I think he may be the one who wrote them. So you see, he had links to both victims."

"But you don't know for sure," said Drake.

"I agree it's a long shot," said Taylor. "Still, I'm all in favour of keeping our options open at this stage. We don't exactly have a lot of suspects. Now let's get back to this lesbian love triangle theory. Who could the third person be?"

"The other two women who were close to her were Anne Gregory and Rosemary Rogers," said Drake.

"They both had husbands," said Owen.

Drake scoffed.

"That doesn't rule them out," she said.

"It doesn't," said Taylor. "However, we should be looking for other women who knew them both."

"Susan Sharpe was agent to both of them," said Owen.

Patel smiled to himself. He couldn't imagine Susan Sharpe being involved with either of the victims. There was a considerable age difference between the agent and her former clients but maybe that wasn't important. Perhaps his view was coloured from his lack of experience of same-sex relationships.

"I still think we should be looking for someone with a motive for both murders," said Drake.

"Michael Groves could fit that bill," said Patel.

Drake shook her head.

"I'm still not convinced," she said.

"I agree there's not much to go on," said Taylor. "You dig a bit, Sanjay, and see what you can find."

Patel nodded. It was great that DCI Taylor was backing him. He just hoped he wouldn't let her down. After all, as Drake had pointed out, the events at Cambridge had happened an awfully long time ago.

"Don't you think it's odd that one victim died in a car crash, while the other was hit on the head?" said Owen. "The first appears to be premeditated murder, while the other seems to be a spur-of-the-moment thing, see?"

Taylor turned to face him.

"So you think there's more than one killer then?" she said.

"Could be," said Owen.

"The findings at the scene and the PM results are certainly consistent with Pearl Bailey's killing being unplanned," said Patel. "Actually Pearl Bailey could easily have survived the attack if she'd hit another part of her head on the mantelpiece."

"Exactly," said Owen. "The problem is we don't know who was at Pearl Bailey's house that night."

"Which is why we need the results from forensics," said Taylor. "OK, what about that mobile phone?"

Paul Owen consulted his notebook.

"I'm not finished with it but I'll tell you what I've got so far," he said. "Pearl Bailey didn't make any calls to Dr Rogers during the period leading up to her death."

"Unless she used the landline," said Taylor. "Shelly, did you get her phone records?"

"Yes," said Drake. "There was one call to Dr Rogers' number. It was before the funeral."

"Most probably she was confirming she'd attend," said Taylor.

"And another from Dr Rogers a few days afterwards."

"Thanking her for attending?" said Owen.

"Could be."

"Were there any calls where you couldn't identify the caller?" said Patel.

"One or two," said Drake. "I suppose you think your mysterious Michael might have called her."

Patel was becoming increasingly irritated by Drake's attempts to undermine him.

"He might have done," he said.

"All right, all right," said Taylor. "While we're on the subject, were there any other calls of interest?"

"Nothing obvious," said Shelly. "I'm still working through them."

"Carry on with that," said Taylor. "Anything else, Paul?"

"She'd made a couple of calls to her former agent, Anne Gregory," said Owen. "Both of them were fairly short."

"Maybe she was inviting her to dinner," said Patel.

"Maybe," said Taylor. "They might just as easily have been about something else but we'll keep it in mind."

"I'm still working through the emails on the phone," continued Owen. "On the whole they're pretty routine, mostly communications to and from her agent and publisher. She didn't send or receive many text messages. There was one from Joan Templeton asking if she was going to be at the funeral and a reply from Miss Bailey saying she was. There are also several from her lodger, Helena. They say things like 'I'll be late' or 'Do you need anything from the shops', that sort of thing. The apps on the phone are pretty much what you'd expect. She had several taxi hailing apps. We know she had her own car but it seems she didn't always use it."

Taylor turned to Shelly Drake.

"What did you find out about her will?" she asked.

"I got a copy faxed over," said Drake. "She's worth about three million and, guess what, most of it goes to Helena Cooke."

Tracy Taylor's eyes grew larger.

"Helena the lodger," she said. "That puts a completely different complexion on things. I wonder why she did that?"

167

"I think Helena was Pearly Bailey's lover," said Patel.

"Why do you think that?" said Drake.

"The password for the computer was 'Helena' and she had a lot of photographs of her on it."

"So, now we've got someone with a motive for killing Pearl Bailey," said Taylor.

"The only problem is she doesn't have a motive for killing Joan Templeton," said Patel. "I don't suppose she even knew her."

Chapter Twenty-Nine

Brian Todd came into the office and tossed a pile of files onto his desk.

"I'm whacked," he said. "You fancy a pint?"

"Yeah, all right," said Paul Owen who was in the process of closing down his computer. The chance of a quiet drink with his friend was more appealing than hanging around in the office. Todd was thick as thieves with Brewer but on his own he was a pretty decent bloke.

The bar of the Prince of Wales was almost empty when they arrived and they were soon settled with their beer. Todd took a long swig and replaced his glass on the table.

"That's better," he said.

"Hard week?" asked Owen.

"Frustrating mainly," said Todd. "You probably know Musgrove says it's not him on the CCTV."

"I'd heard," said Owen. "What about the facial recognition thing?"

"We haven't got the report yet."

"I thought it was him when the image came up but I could be wrong," said Owen. "He wasn't exactly close to the camera."

"To be honest even Colin's having second thoughts," said Todd. "I've been over the images several times myself since we spoke to Musgrove. The more I look at them, the more uncertain I am it's him, fuck it."

"Did the bank records show anything useful?" asked Owen.

"Not really," said Todd, scratching his head. "The Musgroves weren't exactly flush before their little windfall, but they were in the black. Their mortgage payments were up to date and all. Obviously they're a lot better off now, so the motive's still valid. Oh yeah, and Mrs Musgrove didn't lose her job, she resigned because of ill health. Some sort of nervous trouble."

"What does Colin want to do next?" said Owen.

"He's had us interviewing bus drivers on the routes from Wimbledon to Kingston," said Todd. "We're not remotely finished but we should get through them all next week."

"Sounds like a big job."

Todd nodded.

"It is, tedious too," he said. "Colin's itching to interview Musgrove again but DCI Taylor says get more evidence first."

"Maybe Musgrove didn't do it."

Todd scoffed.

"Well the fairies didn't bugger the old girl's brakes, so someone must have," he said.

Owen shrugged.

"Maybe it was suicide after all," he said.

Todd shook his head.

"Colin's convinced it's murder and I have to say I agree with him," he said. "Trouble is, there aren't any other suspects."

"No one with an obvious motive anyway," said Owen. "Is Colin enjoying running that part of the investigation?"

Todd smiled broadly.

"Oh yeah, he's like a pig in clover."

"What's it like having him in charge?"

"It's all right," said Todd. "I mean, he can be a difficult sod but he's focussed on the job in hand and he's good at sniffing out the truth."

"I suppose so," said Owen.

Todd took another swig of beer.

"What do you make of Patel?" he said.

170

"I wasn't sure about him at first," said Owen. "He's not your typical copper but that's not necessarily a bad thing."

"Well he got a black mark for missing that garage."

"I missed it too," said Owen ruefully. "I was the one who searched the back bedroom and didn't pull the blind up. I didn't see the need at the time."

"Yeah but he was the one in charge," said Todd. "He didn't say 'Check the garden' or 'Look out of the back bedroom window' so you didn't. Now Brewer on the other hand spotted it on his first visit to the house. That's the difference. He's got experience, local knowledge and all."

"Granted, but Patel's smart."

"Smart arse more like."

Owen frowned.

"Patel's an outsider, see," he said. "Doesn't fit in, but that gives him a different perspective."

Todd grinned.

"You're right there, he doesn't fit in," he said. "What you need in police work is a team, people who understand each other and all pull in the same direction."

"Come to think about it, I'm an outsider too."

Todd patted him on the shoulder.

"OK, you're a taffy," he said. "But you've been here a while. You're one of us now."

Owen smiled.

"Nice of you to say so," he said.

"You don't learn policing at university," said Todd. "All you get there is a load of poncified theories and bollocks like that."

"There's no harm in having education," said Owen. "I wish I had more myself."

"You're better off as you are, believe me." Todd finished his pint. "You want another?" he said.

"Yeah, all right," said Owen.

Todd went over to the bar with the empty glasses.

When he resumed his seat Owen said: "Can I ask you a favour?"

"Yeah, of course."

"Well the thing is, Gemma's chucked me out," said Owen. "I was wondering if I could crash at yours for a bit."

"Oh shit, mate, of course you can," said Todd. "What's going on?"

"She's got another bloke, see," said Owen. "It's been going on for a while, but I didn't know about it until this week."

"That's rough," said Todd. "You'll have to kip on the couch, mind."

"No problem."

Chapter Thirty

Sanjay got up late on Saturday morning. He had spent much of the night turning theories over in his head, trying to make sense of what had happened. It was after four when he finally fell asleep. He went through to the kitchen where Amber was reading the paper over a cup of coffee.

"You were restless last night," she said.

"Sorry, love, I couldn't sleep," said Sanjay.

"You've got to learn to switch off," said Amber. "You've always brought your work home with you, mentally I mean. It isn't healthy."

"I know," he said, running his fingers through his hair. "This case has really got to me."

"Would it help to talk about it?"

"I'm not sure," he said. Seeing her looking at him expectantly he added, "We've got two victims who've known each other for years and lived just a few miles apart, so you'd have thought there'd be a connection, but we can't seem to find it."

"Obviously I only know them from their books," said Amber. "My impression is they were very different people."

"There's no doubt about that," said Sanjay. "The thing is, I found a photograph in Pearl Bailey's study that shows a male fellow student she had sex with when she was at Cambridge in the late sixties."

"Can't see what's remarkable about that," said Amber, as she put her plate and mug in the dishwasher. "When you and I were at university a lot of the other students were at it. I mean I know it was a long time ago but it was the decade that launched the permissive society."

"It's only remarkable because Pearl Bailey was a lesbian," said Sanjay.

Amber turned to face him.

"You're kidding," she said. "What about all the rampant straight sex in her books?"

"Well, she had some, probably not much, experience to base it on," said Sanjay. "Don't forget she was writing fiction, not a sex manual."

"All right, but what's the relevance of all this to her murder?"

"The thing is, she dumped this guy and I've got a hunch they might have met up again recently," said Sanjay. "Maybe he still had a thing for her and lost his rag when she rejected him again."

"Well it all sounds rather far-fetched to me," said Amber. "Still, I think you should go with your instincts."

Talking about it had crystallised the vague notions that had been wandering in and out of his consciousness since he had first seen the photographs and then talked to Rosemary Rogers. It seemed to fit together. Michael Groves was the mystery dinner guest but their reunion hadn't gone well. They had quarrelled and he had hit Pearl Bailey. Probably he hadn't meant to kill her. Of course this was all speculation and evidence was required to prove that Groves was at Pearl Bailey's house. The relative lack of fingerprints at the scene made this more difficult. However, one set of the suspect's prints would be enough. A lot of murderers try to destroy evidence linking themselves to the crime but few are thorough enough to ensure that they have left no trace. Did Michael Groves fall into that category or not?

Amber finished packing the dishwasher and sat down opposite him at the table.

"I hope you haven't forgotten we're going to your parents for lunch," she said.

"Oh shit," said Sanjay. "It's Holi."

"I get confused with all these Hindu festivals," said Amber. "Remind me what this one's all about."

"Essentially it marks the beginning of spring," said Sanjay. "It also celebrates the triumph of good over evil in one of the Hindu legends. In India people throw coloured powder at each other."

Amber made a face.

"Does that mean I should wear old clothes?" she said.

Sanjay laughed.

"No need," he said. "My parents won't be doing anything like that. Holi's a time when families get together for a meal. Usually it's dinner but in our family it's usually been lunch."

"That's a relief," said Amber. "Anyway, you'd better get through the shower."

*

Sanjay's parents lived in a flat above their takeaway restaurant in Upper Norwood. Mr Patel opened the door to them when they arrived. He had an irregular dot of *tilaka* on his forehead and was wearing his best suit, the light-blue double-breasted one with wide lapels and baggy trousers. As usual Amber became aware of the smell of coriander and cumin as soon as they entered the hallway.

"Come in, come in," he said. "Lunch almost ready."

Sanjay's mother appeared in the doorway to the kitchen.

"How are you, Amber?" she said.

"I'm fine, Mrs Patel," said Amber, smiling.

"I told you before, you know, you must call me Sangita," said Mrs Patel, sounding aggrieved. "We are being family now."

Amber cowered in mock fear. Once again she had got off on the wrong foot.

"Sorry, Sangita," she said.

175

They went through to the living room where they found Sanjay's sister, Aashna, laying the table.

"How are you?" said Amber brightly.

The girl gave a shy smile.

"I'm good, thank you," she said. "How's work?"

"Great, actually," said Amber. "We've got a lot of new clients at the moment so it's pretty hectic."

Sanjay's father smiled.

"You want beer?" he said.

"Yes please, Dad," said Sanjay.

"I'm fine just now," said Amber, forcing herself to smile.

"OK, two beer," said Mr Patel.

Aashna put the last spoon and fork on the table and went out of the room, returning shortly afterwards with the drinks. Then she disappeared again.

On the dining table were small wicker baskets containing poppadoms, decorated bowls of mango chutney and pickle and a large serving dish from which pungent aromas were emanating. Amber hoped the curry wouldn't be too spicy. Mrs Patel came in carrying two plates of rice, followed by Aashna with two more.

"It smells great," said Sanjay, smiling broadly.

"Come to table now," said Mrs Patel.

Sanjay and Amber took their seats and Mr and Mrs Patel joined them. Aashna reappeared with another plate and sat down in the remaining place. They helped themselves to food and for several minutes ate in silence.

"How is new job?" asked Mr Patel.

"Good, it's going really well," said Sanjay.

"We glad you are nearer home," said Sangita.

"Yeah, it only took us half an hour to drive here," said Sanjay. "Mind you there wasn't much traffic."

There was an uneasy silence then Sangita said, "I am still wondering why you give up good career and become policeman."

"We've been over this before, Mum," said Sanjay. "I realised I wasn't cut out to be a doctor. This is what I want to do. I won't always be a junior officer. I shall go for promotion as soon as I can."

"Your mother concerned for you," said Mr Patel. "She only want you do well."

"I know that, Dad," said Sanjay.

"Sanjay's good at his job," said Amber. "He can do just as much good for the community as a policeman as he could as a doctor."

"Maybe so," said Sangita. "It seem a shame he doesn't do job he trained for, like you."

"That's different," said Amber. "I always wanted to be a lawyer."

There was another uncomfortable silence during which nobody made eye contact. Amber was fed up with Sangita's obsession with Sanjay's career change. She had a sneaking suspicion she also didn't like the fact that she earned more than her husband. Her conventional view of the world was outdated, but Amber had to concede that it was understandable.

"Where's Dinesh?" said Sanjay.

His father smiled.

"Your brother has gone to girlfriend's house," he said.

"Dinesh has a girlfriend?" said Sanjay. "How long has this been going on?"

"They meet at temple," said Sangita. "We introduce them. She is nice girl from good family."

"Good for Dinesh," said Sanjay. "Do you think it's serious?"

Sangita frowned and wobbled her head from side to side.

"It is a shame you are not more like you, brother," she said.

Here we go again, thought Amber. Dinesh is a successful businessman and now it seems he will soon have a nice Hindu wife. He's always showing up his elder brother, the consummate failure who inexplicably hooked up with a white woman.

"What you working on right now, Sanjay?" said Mr Patel.

"It's a murder investigation," he said.

"I don't know why you are wanting to be involve in such beastly unpleasantness," said Sangita raising her eyes to the heavens.

"Well of course murder isn't nice," said Sanjay. "Still, the perpetrators have to be brought to justice. In any case, for a detective, working out who's killed someone is a challenge, a puzzle to be solved."

"And who is it that has been killed? Some drug seller or other criminal person?"

"No actually," said Sanjay. "We're investigating the suspicious deaths of two writers."

"What sort of writer?" said Sangita. "Are they producing this modern filth?"

"One of them wrote detective stories," said Amber. "Joan Templeton, have you heard of her?"

"Oh yes," said Aashna. "I read one of her books. It was good."

"Which one was it?" said Amber, pleased that Sanjay's sister had finally managed to join in the conversation.

"I can't remember what it was called," said Aashna. "It's about people being murdered and left with no shoes on."

"*Dead Men's Shoes*," said Amber. "It's good, isn't it?"

Sangita scoffed and looked as if she was going to launch into another tirade.

"Will you play cricket this year?" said Mr Patel, before she could speak again.

"Yes, I plan to," said Sanjay. "I'm hoping to join Mitcham Cricket Club."

"Very splendid," said Mr Patel. "They have one of oldest grounds in the country."

As they were leaving Mr Patel took Sanjay on one side.

"Do not mind your mother," he said. "It is only she worry about you."

Sanjay smiled and patted his arm.

"I know, Dad," he said.

*

On the way back in the car Amber said: "I still don't understand your head gestures. What was Sangita trying to say when you asked if Dinesh's relationship was serious?"

"Normally the head wobble means yes, but in this case it was maybe," said Sanjay. "I hope it works out for him. It's about time he flew the nest."

"It's Aashna I worry about," said Amber. "She's stuck serving in that takeaway. She needs to get out so she can meet people of her own age."

Sanjay appreciated Amber's concern about his sister but believed it was best for her not to interfere.

"Don't worry about Aash," he said. "My parents will make sure she gets a husband when she's a bit older."

Amber snorted.

"A husband they approve of," she said. "She should be able to choose her own life partner."

They drove on in silence and Amber looked out of the car window. Sanjay had a question he wanted to ask but was uncertain how she would respond. Eventually he plucked up courage.

"Would you mind if I pop into the station for a short while?" he said. "There's something I'd like to check out."

"Go ahead," said Amber. "I ate so much at lunch that I won't be wanting anything else till much later."

*

There was only the desk sergeant in the reception area of Wimbledon Police Station. Sanjay gave him a wave and went straight to the CID office.

179

He booted up his computer and initiated a search. When the home screen of the criminal records database came up he typed 'Michael Groves'. The next field asked for a date of birth. He didn't know it but he thought there was a good chance he had been born in the same year as Pearl Bailey and Joan Templeton. He typed *.*.1945 and hit enter.

A page loaded and came up on the screen. He stared at it in disbelief. It said: *Crime: Murder, Sentence: Life.*

CHAPTER THIRTY-ONE

When Brewer arrived at Wimbledon Police Station on Monday morning he was met by Brian Todd who was looking rather glum.

"We've got that report, Colin, you know, the image recognition," he said. "They reckon it isn't Musgrove."

"Fuck," said Brewer. "Oh well, we'll just have to keep at it."

"Can we pack in the bus search?"

Brewer shook his head.

"Of course not," he said. "If it wasn't him at the station, chances are he went by bus."

He was well aware that finding a witness who had seen Musgrove on a bus that evening was like looking for a needle in a haystack but they didn't have any other lines of enquiry to pursue.

"Have we got that search warrant?" he said.

"Yes," said Todd, "Pringle picked it up first thing this morning. Surely there's no point looking for that coat if it's not Musgrove at the station?"

"Maybe not but there's still the hacksaw or whatever else was used to cut the brake lines."

"Surely he'll have got rid of it or cleaned it so there's nothing to prove it was used to do it?"

"Maybe, maybe not," said Brewer. "Right, let's get round there then. It'll also give me the chance to lean on Mrs Musgrove while hubby's at work."

Brewer rang the bell and noted with satisfaction that Sarah Musgrove's face fell when she opened her front door to see the three police officers on the step. He thrust the search warrant in front of her face and she reluctantly let them in.

"Right, get on with it," said Brewer, gesturing towards Todd and Pringle. "You know what you're looking for. Meanwhile I'd like a word, Mrs Musgrove."

She showed him into the sitting room and invited him to take a seat. Brewer grimaced as he sat on a wayward spring in one of the armchairs. He shifted his position in an effort to get comfortable. It was a depressing room, he thought, full of old junk and smelling of stale lavender.

"I'll come straight to the point," he said. "I want to clear up the matter of when your husband came home on the night before your aunt died. During his original interview with Sergeant Patel he said he was home before seven."

"That's right, he was."

"My problem is that he was picked up on CCTV at Kingston Station at a quarter to eight. According to my reckoning that means he would have been home by eight o'clock, not seven."

Brewer was banking on the fact that Sarah Musgrove didn't know about the results of the image analysis. His only worry was that the expert acting on behalf of the Musgroves might have submitted his report already. Sarah Musgrove blushed and squirmed a little in her chair, which encouraged him to believe this was not the case.

"There must be some mistake," she said.

"So are you telling me that he was definitely home by seven?"

"Yes, well a bit after maybe."

"How much after?"

"I don't know," she said, looking flustered. "I was getting our dinner ready so I'd have been too busy to check the time."

"So it could have been eight then?"

"No," she said firmly. "I aim to have dinner on the table soon after seven. Alan's always hungry when he gets home."

"If that's the case you have to keep an eye on the time."

"Yes but not every five minutes."

She had a point, he thought, and decided not to labour the matter further.

"OK, let me ask you about something else," he said. "We know you were sent a copy of your aunt's will by her solicitors. Stands to reason you knew you were more or less her only beneficiary."

More squirming.

"I did read the will when it arrived," she said. "Then I put it away and didn't look at it again until she died."

"Your husband says you never even opened it."

"I didn't tell him I'd read it," she said. "It was private, between Aunty and me."

Brewer raised his eyebrows. He had never been married but he was damn sure he would expect a wife to share information of this sort with him if he ever did take the plunge.

"I find it hard to believe you didn't tell your husband you were set to inherit a considerable sum of money," he said.

"Well I didn't. It was family business."

"And your husband isn't part of your family?"

"Of course he is but he didn't need to know about it while she was still alive."

Brewer sat forwards in his chair.

"What, did you think he'd kill her if he knew?" he said.

"No of course not," said Sarah angrily. "You're twisting my words and trying to make me say things I don't mean."

Brewer shook his head.

"I'm asking you some perfectly straightforward questions," he said. "I'd appreciate some honest answers. If you and your husband hadn't been so keen to pull the wool over our eyes we wouldn't be sitting here now."

"I don't know what you're talking about."

"I think you do," he said. "You've been trying to get us to think that she was so depressed about her supposed illness that she killed herself. It makes me think you've got something to hide."

"I only told the other policeman what Aunty said to me," said Sarah Musgrove shaking her head. "I didn't know it wasn't true."

"Lying to the police is a serious offence."

Sarah Musgrove was red in the face and tears were welling up in her eyes.

"I didn't lie," she said.

"I want you to think carefully about what I've said," said Brewer in a gentler tone. "I can appreciate that it's hard for you to accept your husband killed your aunt but all the facts suggest he did. If you want to talk to me again, give me a call."

He offered her his card and she took it reluctantly.

Brian Todd appeared at the door.

"All done," he said.

"Find anything?" said Brewer.

Todd lifted the evidence bag that he was holding in his right hand.

"There was a hacksaw in the cupboard in the hall," he said.

"What about the raincoat?" said Brewer.

"No luck," said Todd.

"No surprises there," said Brewer.

"What raincoat?" said Sarah Musgrove. "What are you talking about?"

"I'm talking about the coat your husband was wearing the evening he cut through the brake lines on your aunt's car."

Sarah Musgrove went very pale but said nothing.

CHAPTER THIRTY-TWO

When Patel arrived in the CID office a large envelope was waiting on his desk. Opening it he found the file on Michael Groves that he had requested. He went through to the incident room, pulled up a chair and settled down to read it.

It was evident that Groves had completed his medical training because he was referred to as 'Dr Groves' in the report. He had also got married somewhere along the line because the woman he had killed was referred to as 'his wife'. At the time of the murder he was working at Orpington Hospital and was living in a flat in the hospital grounds. According to the report, a neighbour had heard noises suggesting a violent struggle coming from the flat across the landing and had called the police. When they arrived and broke down the door they found the body of a woman in her twenties lying on the kitchen floor. She had been hit several times on the head with a blunt instrument, later identified as a domestic iron. It was retrieved from a skip near the block of flats and had the victim's blood on it. Michael Groves' fingerprints were on the handle, as were those of the victim. A third set of prints did not match those from other individuals who were interviewed during the course of the investigation and remained unidentified.

Groves himself was not in the flat but he was arrested later that evening at the hospital's Accident and Emergency Department, where he was on duty. He claimed to have been working at the time of the murder, but a member of the nursing staff said he had popped out for about twenty minutes around the time his wife died because there were no patients who needed his attention. He was arrested and charged with murder. No other suspects were interviewed and no other lines of enquiry were explored.

At the trial his defence council argued that Groves would inevitably have left his fingerprints on the murder weapon because he did his own ironing. His wife was also a junior doctor working long hours and they shared all the chores around the flat. He also pointed out that there was a third, unidentified set of prints that the police had been unable to explain. The barrister painted a picture of a happy marriage in which the only tension was the limited time the couple spent together because of the pressures of their work.

The prosecution argued that Dr Groves had opportunity and that the fingerprint evidence was damning. They admitted that the perpetrator's motive was not entirely clear but presented in evidence a medical report from the accused's time at Cambridge, which described mental health problems that included paranoid ideas and violent mood swings. The university authorities had questioned whether he should be allowed to continue his studies and had sought a psychiatric evaluation. It was the opinion of the examining specialist that there was clear evidence that his mental state had improved significantly following a course of psychotherapy and passed him fit to continue.

Patel couldn't help wondering if his mental breakdown had been precipitated by the collapse of his relationship with Pearl Bailey. He made a mental note to try to establish when during his time at Cambridge his brief fling with her had occurred.

The accused had undergone further psychiatric evaluation prior to the trial and had been passed fit to answer a charge of murder, rather than manslaughter due to diminished responsibility, so the prosecution pressed for a conviction for homicide. After lengthy deliberation the jury found him guilty.

Michael Groves continued to protest his innocence, which led to him being refused parole on several occasions. However, the final entry in the file indicated that he had been released on licence a year previously.

While he had been reading the file Paul Owen had arrived ready for the morning briefing, clutching a thin folder. When DCI Taylor came into the room Patel replaced the bulky file on his desk and gave her his full attention.

"OK," she said. "Where are we with forensics?"

"All the fingerprints from the scene belong to Pearl Bailey or Helena Cooke," said Owen.

"What, all of them?" said Taylor. "I don't see how someone can have a meal in someone's house and not leave a single print."

"Maybe Helena had dinner with her and made up the story about going out with friends to throw us off the scent," said Owen.

"Could be," said Taylor. "Shelly's gone to the Strand to interview the girl this morning. We'll see what she comes up with."

"They found some fibres on two of the armchairs," said Owen. "One set came from the outfit Miss Bailey was wearing when she was killed but they haven't been able to match the other with any clothes in the house."

"Including Helena's?" said Taylor.

Owen nodded.

"How are you getting on with that phone?"

"I've just about finished," said Owen. "I did find one exchange of messages between Miss Bailey and Helena with a slightly sexual flavour but it seems that on the whole they avoided messages that would indicate that their relationship was not simply of lodger and landlady."

"What do you mean by a 'slightly sexual flavour'?" said Taylor.

Owen retrieved a printout from his backpack and leafed through it.

"Here we are," he said. "Pearl Bailey wrote 'When will you be home this evening?' and Helena replied 'Early, I haven't got any lectures this afternoon' to which Bailey replied 'Good, we'll have dinner at home and an early night.'"

Taylor scoffed.

"It's not exactly red-hot passion, but it could be construed as you suggest," she said. "We've been working on the assumption they were at it together. I know it looks likely but we need to be sure. Let's see what Shelly comes up with." She turned to look at Patel. "What's that file in front of you, Sanjay?"

"It's a police report on Michael Groves," he said. "He was convicted of murdering his wife in 1975."

"Is he still in prison?" asked Owen.

"No, he got out a year ago," said Patel.

Tracy Taylor looked pensive.

"So you're suggesting Groves might have killed Pearl Bailey?" she said.

"It's got to be a possibility," said Patel.

"Doesn't sound likely to me," said Owen.

"I agree," said Taylor. "However, since the forensics have failed to indicate a clear suspect, I'd like you to follow up on this for the time being. Where did all this happen, the previous murder I mean?"

"At Orpington Hospital."

"Umm, that's in the London Borough of Bromley," said Taylor. "I suggest we start by giving Bromley CID a ring. Mind you there won't be anyone there who was involved in the case. They'll all be retired."

CHAPTER THIRTY-THREE

Colin Brewer was sitting at his desk with his feet resting on a chair gazing at the ceiling. He was becoming increasingly frustrated by the lack of progress with the case. If he had his way Musgrove would, at this very minute, be cooling his heels in the cells ahead of another session of his rapier-sharp interrogation. But DCI Taylor said there wasn't enough evidence and the lily-livered Cheeseman was going along with her when he really should be putting her firmly in her place.

Opposite him sat Brian Todd opening an envelope. Brewer put his feet down and turned to face him. "Anything on that hacksaw yet?" he asked.

Todd shook his head.

"They only got it yesterday," he said. "It's bound to take a day or two."

"I suppose so," said Brewer. "If they find something incriminating on the blade I think we can charge Musgrove."

"It's odd he didn't get rid of it, don't you think?" said Todd. "You'd have thought it would have been the first thing he would have done after he got home."

"Most criminals make a mistake somewhere along the line," said Brewer. "This is his. I reckon he never thought we'd search the house."

Brewer thought he detected a look of scepticism on Todd's face but decided to ignore it. Brian was a good lad but he lacked experience.

There was a knock at the door and Mike Pringle came in.

"We've got a witness who reckons he saw Musgrove get on a bus in Coombe Lane," he said.

Brewer sat upright and turned to face him.

"And who is this witness?" he said eagerly.

"The bloke who was driving the bus," said Pringle.

Brewer slapped his hand on the desk.

"You see, Brian," he said. "I knew we were on the right lines. I want to set up an identity parade ASAP."

"All right, guv, I'll get on to it right away," said Pringle and left the room.

"I need to speak to Cheeseman," said Brewer, getting to his feet. "I need to get my hands on that phone."

"Do you really think he'll agree to authorise that?" said Todd.

"Well, I'll have to persuade him, won't I?"

*

Superintendent Cheeseman was on the phone waiting for a reply when Brewer burst into his office. He put down the receiver and turned to face the more junior officer.

"Take a seat, Colin," he said. "What can I do for you?"

"I want you to authorise me to get a court order so that I can seize Musgrove's mobile phone and have the contents analysed," said Brewer.

"Have you got some new evidence?" said Cheeseman. "I've discussed all this with DCI Taylor and we've agreed you can't pin the killing on Musgrove until you have something more concrete."

"Oh yes, I've got new evidence all right," said Brewer triumphantly. "A witness has placed Musgrove on a bus in Coombe Lane on the evening before the old girl died. It was going to Kingston."

"I see," said Cheeseman. "That's good news, Colin. I presume you're talking about the witness identifying Musgrove from a photograph, am I right?"

190

"Yes sir. Obviously we'll be having an identity parade to confirm it."

Cheeseman sighed. He couldn't help but admire Brewer's enthusiasm and single-mindedness but he did wish he wouldn't approach every problem like a bull in a china shop.

"It's progress, I'll admit," he said. "If the witness picks Musgrove out, you've probably got enough to arrest him. You could seize his phone in those circumstances."

"I think we've got enough to arrest him as it is," said Brewer.

"I don't agree," said Cheeseman. "Everything you've got is circumstantial."

Brewer looked downcast. Cheeseman wished he could accede to the inspector's request but that would undermine DCI Taylor, whose investigation this was. In any case, his own view was that Brewer was in the wrong on this occasion.

"I suppose that'll have to do," he said.

"I'm sorry, Colin, but I have do things by the book." Cheeseman thought for a moment then added, "Wait a minute, I thought the CCTV showed Musgrove was at Kingston Station that evening."

"The image recognition software said it wasn't him."

Cheeseman groaned inwardly.

"I told you Musgrove, or whoever it was, was too far away from the camera for you to be certain it was him," he said. "This modern technology is supposed to make our job easier. Now it seems it creates more problems than it solves. It's a bloody shame this witness of yours didn't come forward earlier. I'd have saved a useful chunk of our budget if I hadn't authorised that image analysis malarkey."

CHAPTER THIRTY-FOUR

Patel sat in the cosy living room of the bungalow belonging to retired Detective Inspector Jack Healey. Outside the picture window a small well-tended garden could be seen. The room itself was furnished in an old-fashioned style. Healey was a large man with a ruddy complexion and an infectious laugh.

"So," he said, "you want to talk about the Groves case. Why are you interested in it? It all happened years ago."

"I believe it's relevant to a case I'm investigating at the moment," said Patel.

"You think so, eh?" said Healey. "So the top brass aren't convinced. Never mind, son, you got to go with your gut feeling sometimes." He finished lighting his pipe before he continued. "Well, it all happened at Orpington Hospital. Of course, it was a very different place back then. The wards were all old Nissen huts from the First World War. They've all gone now and there's a new building on part of the site."

Patel considered asking Healey to refrain from smoking but he didn't want to antagonise the retired officer. In any case, he was afraid they were getting off the point.

"I'm particularly interested in Michael Groves himself," he said. "What did you make of him?"

Healey exhaled loudly and scratched his head.

"Well," he said, "he was very consistent with his story when we interviewed him. According to him he was in the casualty department when the murder occurred. He said their marriage was happy and he had no reason to want his wife dead. End of story."

"They hadn't been married very long, had they?" said Patel.

"Less than a year," said Healey. "They met when Rita, that was his wife's name, was a newly qualified doctor working at a hospital in London and he was a more senior trainee at the same place."

"So he was older than her?"

"Yes, about five years I think."

The door opened and Mrs Healey came in with a tea tray and placed it on the low coffee table in front of Jack Healey's armchair.

"Shall I pour?" she asked.

"Yes please, love," said Healey.

"Do you take sugar, Sergeant?" said Mrs Healey.

"No thanks," said Patel.

While she poured the tea, Patel examined the elderly couple. They projected a picture of comfortable companionship. He hoped that he and Amber would be like them forty years on.

"I'll leave you to it," said Mrs Healey and withdrew.

"I presume you interviewed people who knew them," said Patel. "How did they see their relationship?"

"They didn't have any close friends at Orpington Hospital, but then they hadn't been there very long," said Healey. "The people they worked with mostly said they seemed happy. There was one nurse who reported seeing them quarrelling when Rita came down to casualty when he was on duty, but let's face it, all married couples have a barney from time to time."

He took a drink from his cup and replaced it on the saucer with exaggerated care.

"We did find one person who'd known Michael Groves for quite a few years," he continued. "It was a schoolteacher. She worked at a local grammar school."

"What was her name?" asked Patel.

"Littleton, no, Templeton," said Healey. "That was it, Joan Templeton."

Patel felt a surge of excitement. He sat forward eagerly in his chair.

"What did she say about Michael Groves?" he asked.

"She'd known him since they were at university together," said Healey. "It was through her we found out about the mental health problems he'd had at Cambridge. Mind you, the shrink who examined him before the trial said he had all his marbles."

"Did she say anything else about him?"

"She appeared as a witness for the defence at the trial," said Healey. "Said Groves was a decent bloke who wouldn't hurt a fly, or words to that effect."

"Did Joan Templeton say anything about another fellow student called Elizabeth Crump?"

"Let me think," said Healey. He finished his tea and relit his pipe. "Blimey, it's such a long time ago. No, I don't think so."

"How many flats were there in the block where Michael and Rita Groves lived?" asked Patel.

"They were in an old house that had belonged to a wealthy local family. I think there were six of them in all. Dr Groves lived on the first floor and there was one other flat on that level."

"Who lived there?"

"It was an Indian doctor and his wife," said Healey. "I can't remember their names. She was the one who called the police. It should be in one of the reports."

"Oh yes, I remember now," said Patel. "It was a Mrs Gupta."

"Yeah, that's right."

Patel took a sip from his cup while he considered his next question.

"Did you think Groves was guilty?" he said.

"Oh yeah, we reckoned we'd got the right bloke."

"What about the other fingerprints on the murder weapon?" said Patel. "The ones that didn't belong to Groves or his wife?"

194

"We didn't think they were important," said Healey. "The thing was, the flat was married accommodation for junior doctors. Like I said before, Groves and his wife hadn't been there long. We assumed the prints belonged to the previous tenant."

"What if they didn't?" said Patel under his breath.

"You what?"

"Sorry, I was thinking out loud."

"Well, I can answer that question," said Healey. "There may have been a serious miscarriage of justice."

"Who was the previous tenant?"

"It was an Egyptian doctor," said Healey. "His name was Werba or Waaba or something like that."

"Did you interview him?"

"We tried but he'd already left the country. Gone home I suppose."

*

As he sat on the train back to London, Patel's mind was racing. Was it possible that Joan Templeton had something to do with the murder of Rita Groves? Could she even have been the real killer? It seemed rather unlikely. But perhaps she had been in love with Michael Groves and not Martin Rogers, as Pearl Bailey had suggested. Groves had been a good-looking young man, so it wouldn't have been surprising. The strikingly statuesque Pearl Bailey would naturally have caught his eye, but not plain, mousy little Joan Templeton. Meeting Michael Groves again in Orpington could have rekindled her feelings for him and she would quite possibly have viewed Rita as the main obstacle preventing her from being with him.

Then there were the unidentified fingerprints on the murder weapon. The police would have had no reason to compare them with Joan Templeton's fingerprints; she was a witness, not a suspect. DNA testing was not available in 1975 but even if it had been a sample would probably not have been taken from Miss Templeton.

If Joan Templeton really did kill Rita Groves and Michael had subsequently come to suspect her of the crime he would have been likely to seek her out when he was released from prison. Perhaps she had confessed or at least failed to allay his suspicions when they met. Surely though he would have killed her on the spot if that was the case, not planned an accident in which she would die, an accident she might in fact survive?

Another problem with this theory was that, like the police, Michael Groves had no reason to suspect Joan Templeton of killing his wife. If he had, he would surely have shared his suspicions with his lawyers and his barrister would have presented this alternative scenario at the trial. And then there was the fact that Joan had appeared as a witness for the defence at his trial, the supportive friend doing all she could to help get him acquitted.

Or had she? It was she who had made the police aware of Michael's mental health problems. Could she have murdered Rita Groves knowing that Michael would be the prime suspect? Could she have smiled to herself as he was convicted, knowing that her revenge on him was complete?

Patel closed his eyes tightly and screwed up his face. The ideas he had been considering were the stuff of a Joan Templeton novel rather than a real-life criminal case. Or were they?

CHAPTER THIRTY-FIVE

Colin Brewer knew he should leave the running of the identity parade to Todd and Pringle but he had an overwhelming desire to be there in person. He wanted to see Musgrove squirm as he stood in the line-up hoping upon hope not to be picked.

He tried to sit at his desk and do some paperwork but he couldn't concentrate. He paced up and down the office for several minutes and then he gave up and went through to the interview room where the witness was to view the identity parade, not bothering to close the door behind him.

"Morning, guv," said Todd when he walked in.

"How's it going?" asked Brewer, trying to sound disinterested.

"The witness should be here in a minute," said Pringle.

"Good," said Brewer, "I'd quite like to have a quick word with him before you start. Meantime I'd like to see the line-up."

Todd restarted the laptop on his desk and a row of similarly dressed men appeared on the screen. Musgrove looked surprisingly relaxed. *Overconfidence*, thought Brewer.

The door opened and a uniformed constable ushered in a large Asian man wearing a tailored jacket with jeans and a woollen scarf.

"Ah, Mr Aziz," said Brewer. "Thank you so much for coming in this morning. I want you to have a careful look at the men we've assembled this morning and tell us which of them was the passenger on your bus on the evening of the twelfth of March."

"No problem," said Aziz in a London accent.

"Come and have a seat over here," said Todd.

Aziz settled himself in front of the screen and studied the row of men for what seemed to Brewer to be an eternity. Then he shook his head.

"He ain't here," he said.

Brewer couldn't believe his ears.

"Are you sure?" he said.

"Sorry, the bloke who got on my bus that day ain't any of these ones."

"But you recognised his photograph."

"That looked like him but, like I said, he ain't here."

"Thank you, sir," said Todd. "We won't take up any more of your time."

Pringle hastily ushered the bus driver out of the room and closed the door.

When Aziz had gone, Brewer exploded.

"That fucker needs glasses," he said. "I've always thought that these video line-ups were a bad idea. You know yourself how different people look on the telly."

"Maybe it really was Musgrove at Kingston Station after all," said Todd. "And maybe he said he'd have taken the bus home if he'd gone to the victim's house to send us off on a wild goose chase."

"Or neither of them is Musgrove and he got home when he said he did," said Pringle, who had re-entered the room.

Brewer sighed. He was beginning to think he'd got it all wrong.

"I suppose you're right," he said. Then his face brightened. "You know what," he said, "we've assumed he went round and buggered the brakes on his way home from work. Maybe he went over there later that evening when it was dark. Yeah, that would make it easier to do it without getting spotted. I don't know why I didn't think of that before."

"How are we going to prove he done that?" said Todd. "His wife says he was at home all evening."

"Well, she would say that wouldn't she?" said Brewer. "She's in on the plot, it might even have been her idea."

"I see what you're saying," said Todd. "Mind you, I've got to say she doesn't strike me like someone who'd have the gumption to plan this."

"Right," said Pringle.

Brewer had to admit they had a point. Sarah Musgrove was the sort of sad cow who couldn't organise a piss-up in a brewery, let alone plan a murder.

"All right, so it was his idea," he said. "Of course, he would have needed her to give him an alibi. So, he tells her he's going out for a while but not where he's going. Then when the old girl winds up dead he tells his missus not to say he was out that night because it would look suspicious."

"OK, but we haven't found anyone who saw him in the vicinity of the old girl's house that evening," said Todd.

Brewer shook his head.

"That's hardly surprising," he said. "If he went over there late there wouldn't have been many people about. In any case, we've been asking people whether they saw anyone near the house during the early evening. I want you lot to go back to Beachcroft Road and interview people living in the nearby streets. Ask them if they saw someone matching his description there after dark, all right?"

Todd nodded reluctantly.

"Right ho, chief," he said.

CHAPTER THIRTY-SIX

When Patel arrived at the station he went to DCI Taylor's office to see if she was in and found her at her desk.

"So what did you find out?" she said, removing her reading glasses and sitting back in her chair.

Patel outlined what Jack Healey had told him and Taylor listened intently, nodding from time to time.

"Well, I agree it's a bit of a coincidence that Joan Templeton was living nearby when Mrs Groves was killed," she said. "But surely it's just that: a coincidence."

"Quite possibly but I'd like to look into it further," said Patel.

Taylor paused and Patel studied her face to see if he could work out what she was thinking.

"What specifically do you want to do?" she asked.

"I know it's a long shot but I'd like to find out if the murder weapon from the Groves case is still available," said Patel. "If it is we can compare the unidentified fingerprints with the ones we've got for Joan Templeton."

"Evidence from a case like this isn't kept indefinitely," said Taylor thoughtfully. "Did Groves appeal against his conviction?"

"Yes, his lawyers appeared before the Court of Appeal but were unable to convince them to alter the verdict."

"When was that?"

"1980."

"I think it's doubtful they'll have kept the weapon this long but I'll look into it," said Taylor. "A request like this would be better coming from me. Of course they might still have the fingerprints on record even if the iron's been tossed. Anything else?"

"Yes, I'd like to interview Michael Groves."

"That shouldn't be a problem," said Taylor. "Again, I think I'd better put in the request myself. If necessary I'll get Superintendent Cheeseman's support. Leave it with me."

Patel breathed an inward sigh of relief. He had been afraid that he would be told to drop the Groves investigation. He was well aware that the scenario he was proposing was supported by next to no evidence but he had a gut feeling that Groves was involved. He smiled to himself. *Perhaps I'm turning into Inspector Tewksbury*, he thought.

"Look at the time," said Taylor. "I was supposed to be meeting with the whole team five minutes ago. Come on."

*

They entered the CID office to find everyone waiting for them. Brewer inspected his watch in a rather theatrical manner. Taylor ignored him.

"Right," she said, "perhaps you'd like to tell us how you've been getting on, Colin."

"Up until now we've been working on the assumption that Musgrove disabled the brakes on his way home from work," said Brewer. "We haven't been able to place him at the crime scene during the early evening and I think that's because he went over there later so he could do the deed under cover of darkness."

"That could make sense," said Taylor. "What do you want to do next?"

"We're going to have another go at finding a witness in the Beachcroft Road area."

Taylor frowned.

"I thought we'd spoken to all the neighbours," she said.

"Most of them," said Brewer. "I'd like to widen the search area a bit. All we need is a sighting of Musgrove near the old girl's house and we've got him."

"All right," said Taylor doubtfully. "Carry on with that for the moment." She turned to Shelly Drake. "Tell them what Helena Cooke had to say."

"She denied having a sexual relationship with Pearl Bailey," said Drake. "She claims to be straight and to have a boyfriend at King's."

"Did you believe her?" said Taylor.

Drake shifted in her seat.

"Not sure," she said.

Brewer was having difficulty keeping a straight face.

"Didn't you pick anything up on your gaydar?" he said.

Drake gave him a filthy look. Taylor raised her hand.

"That's quite enough of that, Colin," she said. "You will treat your fellow officers with respect or I'll be forced to report you to the Borough Commander. Do I make myself clear?"

"Yes, boss, sorry," said Brewer, smirking.

"Right now back to business," said Taylor. "We need to find out if Helena Cooke was lying about her relationship with Pearl Bailey. A team of us are going to King's College to speak to some of Helena's friends, including this alleged boyfriend. I shall go myself and I want Patel, Owen and Drake to come along."

"OK, I understand you think this student killed Pearl Bailey for her money," said Brewer. "But what's the point of trying to find out if she and her landlady were having a thing together? Surely all that matters is she's the main beneficiary in the will?"

"It's the same as with the Templeton case," said Taylor. "Helena has to have a motive. If she didn't know she was getting the money when Pearl Bailey died, why would she have killed her? And if they were having an intimate relationship it's more likely she would have told her about the will."

"Yeah, all right," said Brewer. "But she could have told her she was going to inherit even if they weren't at it."

"I agree," said Taylor. "We still need to work out why Pearl Bailey would have decided to leave her the money if she was just the lodger."

"As I said, what we know is that she left her the money," said Brewer. "The 'why' doesn't seem very important."

Patel could see that Taylor was becoming increasingly angry.

"Again, it's like Musgrove," she said. "If we catch her out in a lie we've got reason to be suspicious of her."

Brewer shrugged but he didn't say anything else. Taylor turned to Patel.

"Tell the others about Michael Groves," she said.

"Michael was Pearl Bailey's lover at Cambridge," said Patel.

"Wait a minute," said Brewer, "I thought she was a lesbo."

Patel was going to respond, but Taylor spoke first.

"It seems it was an experiment," she said. "As far as we know she stuck to women after that."

"The thing is," said Patel, "Groves is a convicted killer who's recently been released on licence."

"What sort of killer?" said Brewer. "Are you saying he's a psycho?"

Patel's mouth was dry and the inspector's eyes seemed to be boring right into him. He hoped his anxiety didn't show in his voice.

"It appears it was a crime of passion," he said. "The victim was his wife."

"And you think he wanted to kill some woman he shagged thirty years ago?" said Brewer. "That sounds like the sort of thing you'd see on the telly, but in real life it doesn't work like that, not in my experience anyway."

"Be that as it may," said Taylor, "we're going to keep all avenues of enquiry open for the time being. Let's face it, we don't have a totally credible suspect for either murder at the moment. You carry on with Musgrove and we'll explore these other possibilities."

CHAPTER THIRTY-SEVEN

As they approached the forbidding concrete frontage of King's College, Patel's mind went back to his own student days. As an ethnic minority student from a South London comprehensive he had felt completely out of place at Queen Mary College. The first few weeks were a blur of unfamiliar faces and locations, but gradually he settled in and made one or two friends.

For the first year he lived at home but before long the lengthy commute by bus, train and underground became irksome. When he was offered a place in a flat within walking distance of the campus he jumped at the chance. His parents took some convincing but he won them over, mainly by pointing out how much he would be saving in travel expenses. For the first time he was living away from home and was free to enjoy the benefits of student life in London.

He was pretty sure his flatmates viewed him as a swot who didn't know how to enjoy himself but they had always tried to include him in what they were doing. So it was that he discovered pubs and booze and girls. He did not indulge in any of these delights to the extent that the others did but, like a nervous bather gingerly dipping a toe in the water, he found this new world surprisingly warm and inviting.

It was during this period that he met Amber. The first time he saw her she was walking across the Mile End Campus with some friends. She had sailed by in a group of laughing, chatting girls, beautiful, serene and obviously unobtainable. When he thought about her, which he did surprisingly often, he tried, with limited success, to dismiss her from his mind. He had to admit to himself that he was attracted to her from the first but he didn't believe she would want to go out with an Indian boy whose family lived over their takeaway restaurant in South London. Fortunately, he was wrong.

She was a law student, so their paths didn't cross very often. He had been admiring her from afar for quite a while before, in an act of what seemed to him to be superhuman recklessness, he plucked up courage to speak to her in the union bar. To his surprise she hadn't made any attempt to get rid of him. On the contrary, she had smiled and moved closer to where he was standing.

*

The college provided a couple of small seminar rooms for the detectives. DCI Taylor told them that she would work with Paul Owen, while Patel was to work with Shelly Drake. Drake grimaced when she made this announcement and Patel's heart sank. Realising he would have to make the best he could of a bad job, he rearranged their room so that there were two chairs on each side of the table which stood on the side of the room furthest from the door.

"We're going to talk to someone called Gemma Harvey first," he said.

"You'd better let me ask the questions," said Drake.

Patel considered this for a moment. He felt he had got off on the wrong foot with Shelly and he was keen to put this right but at the same time he didn't want to appear weak in front of a junior colleague.

"I'll start the questioning and you can chip in as we go along," he said.

"You want to play nice cop, nasty cop, right?" said Drake, grinning defiantly.

"No, but I think we'll get more out of her if we both ask questions. Now, if you wouldn't mind, Constable, I'd like you to ask her to come in."

"Yes, Sergeant," said Drake and walked towards the door at a snail's pace.

Patel gritted his teeth. He knew he had to concentrate on the job in hand and ignore her insolent behaviour but it wasn't easy.

Gemma Harvey was a nervous-looking girl with glasses who explained that she was in Helena's year and, like her, was doing European studies. She said that they had been friends since their first term.

Patel smiled at her.

"Has Helena said anything about inheriting some money?" he asked.

Gemma looked puzzled.

"No," she said. "We never talk about things like that."

"What do you mean by 'things like that'?" said Drake.

"I mean money," said Gemma. "It's none of my business what she has or hasn't got."

Patel fought to control his irritation. It was his view that they would get more out of the witness if they went easy on her, at least at first.

"OK," he said. "Has she told you anything about the place where she lives in term time?"

"Well, I know it's in Wimbledon," said Gemma. "That's about all."

"You haven't been there then?"

"No, she's never suggested it."

"Has she talked about Pearl Bailey at all?"

"I know she lived with her," said Gemma. "She was a writer I think. Helena said she was killed. She was really upset about it."

"Does Helena have a boyfriend?" asked Patel casually.

"Not really, well there is Damian, they go around together," said Gemma. "I mean I don't think they're sleeping together or anything."

"Are you sure about that?" said Patel.

"Not really," she said hesitantly then added, "I think she'd have told me if she was but maybe she kept it to herself."

"Is there anyone else Helena is particularly close to?" said Patel.

"Well, there's Lou and Amy, and I think she spends time with Nadia sometimes. They're both into netball."

"So she likes sport, does she?" said Patel.

Gemma smiled.

"Oh yes, she's really fit I think, not like me," she said.

Drake had been slouching in her chair but at this point she leaned forwards and rested her forearms on the table.

"Has she ever shown any sexual interest in you?" she asked.

Gemma blushed deeply.

"What do you mean?" she said.

"Well, has she ever tried to kiss you, or suggested you might like to sleep with her?" said Drake.

"No, of course not," said Gemma. "Why would you think such a thing?"

"We have reason to believe that Helena is a sexually active lesbian but she denies it," said Drake. "Personally, I think she's lying. You're a reasonably attractive girl so I thought you might be her type."

Gemma looked as if she was going to burst into tears but she controlled herself.

"I don't know why you think that," she said. "Helena's a perfectly normal young woman."

"Oh and lesbians aren't normal, is that right?" said Drake.

Gemma looked at Drake's rotund figure, close-cropped hair and make-up-free face and swallowed hard.

"No of course not," she said. "I only meant that she isn't interested in women, not in that way."

This exchange had clearly unnerved the witness but Patel decided that a change of tack was needed.

"Were you out with Helena and the others last Saturday?" he asked.

Gemma nodded.

"There were five of us," she said.

"Who were they?"

"Helena and I, Lou, Amy and Damian."

"Where did you go?"

"We met up at college and went to a pub."

"Which one?"

"The Wellington."

"Do you remember what time Helena left that evening?" said Patel.

"About ten I think," said Gemma. "The rest of us stayed on and had another round of drinks."

"You're sure she was with you that night?" said Drake.

Gemma frowned.

"Yes, positive," she said. "I don't know why you're trying to catch me out."

"Well, it's like this," said Drake, "if she wasn't with you she might've been in Wimbledon killing Pearl Bailey."

Tears were streaming down Gemma's face. She shook her head.

"She was with us, like I told you," she said.

Drake sat back in her chair.

"Lying to the police is a serious matter," she said.

"I'm telling the truth."

Patel decided that it was time to call a halt.

"All right, Gemma," he said. "That will be all for now."

When she had left the room Drake said: "You see, nice cop, nasty cop, always works."

Patel was on the point of losing his temper but managed to avoid raising his voice.

"I'm not convinced we got as much information out of her as we might have done," he said. "Still, we can always talk to her again if necessary." He took a deep breath. "OK, let's see what Damian Fisher has to say for himself."

Drake ushered a tall young man with a shock of curly hair into the room and invited him to take a seat. He stared at the two policemen like a rabbit caught in headlights.

"OK, Damian," said Patel. "Are you doing European studies as well?"

"No, I'm reading Spanish," he said.

"So how do you come to be friends with Helena then?"

Damian shrugged.

"I mix with a lot of students on different courses," he said. "It's part of the fun of university life."

"It is, isn't it?" said Patel, nodding and smiling. "Were you at the Wellington with the others last Saturday?"

"Yes, I was there."

"Was Helena with you?"

"Yes."

"What time did she go home?" said Drake.

"Early," said Damian. "About ten I think."

"Why was that?" said Patel.

"She said she was tired," said Damian. "Actually I think she was pissed off that Amy was the centre of attention."

"Was she flirting with you? Amy, I mean," said Drake.

Damian gave a little laugh.

"No, of course not," he said.

"Why do you say of course not?"

"Amy doesn't fancy me, she's got a boyfriend," said Damian. "He's not a student, he's at work."

"When you said 'Amy was the centre of attention', what did you mean exactly?" asked Patel.

"Amy's a total extrovert," said Damian. "She talks non-stop and sometimes it gets on Helena's nerves."

"I see," said Patel. "Why didn't you leave with Helena?"

Damian shrugged.

"She said she was going straight to bed when she got home," he said. "I wanted to stay on with the others."

"Is Helena your girlfriend?" said Drake.

"Yes, well sort of."

"What does that mean?"

Damian's face turned bright red.

"We go out together sometimes, you know for drinks or the cinema," he said.

Drake fixed him with her most penetrating stare.

"Are you sleeping together?" she said.

"No."

"Why's that?" said Drake. "Don't you fancy her in that way?"

"Oh God, this is so embarrassing," said Damian. "I'd like to but she won't let me."

"What about kissing?" said Drake. "Is she up for a good snog?"

Damian didn't answer at first and his face was contorted, Patel presumed, by inner conflict.

"I've kissed her," he said at last. "She's, well, she's not very responsive, not like other girls I've known."

"Maybe she prefers girls," said Drake.

"No, I don't think so," said Damian. "She's not that type."

"What do you mean, 'that type'?"

"Well you know, the butch, mannish type."

"Well, I've got news for you," said Drake. "That's a stereotype bandied about by homophobic ignoramuses. Girly girls like Helena are just as likely to be gay."

Patel coughed loudly.

"Did Helena ever invite you to visit her in Wimbledon?" he said.

"No, she didn't," said Damian.

"Why do you think that was?"

Damian frowned.

"I don't know," he said. "She just didn't."

"Are you sure she was with you at the pub that night?" said Drake.

"Yes," said Damian. "She was definitely there."

"If we find out you've lied to us about that you'll be in serious trouble."

Damien looked Drake straight in the eye.

"She was there," he said.

"All right," said Patel, "that's all for now."

When he was gone, Patel considered what they had been told. If the two students were telling the truth then it was clear that Helena did not have dinner with Pearl Bailey on the night she died. However, the dinner guest might have left before she returned from the pub and Helena could have seen the chance to kill her landlady and throw suspicion on whoever had been at the house earlier in the evening. Having done the deed, she had phoned the police to reinforce that perception. The only odd thing that didn't fit was the obvious care that had been taken to remove any fingerprints left by the dinner guest. It would have been in Helena's best interests to ensure that there was plenty of evidence to allow the identification of that person. That was unless she was keen to keep their identity secret for some reason. It was hard to imagine why that might be.

They interviewed two other students who were friendly with Helena, both of whom confirmed what they had already been told. They were unable to extract any useful additional information from either of them. When DCI Taylor and DC Owen came through to their room after the last witness had left they reported that Lou and Amy had confirmed that Helena stayed at the Wellington until around 10pm on the night of the murder and then announced she was going home to bed.

"It all seems to fit," said Taylor. "It would have taken her about an hour, give or take, to get back to Wimbledon." She turned to Patel. "What did the boyfriend have to say?"

211

"He says they were going out but not having sex," he said. "That was sort of confirmed by the first girl we interviewed, Gemma Harvey."

"Maybe Helena put them up to saying she was with them that night," said Drake.

"That's pure speculation," said Patel. "The evidence suggests she didn't get back to Wimbledon until after eleven. In any case why would they agree to lie for Helena in these circumstances?"

"Even if she didn't get home until then she could still have done it," said Taylor. "We have some reason to believe that Helena lied to us about her relationship with Pearl Bailey and she certainly had motive and opportunity. We'll get her in and interview her under caution."

CHAPTER THIRTY-EIGHT

Tracy Taylor sat down in front of the Cheeseburger's desk. She noted that the superintendent was wearing a different suit from the usual one. That was a first. Still, he'd somehow managed to make it look as if he'd been sleeping in it. Tracy wondered whether Cheeseman's wife worried about his lack of sartorial *savoir faire* and came to the conclusion that she didn't, or that more likely she had decided he was a lost cause long ago.

"I'll come straight to the point," said Cheeseman, picking up a letter that was lying on his desk. "I've had a complaint from a solicitor acting for your suspect Alan Musgrove. It's concerning the behaviour of Inspector Brewer, but I thought I should speak to you first as you're the senior investigating officer in this case. The lawyer says that Mr Musgrove and his wife have been quote: 'harassed by DI Brewer'. He says that we have been investigating him for the possible murder of his aunt, despite the fact that we have quote: 'not the slightest shred of evidence against him'."

"I don't think that's entirely fair, sir," said Taylor.

"Maybe not," said Cheeseman. "I've spent the morning going through all the evidence you've collected again and I have to say that I'm not impressed. Granted, the brakes on the lady's car were tampered with but you haven't come up with anything that confirms that Musgrove did it."

"I'd like to point out that the Musgroves haven't been entirely honest with us," said Taylor. She realised, somewhat to her surprise, that she was effectively defending Inspector

Brewer's conduct, not a situation she had imagined she would find herself in.

"OK, they were less than open about the will," said Cheeseman. "You've attempted to establish that they lied about when Alan Musgrove got home, but I have to say, what you've come up with doesn't convince me."

"I accept what you say," said Taylor. She thought for a moment then added, "Surely though it's for a jury to decide if Musgrove's guilty?"

The Cheeseburger scoffed.

"I can't see the CPS agreeing to go to court with the evidence you've got at the moment," he said. "You've had a team of detectives on overtime interviewing bus drivers and you've come up with nothing."

"The fact remains that we still don't know how Miss Templeton's brakes were disabled," said Taylor. "And we haven't got the forensics on the hacksaw from Musgrove's flat."

Cheeseman got up and walked round to the front of his desk. Perching on its corner he said: "Look, Tracy, I know there are loose ends but we can't be expected to get to the bottom of everything that goes on in this borough. We've expended a lot of police time on this and got nowhere. In this age of PR and PC and P-bloody everything else I have to try to look at things objectively. I think this complaint is total bollocks and I'll write a response to all the points they raise. However, I'm suspending the investigation into Musgrove unless and until some new evidence comes to light. The Templeton case remains open of course and you'll continue to explore other lines of enquiry but there will be no further action with regard to Mr and Mrs Musgrove. Do I make myself clear?"

"Yes, sir," said Taylor, shifting in her seat. "Who's going to tell DI Brewer?"

Cheeseman frowned.

"You are, of course," he said.

"Wouldn't it be better coming from you?" she said, realising as she spoke that this question made her appear weak.

Cheeseman's face turned a nasty shade of purple.

"You're in overall charge of this investigation and it's your job to deal with the officers under your command," he said. "I know Brewer can be an awkward sod, but he has to take orders from his superiors like the rest of us. I supported your assignment to the Major Investigation Team because I thought you had the leadership skills required for the job. Please don't prove me wrong, all right?"

"Of course, sir, I'll speak to him as soon as possible."

"Right then," said Cheeseman. "What about this other murder? Do you think the two are linked?"

"We are pursuing several lines of enquiry," said Taylor. "At present we don't have concrete evidence of a link."

"All right then, keep me posted."

Cheeseman's assertion that he had supported her appointment as head of the Major Investigation Team came as a surprise to Taylor. Her impression had always been that he had fought it tooth and nail and had only reluctantly acquiesced to her being given the job when pressured to do so by those above him. But was it true? She found it hard to imagine Cheeseman being on her side, especially as there had been a well-qualified local candidate on the shortlist. But, if it wasn't true, why had he said it?

*

Taylor went through to the incident room. Its only inhabitant was Brian Todd who was working at his computer.

"Is Colin about?" she said.

"He's gone to take another look at the victim's car," said Todd. "He reckons we've got to go back to square one and start again."

"What are you doing this morning?"

Todd put down his pen and swivelled round in his chair.

"I'm making a list of taxi firms that operate in the area around the victim's house," he said. "This afternoon we're going to go round them and show them Musgrove's picture in case any of the drivers remember picking him up. Colin reckons Musgrove got a taxi to Kingston Station and then walked home to make it look like he'd used the train."

Taylor sighed.

"You might as well pack it in because Superintendent Cheeseman has suspended the enquiry into Musgrove," she said. "He reckons it's going nowhere."

"You're kidding? DI Brewer will be gutted."

"I know, but there's nothing I can do about it."

*

Brian Todd and Colin Brewer were sitting in a booth in the Prince of Wales with two half-empty glasses of beer in front of them. Todd could see that the inspector was seething with anger.

"We were so fucking close to nailing that bastard," said Brewer. "I only needed another few days."

"They shouldn't have closed us down but quite frankly we didn't have enough to charge Musgrove," said Todd.

"I know that," said Brewer. "The thing is, my gut feeling was he's our man. It drives me mad when the guilty get away with murder, literally in this case."

"Yeah, well, it's out of our hands now."

Brewer emptied his glass and said, "Same again?"

"Yeah, all right."

When Brewer returned with the drinks he said, "I blame that fucking bitch Taylor. She should have stood up to Cheeseman and insisted we carry on."

"Maybe he'll knock the whole thing on the head," said Todd. "Not bothering to investigate crime seems to be all the rage now."

"Maybe," said Brewer. "I'll tell you one thing, this wouldn't be happening if I was in charge of this investigation rather than her."

It was not the first time that Brewer had spoken to Todd about his unsuccessful appearance in front of the promotion board for chief inspector and he was well aware of his friend's ambition to be head of the Major Investigation Team. He also knew it was a job for an experienced chief inspector and the obvious local candidate when Taylor was appointed was DCI Alan Cook, who was liked and respected around the station. Most people had thought he was a dead cert to take over the Major Investigation Team but it seemed that the powers that be had wanted new blood. In any case if Brewer had become a DCI he would have ceased to be a member of the team. He knew from experience that the best thing to do in these circumstances was to humour Colin.

"Quite frankly I was gobsmacked when you didn't get promoted," he said, "and I thought Alan Cook would take over from Jack Richards."

"Yeah, well, it's fucking typical of the way things are going," said Brewer. "They're shit-scared not to appoint a woman when there's one on the shortlist."

"Yeah," said Todd. "Mind you, she is good at the job."

Brewer grunted. Todd wondered if he'd spoken out of turn but Brewer looked thoughtful. They drank in silence for several minutes then Brewer put down his glass.

"I heard something about our precious DCI the other day," he said. "I was at a home game up at Craven Cottage and I met a geezer who used to work with her in Newham. Apparently they called her 'Tracy the Tramp' up there."

Todd was relieved that the subject had been changed. On top of that this sounded interesting.

"Why did they call her that?" he said.

"It seems she had a bit of a reputation for having it off with fellow officers," said Brewer. "This bloke reckoned a lot of what people said about her was probably bollocks but, as he put it, there's no smoke without fire. Apparently she got divorced around the time she moved to Newham. The husband was another serving officer. I don't know what happened to him; presumably he stayed put and she moved so they wouldn't have to meet during the course of their work. She'd been working somewhere outside London apparently. This bloke didn't know where exactly. Anyway she put it about a bit, by all accounts."

"You wouldn't expect her to be short of offers in that department," said Todd. "That doesn't mean she isn't a good copper."

"Granted," said Brewer. "The guy I'm talking about said as far as he was concerned she was a good gaffer but a lot of the blokes resented her being a chief inspector. There are a lot of tough old-school coppers in that area and they didn't like having a woman tell them what to do. Mind you, according to this bloke, she got herself a reputation for clearing up crimes. Said there are a lot of villains in Newham and she collared quite a few of them."

"There you are," said Todd. "I said she was good at the job."

"Might have been luck," said Brewer. He leaned closer to Todd and dropped his voice. "It seems she was screwing the superintendent she was working with. They had a lot of 'evening meetings' to discuss the progress of an investigation they were working on. It turned out they were held in her bedroom."

Todd laughed.

"Well, there's one thing," he said. "I can't see her doing that with the Cheeseburger."

"Right on," said Brewer grinning broadly.

"Mind you, she seems keen on our new DS," said Todd.

"Oh yeah, she's all over Wonder Boy." Brewer drained his glass. "Maybe she's at it with him," he said.

"It's possible," said Todd. "Maybe she likes the lick of the tar brush."

"It's more than a lick in his case," said Brewer. "Right, you want another?"

"I'd better be going in a minute so I'll pass," said Todd. "What do you make of Patel?"

"I've seen his type before," said Brewer. "They think because they've had a fancy education they're better than the rest of us. You've heard all his half-baked theories about who killed the victims in this case. I'd like to see him produce some real evidence, but of course he won't. That would involve hard graft and that's beneath him."

Chapter Thirty-Nine

Helena Cooke was already in the interview room when Patel and Taylor entered. Patel noted that she looked deathly pale. It was only natural, he thought; being interviewed under caution is stressful even if you are innocent.

Beside her sat her solicitor, a balding man wearing a pinstripe suit and a spotted bow tie. Before the two officers had taken their seats he began speaking.

"I would like to make it clear at the outset of these proceedings that I consider your decision to interview my client in these circumstances unnecessarily heavy-handed," he said. "She did her public duty by reporting the discovery of the body of the deceased in a timely manner and, as I understand it, has answered all the questions put to her fully and truthfully."

"Good morning," said Taylor as she took her seat. "I am Detective Chief Inspector Taylor and this is my colleague Sergeant Patel. We have reason to believe that your client has not answered our questions fully and truthfully."

"You'll need to be more specific," said the lawyer, looking down his nose at Taylor.

"I intend to be," she said. "If you don't mind I will direct my questions to your client, but first I will ask Sergeant Patel to commence a recording of these proceedings and read Miss Cooke her rights."

While Patel was doing this, the lawyer regarded him with

apparent disgust. When he had finished DCI Taylor turned to Helena and smiled.

"Why do you think Pearl Bailey left her money to you in her will?" she said.

"I don't know," said Helena. "It's awfully kind of her but I can't see why she picked me. I mean, I know she had no family but surely there must have been someone else who was important to her."

"Why do you think she didn't marry?"

"I don't see the relevance of that question," said the lawyer. "In addition I cannot see how my client could possibly know the answer to it."

Taylor sat back in her chair and folded her arms.

"Oh I think she knows the answer," she said. "We know that Pearl Bailey was a lesbian and we believe Helena knew it as well."

"What precisely are you suggesting?" said the lawyer.

Taylor smiled and glanced at Patel.

"We believe that Miss Bailey and Miss Cooke were lovers," he said.

Helena swallowed hard and the lawyer scoffed.

"What grounds do you have for this extraordinary assertion?" he said.

"Pearl Bailey kept a photograph of Helena on her mantelpiece," said Patel. "She also used Miss Cooke's name as the password to access her computer and we found a message on the deceased's phone that suggested they were having regular sex."

The lawyer looked as if he were about to explode.

"This is preposterous," he said. "I have acted for Miss Cooke's family for many years and I have known her since she was at school. I really don't think it is likely she would become involved in a relationship of the sort you are suggesting. And even if what you say is true, same-sex relationships are not a criminal offence."

"No indeed," said Taylor. "I am not interested in whether or not your client was having sex with the deceased. What I want to discuss today is whether or not she killed her lover in order to inherit her fortune."

The lawyer narrowed his eyes.

"What evidence do you have to support this ridiculous notion of yours?" he said.

"Miss Cooke had motive and opportunity," said Patel. "In addition her fingerprints were found at the scene of the crime."

"Well, of course you found her fingerprints at the scene," said the lawyer. "She had been living in the house for the best part of a year and a half."

"Granted," said Taylor. "The point is we didn't find any fingerprints other than those belonging to the deceased and Miss Cooke."

"So, the murderer wore gloves. I'm sure I would if I was going to commit such a crime." He paused then added, "Are my client's fingerprints on the murder weapon?"

Patel winced inwardly. The lawyer had put his finger on the major weakness in their case.

"We haven't found a murder weapon as yet," said Taylor.

"In that case you have no substantial reason to accuse my client of this crime."

"We'll have to beg to differ about that," said Taylor. "I would like to hear what Miss Cooke has to say about what happened that night."

Helena Cooke looked at the lawyer, as if imploring him to deny the request. He turned to face her.

"I am sure you have already answered questions about all this, my dear," he said. "However, I think it would be in order for you to give an account of your actions on the night in question."

Helena sighed and sat upright in her chair.

"Like I said, I went out for a drink with some friends," she said. "I left the pub about ten and came back to Wimbledon."

"How did you travel?" asked Patel.

"I got a minicab."

"When we first met you said you travelled to and from Wimbledon by Tube," said Taylor.

"When I'm going to college, yes," said Helena. "Late at night I prefer to take a cab."

"Fair enough," said Taylor. "When you arrived at the house, did you see anyone? Someone leaving the house or walking along the street perhaps."

Helena shook her head.

"All right, carry on."

"When I got home I called to Pearl to tell her I was back but there was no reply. I went through to the sitting room and there she was lying on the floor."

At this point tears started to stream down Helena's face. The lawyer laid a reassuring hand on her shoulder and Patel pushed a box of tissues across the table towards her. When she had recovered herself she continued.

"I looked closer to see if she was alive and then I took out my mobile and dialled 999."

"Did you ask for an ambulance or the police?" asked Patel.

Helena didn't reply immediately.

"Umm, police," she said at last.

"Why didn't you request an ambulance?" said Patel. "We've been told that Miss Bailey's life might have been saved if she'd received early medical treatment."

"She was dead."

"How do you know?"

Helena looked confused.

"She didn't have a pulse," she said.

"So you took her pulse?" said Patel.

"Yes," said Helena. "I've done first aid so it was the obvious thing to do."

"And you felt you were able to decide she was dead without seeking a professional assessment of her condition?"

"Yes."

Patel shook his head. Helena glanced at the lawyer who gave her a reassuring smile.

"Someone had dinner with Pearl Bailey the night she died," said Taylor. "You've told us she didn't tell you who it was, but do you have any idea who it might have been?"

"None at all, honestly."

"Did she often have people over for dinner?" asked Patel.

"No she didn't," said Helena. She paused then added: "There was someone a couple of weeks ago."

"Who was it?" said Patel.

"A friend called Rosemary something or other."

"Rosemary Rogers?"

"Yes, that was it."

This was unexpected. Patel thought back to his interview with Dr Rogers. What was it she had said? 'I can't remember the last time I went to Liz's house.'

"Did you have dinner with them?" he said.

"No."

"Did Miss Bailey say anything about that evening after the event?" said Taylor.

"No," said Helena. "I didn't ask about it and she didn't volunteer any information."

"Is it possible that Rosemary Rogers had dinner with Miss Bailey on the night she was killed?"

"I suppose so, but why would she come again when she'd been two weeks before?"

It seemed to Patel to be a reasonable assumption, unless Rosemary Rogers was a regular visitor to the house. If she was, that could be significant, or it might be completely irrelevant. Either way it was something Dr Rogers had failed to mention when he interviewed her. It seemed that Taylor was thinking along the same lines.

"Had Rosemary Rogers been to the house before, during the period you've been living there?" she said.

"Not as far as I'm aware," said Helena. "Of course Pearl didn't tell me about everything she was doing and everyone she was meeting. Why would she?"

"Where were you the evening Rosemary Rogers came to dinner?" said Patel.

"At a party. I left before this Rosemary person arrived and didn't get home until after midnight, by which time she'd gone home."

"Where was the party?" said Taylor.

"At a friend's house in Barnet."

"I'll need the name and address of the host, so we can check you're telling the truth."

"I really don't think that's necessary," said the lawyer.

"That's all right," said Helena and wrote the details using pen and paper proffered by Patel.

"Any more questions?" said the lawyer.

"That's all for now," said Taylor. "I have to tell you, Helena, that you remain under suspicion but we will be taking no further action for the time being."

The lawyer pushed his chair back and got to his feet.

"I very much hope you will identify the real culprit in the near future. My client has suffered quite enough. Good morning."

When they had left, Taylor turned to Patel.

"Good work, Sergeant," she said. "In view of what we've just heard, I think we'd better have another word with Dr Rogers. You and Owen can go round there."

CHAPTER FORTY

Rosemary Rogers opened the door to the two policemen and invited them to come in. On this occasion she was wearing a black sweater with a tweed skirt. Patel couldn't help wondering if fibres from it would match those found at the murder scene. If so they weren't from a garment worn by the killer, which would make getting a conviction more difficult.

"So, what can I do for you this time?" she said, when they were seated in the living room.

"Last time I was here you said you hadn't been to Pearl Bailey's house for dinner in the recent past," said Patel. "We have reason to believe you went there shortly before the night she was killed."

Dr Rogers reddened a little.

"Oh yes, I'm sorry about that," she said. "I did have supper with her soon after Martin's funeral. I should have told you but it slipped my mind."

"When was this arranged?" said Patel.

"At the funeral," said Dr Rogers. "She invited me and we got our diaries out then and there."

"Did you meet her lodger, Helena Cooke, when you were there?"

"No, she was out for the evening. Mind you, Pearl talked about her quite a lot. I got the impression she was very fond of her."

"Would it surprise you if I told you that Helena Cooke is going to inherit all Miss Bailey's money?" said Patel.

"Goodness, yes it would," said Dr Rogers. "I didn't think they were related."

"They aren't," said Patel. "We understand that her parents were friends of Miss Bailey's."

"Did the young woman know she was going to inherit when Liz died?" said Dr Rogers.

"She says she knew nothing about it."

"Oh dear," said Dr Rogers. "It reminds me of Julie Palmer."

"Who's that?" said Patel.

"Liz met her at a book festival somewhere or other and they sort of clicked," said Dr Rogers. "She moved in with her for a while and Liz decided to make her the main beneficiary of her will. She told Martin and I about it and we tried to talk her out of it. She said we should mind our own business. Anyway, in due course Julie showed her true colours. Liz found out she was seeing someone else. Worst of all, it was a man. She sent her packing and changed her will."

"Do you think it's likely that Miss Bailey would have told Helena Cooke that she was going to inherit?" said Owen.

"Based on the Julie Palmer episode, I'd say so," said the doctor. "I know she told Julie about it. It seems strange to say this, because Liz was always outwardly so confident, but I honestly think that she used the promise of an inheritance to make the girl stay with her. She always seemed insecure in her relationships. I think that's partly why they tended not to last."

"How old was Julie Palmer?" said Owen.

"Early thirties I should think," said Dr Rogers, crossing her legs. "This was about ten years ago, so Liz was in her late fifties."

"I'm sorry to bring this up again," said Patel. "I need to confirm that you didn't have dinner with Miss Bailey the night she died."

"As I told you before, I wasn't with Liz that night," said Dr Rogers. "I can prove it if you'd like. I was at a concert at the Wigmore Hall and I still have my ticket. Would you like to see it?"

227

"If it wouldn't be too much trouble."

Dr Rogers got up from her armchair and went across to a bureau on the other side of the room. She opened a drawer and took out a ticket stub, which she proceeded to give to Patel.

"Thank you," he said. He checked the date on the ticket. It was for the evening of the murder. He hadn't really thought that Dr Rogers was a suspect but couldn't help feeling disappointed. *Another blind alley*, he thought. "We won't take up any more of your time," he said. "Before we go we'd like to take your fingerprints and a DNA sample."

For the first time Dr Rogers looked uneasy.

"I'm getting the distinct impression I'm a suspect," she said.

"It's all just to assist us in a process of elimination," said Patel.

*

As they headed back to Wimbledon Police Station with Owen at the wheel, Patel thought about what they had discovered. Dr Rogers had lied about having dinner with Pearl Bailey, or at least had failed to mention it during their first interview. She now admitted having been at the house on that occasion and Helena had previously confirmed that she was there. Dr Rogers continued to deny being at the victim's house on the night she had been killed and appeared to have a cast-iron alibi. In any case it was difficult to understand why she would have wanted Pearl Bailey dead. In fact she had more reason to kill Joan Templeton, based on what they had been told about her behaviour at Martin Rogers' funeral, but Patel couldn't see her manoeuvring her considerable bulk under Miss Templeton's car to cut the brake lines.

The episode involving another of Pearl Bailey's younger lovers suggested that she was likely to have told Helena about her inheritance but didn't prove that she had done so. Helena was the only suspect with motive and opportunity but somehow Patel wasn't convinced that she was guilty.

Brewer, Todd and Pringle had been tasked with speaking to other individuals with links to Pearl Bailey, her lawyer, accountant and so on. Perhaps they would come up with a new suspect. Somehow he rather doubted it.

That left Michael Groves. He just had to hope that DCI Taylor would be able to arrange for him to be interviewed. If this became possible, Patel hoped very much that he would have the chance to speak to the convicted murderer himself.

CHAPTER FORTY-ONE

Patel looked up from his computer to see that DCI Taylor had entered the incident room and walked over to where Brian Todd was sitting.

"How did you get on?" she said. "Did you get anything useful from Pearl Bailey's solicitor, Brian?"

"Not really," said Todd. "There were only two copies of her will, one with the victim and one in the lawyer's office. They're pretty certain no one else had sight of it."

"And the accountant?" she said, turning to Pringle.

"Zilch," he said.

"What about you, Colin, anything to report?"

"I spoke to her editor," said Brewer. "Unfortunately she hadn't been working with the victim for long and couldn't tell me much. She did say Pearl Bailey could be difficult to work with but that's hardly a motive for murder."

"Who was her previous editor?" asked Taylor.

"I got the name, do you want me to interview her as well?"

"Yes please."

Taylor turned to Patel.

"There is one piece of good news," she said. "Michael Groves has agreed to be interviewed."

Patel punched the air.

"That's fantastic," he said.

"I'm going to let you have a preliminary chat with him," said Taylor. "If you get something promising I'll speak to him myself."

Brewer rolled his eyes and exhaled loudly.

"Yes, Colin?" said Taylor.

"It's just that I'm concerned we're going off at tangents," he said. "Also we seem to have given up on the Templeton case."

Taylor gritted her teeth.

"We've put a lot of effort into that investigation and so far we've failed to identify the killer," she said. "With regard to Alan Musgrove, as you already know, Superintendent Cheeseman and I agree that we need more evidence or a new line of enquiry if we're going to take that area of investigation forward. That doesn't mean we've given up on the Templeton case. For a start, Michael Groves is a potential suspect for both killings."

"There isn't a scrap of real evidence he was involved in either of them," said Brewer fiercely.

"Which is why I've asked Sergeant Patel to interview him," said Taylor. "It may get us nowhere but it's a line of enquiry that needs to be pursued."

Brewer had a face like thunder but he said nothing.

"Have we got the forensic report on the hacksaw you took from Musgrove's flat?" said Taylor.

"Not as yet," he said.

"Right then, Pringle can chase that up this morning." She turned to Shelly Drake. "How did you get on at King's College?"

"I spoke to some more students in Helena's year," said Drake. "They couldn't tell me anything we didn't know already. However, as I was about to leave, Helena buttonholed me and said she'd remembered something that might be important. It seems that Pearl Bailey had an ornament on the mantelpiece, an ugly modern sculpture-type thing. It was supposed to be a mother and child apparently. Anyway, when she got back on the night of the murder it wasn't there."

"I don't remember anything like that at the murder scene," said Taylor. "What about you, Sanjay?"

"As far as I can remember there was only a clock and a couple of candlesticks on the mantelpiece," he said.

"So, maybe that's our missing murder weapon," said Taylor. "Paul, have you got her phone handy?"

"I can get it," said Owen and left the room.

He reappeared carrying an evidence bag containing a smartphone. He removed it from the bag and switched it on.

"I want you to look through the pictures," said Taylor. "See if any of them include the mantelpiece in the living room."

Patel went and looked over Owen's shoulder while he scrolled through the images. After a few moments he stopped and made one of them full screen. The detectives gathered around.

"There it is," said Owen. "It is pretty hideous."

In the picture Pearl Bailey was standing next to a middle-aged man. Both were holding glasses of champagne and smiling broadly for the camera. Behind them was the object Drake had described. It appeared to be made of some form of ceramic material and was dark grey in colour.

"It certainly looks substantial enough to be used as a weapon," said Brewer.

"I'd say it's an ideal weapon," said Patel. "By the look of it you could smash it into little pieces and scatter them so we'd never be able to put it back together again."

"Are you suggesting the murder was planned then?" said Brewer.

"No I'm not," said Patel. "Given the circumstances I think it's likely the murderer grabbed the nearest object and was lucky enough to get hold of this."

"I agree," said Taylor. "The question is: where is it now?"

The others shook their heads but Patel looked more closely at the picture.

"Who's the man she's standing next to?" he said.

"He looks a bit like Helena," said Owen. "Maybe they're related."

"Possibly," said Taylor. "Anyway, I'd like you to find out who he is. I suggest you get some copies of this and see if any of our witnesses recognise him."

CHAPTER FORTY-TWO

Bridewell Police Station is an impressive modern building in the centre of Bristol. Its frontage is composed of large windows through which the interior can be clearly seen. Patel entered the large atrium and asked for the contact he had been given, Detective Sergeant Raymond. Lee Raymond was a large dark-haired young man with a ruddy complexion and a broad West Country accent.

"So, you've come to see Michael Groves," he said with a welcoming smile. "We've brought him in like you asked."

"Can you tell me what he's like?" said Patel.

"Not really," said Raymond. "He's supervised by the probation service. I'm just the contact person in the local police force. From what little I've seen of him I'd say he's a bit of an oddball character but maybe that's just because he's been inside so long."

The interview room was small and furnished in a minimalist, contemporary style. When Patel was shown into the room by DS Raymond, Michael Groves was already sitting at the table in its centre. He was barely recognisable from his undergraduate photograph. The tall, upright, good-looking student was now a round-shouldered old man with unkempt grey hair and a wispy beard. The staring eyes that had so struck Patel in the picture were now dull and lifeless. He was wearing a crumpled shirt and a shapeless fleece and was enveloped in an aura of stale sweat. Groves looked up when he heard Patel come in and eyed him suspiciously.

"I'm Detective Sergeant Patel, Merton CID," he said. "I'm very grateful to you for agreeing to see me."

"I don't have much choice in the matter," said Groves in a weak, colourless voice. "I'm not a free man you see. They haven't told me why you want to talk to me. Is it something to do with my wife's murder or some unrelated matter?"

During the train journey from London to Bristol, Patel had rehearsed a number of opening gambits for his interview with Michael Groves. Even now he was uncertain how to begin. He cleared his throat.

"We're investigating the death of someone you knew when you were at Cambridge," he said. "You would have known her as Elizabeth Crump."

Michael Groves frowned.

"Liz?" he said. "What on earth do you think I could tell you about Liz that would be of any value to you?"

"Well, actually I was wondering if you'd seen her at all since you've been out of prison."

"Does she live in Bristol?" said Groves.

"No," said Patel. "She lived in London."

"Well, you see, I haven't left Bristol since they brought me here," said Groves. "Apart from anything else I don't have the funds to travel around the country whenever I feel like it."

"The thing is, Pearl Bailey, I mean Elizabeth Crump, has been murdered."

Michael Groves closed his eyes and sighed.

"I see, and you thought a homicidal maniac who knew her forty years ago might have done it," he said. "Sorry to disappoint you, Sergeant, but you're not going to be able to pin this one on me."

It seemed that the present line of questioning was getting him nowhere, so Patel decided to change tack.

"I believe you also knew Joan Templeton in your student days," he said.

"Oh yes, Joan was a friend of mine," said Groves. "We kept in touch for a while after Cambridge, until I was wrongly convicted of murder that is."

"I'm sorry to have to tell you that she's also died in suspicious circumstances."

Groves shook his head and then laughed mirthlessly.

"Oh I see," he said. "You think I might be next."

This wasn't what Patel had been thinking but it opened up a new line of questioning.

"We don't have any reason to think your life's in danger," he said. "We do wonder if the two deaths might be related. I was wondering if you could think of anyone who might have wanted them both dead."

"Come on, officer, I haven't seen either of these ladies for forty years," said Groves. "I know nothing about them."

"We know that you wrote to Joan Templeton from prison," said Patel.

"I did for a while," said Groves, nodding his head sadly. "She was the only one who was there for me when my wife was killed."

"Why did you stop?"

"There didn't seem much point carrying on. Quite frankly I'd run out of things to say. Mind you, she carried on writing. Dear Joan, I think she was quite fond of me."

"Did she write you love letters?"

Groves laughed again and then burst into a fit of coughing.

"Good Lord, no," he said when he had recovered himself. "It was mostly pretty mundane stuff about what she was doing. She told me about the books she was writing of course. Fancy little Joan writing about violent death, she was such a mild-mannered person. In any case, the person she was mad about when we were students was Martin Rogers. Unfortunately for her, he didn't feel the same."

Michael Groves appeared to be confirming what Pearl Bailey had said about Joan Templeton and Martin Rogers. Rosemary

Rogers had dismissed the notion that Joan Templeton had loved her late husband and that this explained her distress at his funeral. Patel had been more inclined to believe the doctor's account but now he wasn't so sure. Could this have been the motive for murder after all? He didn't think so. Joan Templeton's feelings for Martin Rogers would have been an issue for his wife while her husband was alive but surely they were irrelevant now he was dead?

"Did you ever think it was possible that Joan had something to do with your wife's death?" he said.

"Well, you're the first policeman who's suggested I didn't do it," said Groves, a ghost of a smile passing momentarily across his face. "That's something I suppose. But the idea that Joan could have killed Rita is frankly preposterous. For a start, why would she have done it?"

"Because she was in love with you," said Patel.

Groves sat with his mouth hanging open for several moments before he replied. Then he gave a wheezy laugh.

"I think you're in the wrong job," he said. "With Joan gone there's a gap in the market for a crime writer who can come up with stuff like that."

Patel could feel himself blushing.

"You said yourself she was fond of you," he said.

"She was a good friend," said Groves. "I hate to demolish your little fantasy but the fact is Joan was only ever in love with Martin Rogers. OK, she was bisexual. She and Liz slept together regularly during our second year at Cambridge I believe. As far as I know she didn't have any other same-sex relationships after that. She was too busy making eyes at Martin. I have no idea what she got up to after Cambridge, relationship-wise. All I can tell you is that she never mentioned relationships or sex when she wrote to me."

"You slept with Liz Crump as well, didn't you?" said Patel.

"That was a disaster," said Groves, rolling his eyes. "I'd never had sex before so I was pretty inept. I've always thought I might have turned Liz gay, but almost certainly I only helped to confirm what she already thought about her sexuality."

"Were you upset when she broke up with you?"

"Relieved, more like," said Groves. "I was glad to put the whole sordid episode behind me."

"Did you sleep with Joan Templeton?"

"God, you've got sex on the brain," said Groves. "No I didn't. She just wasn't my type."

"Are you aware that there were fingerprints on the weapon that was used to kill your wife that were never identified?" said Patel.

"Of course," said Groves. "That was an important part of my defence. Not that it got us anywhere. The jury bought the idea it had been left by one of the previous tenants in our flat."

"I've been told the police didn't manage to get the fingerprints from the previous tenants."

"They couldn't," said Groves. "Dr and Mrs Wahba had buggered off back to Egypt and couldn't be traced. It was convenient for the police and the prosecution because it meant they could avoid trying to find out whose fingerprints they actually were."

Patel felt he was getting nowhere. The idea that Michael Groves had anything to do with the killings of Joan Templeton and Pearl Bailey now seemed ridiculous to him. Groves was clearly a broken man but as far as he could tell he was perfectly sane. In any case he had been naïve to imagine that Groves would confess to either murder. He should have looked for evidence to link him to the crime scenes, or at least to establish he had met one or other of the victims in the recent past. The trouble was he had no idea where to begin.

"Thank you for your time," he said as he got up to leave.

Groves grabbed his arm.

"I didn't do it, you know," he said.

"I'm sorry?"

"I didn't kill my wife."

Patel returned to the CID office where he found Lee Raymond sitting at a computer.

"How did you get on?" he said.

"To be perfectly honest, I got nowhere," said Patel. "One thing I would like to ask though, do you know whether Groves has been outside Bristol since he left prison?"

"According to the probation service, Michael hasn't left Bristol since his release," said Raymond. "Mind you, he probably wouldn't have told them if he had."

CHAPTER FORTY-THREE

As Patel sat at his desk in the CID office at Wimbledon Police Station he felt extremely dejected. He was all too aware that it was his suggestion that Michael Groves should be investigated and it was his crackpot theory that implicated him in the murders of Joan Templeton and Pearl Bailey. Inspector Brewer had made it very clear that he was sceptical about the idea from the first but DCI Taylor had given him the go-ahead to proceed. As a result he had wasted a whole day going to Bristol, time that could have been better spent on other lines of enquiry. He couldn't help wondering why Taylor had allowed him to do it. Perhaps it indicated that she trusted his judgment, but on the other hand it could be that she was giving him enough rope to hang himself. She seemed supportive but perhaps she really wanted him out of the Major Investigation Team, like most of its other members.

The door opened and Paul Owen came in. Seeing Patel, he came over to his desk.

"How did you get on with Michael Groves?" he asked.

"To be honest, it was a wasted journey," said Patel. "I'm pretty certain Groves had nothing to do with the murders. Have you found out who the man in that photograph is?"

"Yes, it's Helena's father, Miles Cooke," said Owen. "He's the CEO of Amethyst Press, the firm who published Pearl Bailey's stuff. There's something else as well: before he took over at Amethyst he worked for a number of other companies including Romulus, who were Joan Templeton's publishers."

"So he probably knew them both then."

"No question," said Owen. "For a time he was directly involved in marketing the Inspector Tewksbury novels."

"Mind you, that doesn't give him a motive for killing her."

"Ah well, maybe it does," said Owen. "Colin Brewer reckons he might have killed Pearl Bailey because she had seduced his darling daughter."

Patel considered this theory. Superficially it seemed to make sense but would an unprovoked assault really have been the reaction of an overprotective father who had discovered his daughter was having a sexual relationship with a much older woman? He wasn't quite sure. It was certainly perfectly possible that Pearl Bailey would have invited Miles Cooke to dinner on the night she died but surely she would have told Helena he was coming? On the other hand, perhaps the dinner guest had requested that his visit was kept from her, but if so, why?

"What's the plan?" he said.

"Brewer and Todd have an appointment with Mr Cooke tomorrow," said Owen. "Meanwhile we're supposed to try to confirm Helena really was sleeping with Pearl Bailey."

"How are we going to do that?"

"Talk to some more students," said Owen. "Probably have another go at Helena."

Patel was not convinced that this approach would be successful but he said nothing.

"One other thing," said Owen. "We got the forensic report on that hacksaw."

"Hacksaw?" said Patel.

"Yes, you know the one Brian found at Musgrove's flat."

"Oh yes."

"There weren't any residues from brake lines on it," said Owen. "Of course they found Alan Musgrove's fingerprints but you'd expect that. I thought Brewer would have been gutted but I think even he's accepted he didn't do it."

"The question remains," said Patel, "who did?"

"That's the million-dollar question."

Patel sat back in his chair with his hands behind his head and looked at the ceiling.

"What we need is the motive," he said. "It seems to me that you have to have a very good reason to kill someone, assuming you're not a lunatic or a psychopath. OK, the Musgroves are short of money but they're coping, just about. They were in a position to wait until Joan Templeton died of natural causes. If what Sarah Musgrove told us was true, they expected her to die sooner rather than later. The bottom line is they probably don't have a motive after all, never did. What we need to do is find someone who does."

"You may be right," said Owen. "Mind you I think some murders occur in a moment of madness. A situation arises and a perfectly sane person loses it for a few minutes. Pearl Bailey's killing looks like that to me. I don't think the perpetrator meant to kill her. He or she probably regrets it now, but it's too late."

"It still comes down to motive," said Patel. "Once you understand that, you can work out who the killer is."

Chapter Forty-Four

DCI Taylor sat at the head of the table in the incident room with her arms folded. Patel had given an account of his interview with Michael Groves and indicated that he didn't think he was involved in either murder. Brewer had grinned broadly when he heard that.

"OK, Colin, let's hear what you've found out," said Taylor.

Brewer was clearly enjoying being the centre of attention for once.

"We went to see Cooke at his office," he said. "It's in a swanky new block in Hammersmith. He's a smarmy bastard with a 500-quid suit who thinks he's a cut above the rest of us. Before I could ask him anything he launched into a tirade about us harassing his daughter and shit like that. Anyway, I asked him if he'd been to dinner at Pearl Bailey's house recently and he said no, without hesitating. Now I realise there's been publicity about her death, so I put it down as a prepared answer.

"Next I asked if he knew that his daughter and the victim were sleeping together. He said they weren't, so I told him we had evidence they were. He said he'd asked her about it and she'd told him there was nothing in it. He claims he believed her. I looked for tell-tale signs he was lying but he wasn't giving anything away.

"When I asked him where he was on the night of the murder he didn't answer right away. Said he'd have to check his diary. When he'd done it he said he was at home. I asked if anyone could verify that and he said his wife was out so, basically, no. So I asked what he did that evening. He made a big show of trying to remember and then said he watched the telly. Couldn't tell me most of what he watched but said he went to bed after *Match of the Day*. Then he got all indignant and asked why we wanted to know all this. I told him he was a suspect in a murder enquiry. That shut him up."

"So we can't rule him out," said Taylor.

"Not in my book," said Brewer. "Our Mr Cooke is the sort of slimy piece of shit who thinks he's above the law."

Patel was itching to speak but was afraid what he had to say would be met by a barrage of abuse from the detective inspector. He took a deep breath.

"I'm not sure he's got a credible motive," he said.

Brewer swung round and glowered at him.

"Go on," said Taylor.

"Helena's a woman, not a child," said Patel. "Her sex life is her own business."

Brewer scoffed.

"You may think it's all right for young women to be corrupted by elderly dykes," he said. "There are still people around who take a dim view of that sort of thing."

"How old is Miles Cooke?" said Taylor.

"Oh, I don't know," said Brewer. "About fifty I should think. What do you reckon, Brian?"

"About that," said Todd.

"Not having met Mr Cooke it's hard for me to say," said Taylor. "He might be homophobic and he might see what Pearl and Helena were up to as a betrayal of trust, especially as it was through his relationship with Pearl Bailey that she came to be living there."

"That's how I see it," said Brewer, nodding vigorously. "I reckon he went round there for dinner and saw the photograph of Helena on the mantelpiece. He asked the Bailey woman if they were at it and she confirmed they were. At that point he lost his rag and grabbed the nearest thing to hand and bashed her with it. He cleaned up so we wouldn't be able to find his prints or DNA and then got a train to Brighton."

"Is that where he lives?" said Taylor.

"That's right," said Brewer.

"Where do the trains from London to Brighton go from?" she asked.

"Just a minute," said Todd.

He took out his phone and did a quick search.

"Victoria or London Bridge," he said.

"You better find out what time the last train is," said Taylor. "Right, I want Colin and his team to find out more about Mr and Mrs Cooke. Oh yeah and you'd better check to see if he's got a place in London as well."

"He said he commutes to work on the train," said Todd. "Rather him than me." He hesitated, then added: "I'll double-check."

"Might be worth having a word with the force down there as well," said Taylor. "You never know, Cooke might be known to them. Probably not but it's worth a try. I'll give them a call. Assuming he did go to Pearl Bailey's house that night, how do you think he would have travelled to Wimbledon?"

"My guess is he'd have got a cab," said Brewer. "It's less likely for someone like that, but he might have taken the train or Tube."

"You'd better check on both," said Taylor. "If we can prove he was in Wimbledon that night, or even that he was in London, it would show he was lying."

Taylor looked around the table.

"We've spoken to everyone else Pearl Bailey had regular contact with haven't we?" she said.

"What about her agent?" said Patel.

"Susan Sharpe?" said Brewer. "We've had a word with her."

"She hasn't been working with her for very long," said Patel. "It's likely that her previous agent, Anne Gregory, could tell us more about her than Mrs Sharpe."

"Has anyone spoken to her?" asked Taylor.

"We interviewed her following Joan Templeton's death," said Patel. "She was the one who suggested we speak to Pearl Bailey."

"Oh yes, I remember now," said Taylor. "OK, well you and Owen can have another word with her. It may get us nowhere, but in the circumstances we can't afford to ignore any leads, however tenuous."

Brewer gave a barely audible groan.

"There were phone calls between Anne Gregory and Pearl Bailey not long before the murder," said Owen.

"Oh yes, so there were," said Taylor. "You two had better get over there as soon as you can."

She turned to Drake.

"Anything new at your end, Shelly?" she said.

Drake shook her head.

"Right then, get to work."

As the team went their separate ways, Taylor stopped Patel and invited him into her office.

"You seemed pretty certain you were wrong about Michael Groves just now," she said.

"I suppose I was expecting him to be a psychopath who would think nothing of killing former acquaintances," said Patel. "The thing is, he was nothing like that. OK, I know I've only got his word for it, but it really seems he had nothing against either victim."

"Like I said earlier, we'll leave it for the time being," said Taylor. "That doesn't mean I think it was a daft idea, all right?"

Patel smiled.

"Thank you, ma'am," he said.

CHAPTER FORTY-FIVE

"I suppose this is about Pearl Bailey," said Anne Gregory as she led Patel and Owen into her sitting room.

"Yes, that's right," said Patel.

"Did you speak to her after you came to see me the first time?" she asked.

"We did."

"Did you find what she had to say helpful?" said Anne Gregory as she subsided into an armchair.

"Actually some of what she told us was at odds with the testimony of another witness," said Patel.

"She could be extremely economical with the truth," said Mrs Gregory with a half smile. "I suppose I should have told you that the last time you were here."

Patel wondered which of the witnesses was to be believed with regard to Joan Templeton and Martin Rogers. Rosemary Rogers was the most credible. Michael Groves didn't inspire confidence and Pearl Bailey's reliability had just been questioned by Anne Gregory, another credible witness. He wasn't entirely sure how to proceed with the questioning but decided to come at the object of their visit from an angle.

"Did you admire Pearl Bailey's writing?" he said.

"I don't think she was a great novelist but she was a very successful author in terms of sales," said Mrs Gregory. "Publishing is a business, Sergeant. An agent always has to consider the commercial potential of a book as well as its artistic merit.

We don't always get it right of course." She smiled. "One of my colleagues at Parker Nesbitt once wrote to a first-time author to say that his novel was very well written but was far too weird ever to be published. It was published and was a great success. That author went on to have a long and, some would say, distinguished career."

"Did you spot Pearl Bailey's talent when you first read something she'd written?"

Anne Gregory smiled to herself.

"I think what I saw was potential," she said. "She was an experienced journalist and quite clearly knew how to write and I thought her style was what the market was looking for at the time. In that regard I was proved right."

"Did you get on well with her on a personal level?"

"I found her easy to get on with," she said. "She was knowledgeable and well read and a stimulating person to talk to. I can't say that about all my former clients."

"Did you like her?"

Anne Gregory sighed and seemed to shudder almost imperceptibly.

"Yes I did," she said.

"Her death must have come as quite a shock then," said Patel.

"It did, especially because it came so soon after Joan's."

"On the night she died someone was at her house for dinner," said Patel. "Was that you by any chance?"

"Me?" she said incredulously. "No, I wasn't there."

"Do you know who the guest might have been?" said Owen.

"I have no idea," she said.

"What did you do that evening?"

"I was at home as far as I can remember," said Mrs Gregory. "I don't go out much in the evening these days. I usually watch TV and go to bed early."

"Can anyone confirm that?" said Owen.

"I'm afraid not," she said shaking her head. "That's one of the drawbacks of living alone."

"You're sure you didn't go to see Pearl Bailey?"

"Absolutely. Pearl and I have only met occasionally since I retired."

"Why did you retire?" asked Patel.

"It was to take care of my husband," said Mrs Gregory. "He had been in increasingly poor health for a number of years. I wanted to care for him at home rather than put him into an institution of some sort. Anyway, he died last year."

"I'm sorry to hear that," said Patel. A thought struck him and he added, "Have you thought of returning to work by any chance?"

"Oh yes, I've considered it," she said, nodding sadly. "However, in the end I decided I was too out of touch."

"Did any of your former clients encourage you to take them on again?"

"Joan Templeton did."

"And Pearl Bailey?"

"No, we talked about it but she wasn't interested."

"Why not?" said Patel.

"She was happy with Susan Sharpe," she said. "Susan is very good at her job."

Owen produced the printout of Pearl Bailey's mobile phone records.

"You had a couple of phone conversations with Miss Bailey in the weeks before her death," he said. "May I ask what you talked about?"

Anne Gregory looked startled and for a moment she didn't answer. Then she said: "Sorry. It was about Joan actually. I asked if she was going to the funeral and she said she'd get back to me."

"Did you both go?" asked Owen.

"Actually in the end I couldn't," said Mrs Gregory. "Something came up."

"That explains one of the calls," said Owen. "Another was made after Joan Templeton's funeral."

Anne Gregory looked surprised. Then she smiled.

"Oh yes," she said. "I called to ask her how it went and to apologise for not making it. I thought it was the least I could do."

"Do you have any idea who might have wanted Pearl Bailey dead?" said Patel.

"Well, she was someone who rode roughshod over people's feelings," she said. "I've no doubt she's upset a few people but I doubt any of them would go as far as killing her."

"Thank you," said Patel. "We won't take up any more of your time."

When they were back in the car Owen said: "Well, that didn't get us very far."

"I don't know about that," said Patel. "There were one or two things she said that made me wonder if she might have killed Pearl Bailey."

"What, you mean because she didn't want her to be her agent?" said Owen. "That doesn't seem to be a very convincing motive."

"It wasn't that," said Patel.

"What about Joan Templeton, then, do you think she could have killed her as well?"

"Not really. To be honest I'm not sure about Pearl Bailey either."

Owen frowned and started the car.

Patel felt a little foolish. Once again he had verbalised the germ of an idea that he should have kept to himself. He didn't want to get a reputation for wild speculation.

Chapter Forty-Six

The block of flats was obviously new, its brickwork so far relatively free of urban grime. It was in a desirable part of Fulham, close to the river. Brewer scanned the entryphone keypad.

"It's number fourteen isn't it?" he said.

"Yeah," said Todd. "That's according to the girl at the publishers Pringle spoke to."

Brewer pressed the button and waited. Slightly to his surprise, a female voice with a heavy foreign accent answered.

"Police," he said. "We want a word, can you let us in?"

There was a pause and then the girl said, "OK."

There was a loud buzzing sound and the door yielded to Brewer's pressure and opened. They went up in the lift to the third floor and made their way down the corridor to number fourteen. Brewer knocked at the door and it opened to reveal a slim woman in her twenties with long blonde hair. They followed her into the open-plan living room and kitchen and took their seats opposite her on a leather settee.

"Can I ask your name, madam?" said Brewer.

"It is Natasha," said the girl. "Natasha Dabic."

"It's our understanding that this flat belongs to a Mr Miles Cooke," said Brewer. "Is that correct?"

"This is so," said the girl. "I am take care of it for him."

"I see," said Brewer. "Does he spend much time here?"

"He comes if he must work late," said Natasha. "Sometimes he stays at weekend also."

Brewer glanced around the room. It was not very large but the furniture and fittings looked expensive.

"Nice place you've got here," he said.

"I like," she said.

"Where are you from?"

"Bosnia."

Brewer narrowed his eyes.

"How long have you been here?" he said.

Natasha looked uneasy.

"Six month," she said weakly.

"And what exactly is it that you do?"

"I am student."

The girl's outfit was not typical of the students Brewer had come across in the past. He decided to press her further.

"What are you studying?" he said.

"English."

"Where?"

"Sloane Language School."

"Well I must say it's very kind of Mr Cooke to put you up here," said Brewer. "How do you come to know him?"

"We meet online," said Natasha. "I say I want to come to England and he say I can stay in flat."

"You said he sometimes stays at the weekend," said Brewer. "Did he have stay on the weekend of April the eighteenth and nineteenth?"

"I not sure."

"Come on now, it's only two weeks back," said Brewer. "Maybe you've got a note of it on your phone."

Natasha became aware of the phone that was lying on a coffee table in front of her and blushed. Reluctantly she picked it up and started to peck at it. Todd went over and sat beside her but she turned the screen away so that he couldn't see it.

"Yes he come that weekend," she said. "He have dinner appointment on Saturday evening."

The two policemen exchanged glances.

"Did you go with him?" asked Brewer.

"No, it was business event."

"What time did he get back here?"

Natasha fumbled as she put her phone into a handbag that was on the floor beside her.

"I not sure," she said.

"Were you in bed when he got back?"

Natasha picked up a packet of cigarettes from the coffee table, took one out and lit it.

She inhaled deeply. Brewer folded his arms and fixed her with a steady stare.

"I was asleep," she said.

"And what time did you go to bed?"

"I not remember."

Brewer leaned forwards.

"I'd like to see your passport," he said.

The girl looked alarmed.

"Why? Why you want passport?" she said.

"Well, it's like this," said Brewer. "I want to see if you have a valid visa for the UK."

Natasha stubbed out her cigarette violently in the ashtray.

"I have visa," she said.

"Why won't you let me see it then?" said Brewer. "If you have nothing to hide, what harm can it do?"

"You are not immigration."

"No I'm not," said Brewer. "Quite frankly I don't give a shit whether you've got a visa or not, but if you don't cooperate I will speak to the immigration people and get them to investigate you. On the other hand, if you answer my questions truthfully I shall say no more about it."

The girl considered this for a few moments. She looked first at Brewer and then at Todd.

"What you want to know?" she said.

"I want to know what time Miles Cooke got back here on the eighteenth of April," said Brewer. "It's my belief that a man who was paying for you to live in this nice flat would expect you to be awake and ready to, shall we say, meet his needs when he got back."

Natasha sighed.

"He come home eleven thirty," she said.

"Did he say how he got here?" said Todd. The girl looked blank. "Did he take the Tube or get a cab?"

"I not know."

"How did he seem when he arrived?" said Brewer.

"I not understand."

"Well, was he his normal self or did he seem anxious or upset?"

"I think normal," she said. "He say he is tired, so I make him drink and then we go to bed."

"What about his clothes?" said Brewer. "What was he wearing?"

"He wear suit."

"Was it torn or untidy-looking?"

The girl shook her head.

"It normal," she said.

*

Back in the car Brewer rubbed his hands together gleefully. It seemed that the pieces of the puzzle were falling into place.

"We need to work out how long it would have taken him to get from Wimbledon to Fulham," said Todd.

"Agreed," said Brewer. "My guess is he took a cab. Like I said before, I can't see Mr Miles Cooke going on public transport. Check the cab companies first. If we get no joy we'll look at the CCTV on the Tube."

Chapter Forty-Seven

Patel was first in the incident room the following morning. He had spent most of the previous night lying awake going over his interview with Anne Gregory. Her behaviour had seemed odd to him, as had some of her answers. Perhaps Anne Gregory's marriage was not all it appeared to be. Perhaps her relationship with Pearl Bailey had not been purely professional. He had no real evidence to support any of this, only a growing feeling that the former agent was somehow mixed up in the murders.

The door opened and DCI Taylor came in clutching a paper cup of coffee. She sat down on the chair at the head of the table and took a sip from her cup.

"How did you get on yesterday?" she asked.

Patel described his encounter with Anne Gregory and Taylor listened, nodding from time to time.

"I think we need to investigate her further," he said in conclusion. "I think she could well have been the dinner guest the night Pearl Bailey was killed."

"She denied being there, right?" said Taylor.

"Yes, but I don't believe her."

"How would she have travelled to Wimbledon, do you think?" said Taylor.

"Probably the train," said Patel. "I've been to her place twice now and didn't see a car parked outside the house on either occasion."

"It sounds like it's worth following up," said Taylor. "Still, I think we should see what Colin's team have come up with before we make any definite plans."

When the team had assembled, Taylor asked Colin Brewer to report his progress with the investigation of Miles Cooke.

"Mike Pringle managed to sweet-talk a disgruntled employee at Amethyst Press and she told him Cooke has a flat in Fulham which he uses when he needs to stay over in London," said Brewer. "She also told him there were rumours he was keeping a mistress there."

"Good work, Mike," said Taylor. "So, Colin, what did you find when you went round to the flat?"

"A Bosnian girl who's almost certainly in the country illegally," said Brewer. "She claims to be studying English. We checked with the language school she said she was attending and they have no record of her. I think Miles Cooke has been giving her some very personal tuition."

Todd laughed and Brewer grinned at him in response.

"OK," said Taylor. "So we now know that Mr Cooke didn't have to get back to Brighton on the night Pearl Bailey was killed, but that doesn't mean he was her dinner guest."

"Well, we know he spent the weekend in London," said Brewer. "Miss Dabic confirmed that. She also said he went out for dinner on the Saturday night and came back about eleven thirty. She didn't know where he had dinner, or at least she said she didn't know."

"How long would it have taken him to get from Pearl Bailey's house to the flat?" said Taylor.

Brewer turned to Brian Todd.

"You tell her," he said.

"Most likely he took a cab," said Todd. "Once he'd got one the journey would take no more than twenty minutes, assuming there was light traffic as you'd expect at that time of night. If he took the Tube it's probably more like half an hour, assuming there was a train ready to depart when he got to the station, longer if there wasn't."

"Why do you think he took a cab?" said Taylor.

"Mainly because he's the sort of bloke who doesn't use public transport," said Brewer. "Also, if he was thinking straight, he'd have wanted to avoid the CCTV at the station and on the Tube train."

"Fair enough," said Taylor. "Taking a cab is risky as well, assuming we're able to track down the driver. If he used an app to get a minicab the details of his journey would be on his mobile phone."

"Well, obviously we can check on that when we arrest him," said Brewer. "Mind you if I was him I'd have walked to the station and got a cab from the rank there. That way his cab journey doesn't begin at the murder scene."

"That makes sense," said Taylor. "However, he may not have been thinking straight, if we assume he didn't plan the murder. Did the Bosnian girl know how he arrived at the flat?"

"She couldn't or wouldn't tell us how he travelled," said Brewer. "That's why we had to look at all the possibilities."

Patel could see that Brewer was building a convincing case. He had previously proposed the motive for the crime and was now able to demonstrate opportunity. And yet he was still doubtful that Miles Cooke was the killer.

"Is it possible that Miles Cooke went to a dinner related to his work that evening?" he said.

Brewer swung round to face him.

"It's possible," he said. "But I think it's more likely he went to Pearl Bailey's house."

"I think you need to find out if he had a work-related dinner that night," said Taylor. "Perhaps Mike could see if his contact at Amethyst Press can get access to Mr Cooke's diary."

"I'll see what I can do," said Pringle.

"All right then, Colin," said Taylor. "What do you want to do next?"

257

"Bring him in and question him under caution."

"I think we'll see what Mike can find out first," said Taylor. "It seems odd to me that he would have gone to dinner with Pearl Bailey and not told his daughter about it. Apart from anything else, there was a risk that she'd be at the house when he arrived or would come back before he'd left."

"I take your point," said Brewer. "The fact that he didn't tell the kid about it could mean he went to the house with the intention of killing the Bailey woman."

Taylor frowned.

"If that was the case, surely he'd have killed her when he got there and not have waited until after dinner," she said.

"Maybe, maybe not," said Brewer. "In any case he may not have had dinner with her. The stuff in the dishwasher could be from earlier in the day or even from several meals over a day or two. All we know for sure is they had a drink together."

Patel had to admit that this was a fair point. He had jumped to the conclusion that the contents of the dishwasher were from dinner but there was actually no evidence to support that view. Perhaps he had been influenced by what Amber had told him about the Joan Templeton novel called *Deadly Reckoning*.

"If he was there," said Taylor. "See what Mike comes up with, OK?" She turned to Patel. "Right, Sanjay, can you fill us in on Anne Gregory?"

As Patel described his interview with the former agent he was conscious that Brewer was fidgeting and clicking his biro. From time to time he exhaled loudly.

Eventually he said, "Why would this woman have wanted Pearl Bailey dead? They worked together for a number of years, right?"

"That's true," said Patel. "Pearl Bailey was one of her first clients. She says she offered to act as her agent again after her husband died and was turned down. She seemed pretty upset about it."

"This is basic stuff," said Brewer, tossing his pen onto the table. "A killer has motive and opportunity. Quite frankly, your witness had neither."

"If she was the dinner guest, she had opportunity," said Patel. "I don't know for sure what her motive was but my best guess is that her relationship with Pearl Bailey was not purely professional."

"You don't have any evidence to support either of those suggestions," said Brewer. "It's pure speculation."

"The same could be said about your case against Miles Cooke," said Taylor.

"We know that Cooke went out for dinner on the night of the murder," said Brewer. "And we know he returned to the flat in Fulham after Pearl Bailey was dead. I also have to say that the motive I've suggested makes a lot more sense than the one Patel's come up with."

Patel was about to respond to this but Taylor spoke first.

"A lot of what we've discussed this morning isn't supported by hard evidence," she said. "That's why we need to get out there and find some, rather than sitting here arguing. While Mike is speaking to his contact at Amethyst Press I want Todd to look into Miles Cooke in more detail. Find out who his colleagues are, whether the publisher's doing well or not, that sort of thing. Colin, you can get down to Brighton and speak to Mrs Cooke. We don't know whether or not she knows about the Fulham flat, so you'll need to tread carefully. Ask her about Helena. She may know things about her that Mr Cooke doesn't.

"We also need to find out more about Anne Gregory. Owen can look into her professional life and find out more about her late husband. Sanjay, I want you to have another word with Susan Sharpe. I'd like to know if she's aware that her predecessor was trying to steal a couple of her clients for a start.

"I know we talked to the neighbours directly after the murder and no one said they saw anyone arriving at or leaving the house on that night. Shelly, I want you to go back and have another go at finding a witness who remembers seeing someone walking nearby Pearl Bailey's house that evening."

Brewer was red in the face.

"I still think we should pull Cooke in now," he said.

"All in good time, Colin," said Taylor. "Now come on, get to work."

CHAPTER FORTY-EIGHT

Susan Sharpe invited Patel to take a seat in her office but she looked none too pleased to see him.

"I've already had one of your colleagues here asking questions since you last came round," she said. "I can't imagine what you want from me this time."

"It's about Anne Gregory," said Patel. "I interviewed her again recently and I wanted to ask you about some of the things she said. Have you seen her recently?"

"No I haven't," said Sharpe. "I know I told you she drops in from time to time but the most recent occasion was last year."

"Have you ever worked with her, I mean were you at Parker Nesbitt when she retired?"

"I was a commissioning editor at Amethyst Press before I came here," said Sharpe. "I'd always wanted to be an agent so I jumped at the chance when they asked me to replace Anne here at Parker Nesbitt. There was a brief handover period when she came in to show me the ropes, but that's all."

The mention of Amethyst Press made Patel change his mind about what his next question should be.

"Does that mean you know Miles Cooke?" he said.

Susan Sharpe frowned and blushed a little.

"Yes I know Miles," she said.

"We've spoken to Mr Cooke in connection with the murder of Pearl Bailey," said Patel. "Of course we know he was her publisher, but I was wondering if they had a personal relationship as well?"

Susan Sharpe laughed and put her hand up to her mouth.

"Miles has relationships with lots of women, inside and outside the company," she said. "He uses and abuses his position. Quite frankly I was glad to get away from there so I wouldn't have to put up with his unwanted attention." She chuckled again. "But the idea that he would have made a pass at Pearl Bailey is frankly ludicrous."

"I wasn't really suggesting that," said Patel. "I really wanted to know if it's likely that she would have asked him to dinner at her house?"

"I'd say it was highly unlikely," said Sharpe.

Patel remembered the photograph of Miles Cooke and the author taken in her living room that Owen had found.

"There was a photograph of them together on her phone," he said. "It was taken in her sitting room."

Susan Sharpe frowned and adjusted her spectacles. Then her face brightened.

"That was the party," she said. "Pearl had us all round when she sold the millionth copy of her books. Miles was there and she got someone to photograph them together with her phone. Come to think about it she was all over him that night. She was clearly after something but I couldn't work out what it was."

Patel's immediate thought was that she was preparing the ground for revealing her relationship with Helena but he realised there could be other reasons.

"When was this party?" he said.

"About three years ago I think."

So he was wrong; Helena hadn't moved in with Pearl at that time.

"Was there any risk Amethyst would stop publishing Pearl Bailey?" he asked.

"Not likely," said Sharpe. "She was making them too much money. In any case, if they did, another publisher would snap her up in no time."

The interview was not going as Patel had expected, but in a good way. He was unconscionably pleased that Brewer had failed to make the connection between Susan Sharpe and Miles Cooke when he had interviewed her. Clearly his rather boorish approach to investigations had its limitations.

"Do you know how Mr Cooke feels about same-sex relationships?" said Patel.

"I doubt he's bothered," said Sharpe. "Most people in publishing are pretty open-minded about that sort of thing."

"What if his daughter was involved?"

Susan Sharpe sat back in her chair and tapped her teeth with a ballpoint pen.

"That might be a problem," she said. "He's very protective of Helena. Still, she's grown up now isn't she?"

"Third year at university," said Patel.

"Look, I'm only guessing but I think he'd be OK with it."

Patel wanted to ask whether a relationship with Pearl Bailey would be OK but that would involve divulging personal information about Helena Cooke, information that hadn't been verified. Instead he decided to revert to his original line of questioning.

"Did you know that Anne Gregory offered to act as Pearl Bailey's agent after her husband died?" he said.

Sharpe sat up straight and blinked vigorously.

"You're joking," she said.

"She claims that she approached both Pearl Bailey and Joan Templeton," said Patel. "Bailey said no but Templeton was up for it."

"Neither of them spoke to me about it," said Sharpe.

"I got the impression it was Pearl Bailey she really wanted to work with," said Patel. "Anyway it's academic now."

"It's interesting you say that," said Sharpe. "I got the impression that Anne was fond of Pearl. There was always a certain tone in her voice when she talked about her. That wasn't the case with her other authors."

"You knew both these authors through working with them," said Patel. "Do you have any feel for how they viewed Anne Gregory?"

"They both valued her professionally," said Sharpe. "Joan was clearly upset when Anne retired. I found it quite difficult to get on with her in the early days, until she'd got used to me. But I think she was someone who didn't like change. Working with me was outside her comfort zone. Pearl on the other hand accepted me right away."

It occurred to Patel that Paul Owen might have been right when he suggested that they were dealing with a lesbian love triangle, and that the third member was Anne Gregory. He had become far too focussed on what had happened in Cambridge more than forty years ago whereas he should have been concentrating on the two authors' recent past. If Pearl Bailey had murdered Joan Templeton, then perhaps Anne Gregory had killed Pearl. Somehow this didn't seem likely. From what Susan Sharpe had said, it was more credible that Anne Gregory had had a sexual relationship with Pearl Bailey. If that was so and she had discovered that Helena Cooke and Bailey were lovers, Anne could have murdered Pearl, while someone else could have been responsible for Joan Templeton's death. This seemed to make more sense.

"Did you want to ask me anything else?" said Susan Sharpe.

"Sorry," said Patel, "I was miles away for a moment there. Do you think there's any chance that Anne Gregory's relationship with Pearl Bailey was more than just professional?"

"What are you getting at exactly?"

"Could they have been lovers?"

Susan Sharpe snorted with laughter.

"What a weird idea," she said. "Anne was devoted to her husband. For God's sake, she gave up work to look after him."

"It was just a suggestion," said Patel. He was taken aback by the vehemence with which this reply was delivered but he remained suspicious of Anne Gregory. After all, the truth was that Susan Sharpe didn't know Anne Gregory well. "You've been really helpful," he said.

Susan Sharpe frowned.

"I'm not sure I understand why you say that," she said.

Patel stood up and smiled.

"I think the picture is finally becoming clearer," he said.

Chapter Forty-Nine

"Miles Cooke had dinner with a client that Saturday evening," said Brewer. "However, it was over by eight because the bloke had a plane to catch that evening. They met at a hotel near Heathrow. We reckon Cooke had time to get to Wimbledon, kill the old girl and be back at his flat by eleven."

"OK," said Taylor. "But if that's the case, who had dinner with Pearl Bailey?"

"Like I said before, maybe no one," said Brewer. "The stuff in the dishwasher might have been from lunch. All we actually know is that Pearl Bailey poured two brandies and maybe the killer deliberately didn't touch his glass so as not to leave fingerprints."

Taylor sat back in her chair and closed her eyes while she digested this new information. Then she opened them again and consulted one of the reports on the table in front of her.

"What about the wine bottles?" she said. "Surely they suggest it was dinner?"

"We've no reason to be certain they were drunk that evening or that day," said Brewer. "Maybe she was collecting them with a view to recycling them when she had a few."

"OK, let me get this straight," said Taylor. "You think Miles Cooke went round to visit Pearl Bailey after his dinner with the client, they had an argument and he hit her with the ornament from the mantelpiece, am I right?"

"That's it," said Brewer. "I think he saw the picture of Helena and challenged her about it. I also think he was already suspicious about what was going on and went round there to find out the truth."

"It sort of makes sense," said Taylor, nodding her head.

"I have a witness who says Miles Cooke wouldn't have been bothered about his daughter being in a same-sex relationship," said Patel.

Brewer glowered at him.

"Who the fuck's that?" he said.

"Susan Sharpe, Pearl Bailey's agent."

"How does she know anything about Miles Cooke?" said Brewer.

"She used to work at Amethyst Press."

This seemed to knock the wind out of Brewer's sails but he soon recovered.

"It's only an opinion," he said, shaking his head. "She can't really know one way or the other."

"That's true," said Taylor. "But there is a difference between her having a fling with another student and sharing the bed of a woman old enough to be her grandmother."

Brewer grinned and nodded.

"Too right," he said.

"By the way," said Taylor, "what did Mrs Cooke have to say when you spoke to her?"

"She confirmed her husband spent the weekend in London because he had a business meeting. She said they were grateful to Pearl Bailey for taking Helena in and denied they were having a sexual relationship."

"Not much help then," said Taylor. "This might be a good moment for you to report back on your interview with Susan Sharpe, Sanjay."

Patel consulted his notes.

"Susan Sharpe thinks Anne Gregory was very fond of Pearl Bailey," he said. "I think she was the one who resented her involvement with Helena."

"Pure speculation," said Brewer.

"Go on," said Taylor.

"I think she was the dinner guest on the night she died and, as DI Brewer has suggested with regard to Miles Cooke, she saw the photograph on the mantelpiece and put two and two together."

"So, we have two suspects," said Taylor.

Brewer scoffed and tossed the file he was holding onto the table.

"We have two suspects," Taylor repeated firmly. "I think it's time I interviewed them both under caution. Colin, you can bring Mr Cooke in and Sanjay can get hold of Anne Gregory. You can take uniform for backup because I need the rest of the team for other jobs. I want forensic teams to go over Anne Gregory's bungalow and Miles Cooke's flat. If we can match the wool fibre with garments in either location we'll be almost home and dry." She turned to Patel. "Which line is Thames Ditton on?"

"The one to Hampton Court."

"Right, so she'd have arrived on platform five, unless I'm mistaken." Taylor turned to Owen. "I know it's not your favourite job, Paul, but I want you to look at the CCTV from that platform," she said. "Obviously we don't know when she arrived so you'll need to look at it from the afternoon to the middle of the evening. As far as we know Anne Gregory doesn't have a car. What about Miles Cooke, Colin?"

"There is underground parking at the flats," said Brewer. "We didn't check to see if he makes use of it. My guess is not because he isn't living there all the time."

"We can look into that later if necessary," said Taylor. "I know you guys don't think he would have taken the Tube but I'd like Todd to look at CCTV for that section of the station. The cameras should cover people arriving and departing. The other possibility is that he travelled by taxi or minicab. Brian has already started talking to cab companies and I want Pringle to take over, OK?"

Pringle nodded.

"I want you to concentrate on companies that operate in this part of London. Ask them if any of their drivers took someone to Pearl Bailey's house that evening. Shelly, you give him a hand. We need pictures of both suspects so we can show them to any drivers who dropped a fare anywhere close to where she lived."

CHAPTER FIFTY

As they entered the interview room Taylor immediately recognised the solicitor who sat beside Miles Cooke as the one who had acted for Helena Cooke. *Pompous arse*, she thought. As she took her seat opposite the suspect and his lawyer she smiled sweetly, but there was a look of contempt in his eyes.

"Thank you for coming in today," she said. "I am Detective Chief Inspector Taylor. Mr Cooke has already met my colleague Inspector Brewer. Can you commence the recording of this interview, Inspector?"

When this was done Taylor read the suspect his rights before posing her first question.

"I want to ask you some questions about the evening of April the eighteenth," she said. "When you spoke to Inspector Brewer recently you said you were at home then, but that wasn't true, was it?"

"It was a misunderstanding," said Cooke. "When I said 'home' I meant my flat in London, not my house in Brighton."

"I see," said Taylor. "But you weren't there all evening, were you?"

"Well no, I had a meeting with a client in the early part of the evening."

"I understand the meeting finished about eight o'clock but you didn't get to the flat until after eleven."

Cooke shifted in his seat.

"I don't think it was as late as that," he said.

"Miss Dabic, who lives in your flat, said you came back at eleven thirty," said Brewer.

"Natasha isn't good with time," said Cooke. "I remember looking at my watch and it was more like nine thirty."

"What did you do between the end of the meeting and arriving at the flat?" said Taylor.

"Well you see, the meeting was near Heathrow and I got a minicab back."

"It only takes thirty to forty minutes to make that journey by road," said Brewer.

"The traffic was awful," said Cooke. "We were stuck for ages."

"We checked on the traffic that evening didn't we, Inspector Brewer?" said Taylor.

"We did," said Brewer. "Our colleagues say the traffic was light on that route during the period in question."

"Wait a minute," said Cooke. "I remember now, I stopped off at the office on the way."

"I expect there's CCTV at your office," said Brewer. "There's probably someone on duty in the building as well I should imagine."

"I didn't see anyone," said Cooke. "I only popped in to get a file I'd left behind when I left the office."

"We will be interviewing staff at your offices and looking at the CCTV images, if there are any," said Taylor. "We will also be seeking confirmation that this meeting you speak of actually took place. Where is your office by the way?"

"Hammersmith."

"Well, it is on your way to the flat," said Taylor. "How convenient."

"What do you mean by that?" said the lawyer.

"It's just an observation," said Taylor.

"In that case I suggest we terminate this interview now," said the lawyer. "You now have a complete account of Mr Cooke's movements that evening and I think it's clear that he could not have done whatever it is you are accusing him of."

"We think he went to Wimbledon during the period in question," said Taylor.

"What evidence do you have for that?" said the lawyer.

His face was a picture of righteous indignation. Taylor smiled to herself.

"My officers are compiling that evidence as we speak," she said.

"This is a fishing expedition," said the lawyer. "I'm advising my client to answer no more questions unless you can come up with some actual evidence against him."

"What did you think about your daughter's relationship with Pearl Bailey?" said Taylor.

Cooke was about to answer but the lawyer touched him on his shoulder.

"You have already made accusations concerning this matter in my presence," he said. "Mr Cooke is aware of this and Helena has assured him they are unfounded. The matter is closed."

Brewer was red in the face.

"You may think you can sweep it all under the carpet, but you're wrong," he said. "It must have been a nasty shock when you discovered that the woman you had entrusted with Helena's well-being had taken advantage of her like that. I can totally understand how you felt."

The lawyer tried to stop Cooke from responding but he waved him away.

"Do you have any children, Inspector?" he asked.

"No," said Brewer. "But that's neither here nor there."

Cooke smiled and leaned forwards in his seat.

"If you ever have children you will come to understand that you have to trust them," he said. "Helena has told me that nothing of the sort you're implying went on between her and Miss Bailey and I believe her. It's unfortunate that Pearl decided to leave her money to Helena, because otherwise you wouldn't be suggesting all this nonsense. Pearl Bailey was a sad old woman with no real family and very few friends. She was grateful for Helena's companionship and wanted to reward her for her kindness. That's all there is to it."

It was clear to Taylor that they were getting nowhere but she was reluctant to terminate the interview. A thought came to her.

"How did you arrange your cab journeys that evening, Mr Cooke?" she asked.

"As I always do, by using an app on my phone," he said.

"So perhaps you can prove you made those journeys using the receipts the minicab company sent you then."

"If you're asking my client to give you access to the contents of his mobile phone the answer is no," said the lawyer.

"There's no need," said Taylor. "The companies that provide cab hailing apps often send receipts to their customers by email. I'll give you my email address and you can forward the relevant ones to me."

Cooke glanced at his lawyer who sighed and nodded. Taylor handed him her card, which included her police email address. Miles Cooke took out his phone and did as Taylor had asked.

"I'll log into my account and check the emails you've sent me as soon as I can," she said. "You hang on here for a few minutes and with a bit of luck we can get this cleared up once and for all."

*

Patel looked up when the door of the incident room flew open and Colin Brewer stormed in and collapsed into a chair. Tracy Taylor came in moments later and headed to the nearest computer. She typed her personal login and waited until the home screen appeared. Then she operated the mouse and tapped on the keyboard. A smile spread across her face.

"Thank God for Uber," she said. "It's all here, date, time and location of pickup and time and location of drop-off. It's as he said it was. I'll just check the onward journey."

When she had finished she spun her chair round to face the dejected figure of Colin Brewer.

"OK, it's clear Miles Cooke couldn't have killed Pearl Bailey," she said. "You better call the forensic team and tell them to leave his flat. After that you can get Brian back from the station. There's no point in him wasting his time there any longer."

Reluctantly Brewer picked up a telephone and did as he had been asked.

"I'll be back in a minute," said Taylor and strode out of the room.

When the door had closed behind her Brewer sat forward in his chair.

"What the fuck are you looking at?" he snapped.

"Nothing," said Patel. "I was just wondering what's been going on."

"You'll be pleased to hear a bloody great hole has just been blown in my case," said Brewer. "Now we'll have to go right back to square one and start again."

No one spoke. Pringle and Drake looked away and continued with their phone calls. Patel got up from his chair and wondered over to a computer and booted it up. He didn't have any reason for doing so; he just wanted to escape from Brewer's icy gaze.

When Taylor returned, she spoke to Mike Pringle who had the handset of a phone clamped to his ear.

"How's it going?" she said.

"No joy so far," he replied.

She turned to Drake who was punching a number into the keypad of her phone.

"Nothing," she said.

"Keep at it," said Taylor. "Only concentrate on female fares who were dropped near Pearl Bailey's house."

She turned to Patel.

"Right then, Sanjay," she said. "It's time we had a word with Mrs Gregory.

CHAPTER FIFTY-ONE

When they entered the interview room, Sanjay was struck by the change in Anne Gregory's appearance. The dowdy figure he had spoken to previously had been transformed into a confident-looking woman who was smartly dressed in a trouser suit and had taken trouble over her make-up. The set of her jaw was defiant but her hands, which lay in her lap, were trembling, almost imperceptibly. Beside her sat a young lawyer wearing a dark blue suit. Taylor introduced herself and sat down opposite them. Patel read the suspect her rights and started the recording of the interview.

"Now, Mrs Gregory," said Taylor, "there are a few points I'd like to clarify with you today. First of all, when did you last see Pearl Bailey?"

"It was a couple of months ago," said Anne Gregory, without a trace of nervousness in her voice. "We met at her house to discuss the possibility of my becoming her agent once again."

"How did the meeting go?"

"Badly from my point of view," she said. "She told me she didn't want to part company with her current agent."

"Did you quarrel?"

"No we did not," said Mrs Gregory firmly. "It was an amicable discussion over a bottle of Prosecco."

"How did you travel to Wimbledon that day?" said Taylor.

"By train," said Anne Gregory. "I don't own a car. In any case it's quick and convenient."

"How long were you at her house on that occasion?" said Taylor.

"A couple of hours I should think."

"What time of day was it?"

"Afternoon."

"Did you go straight home?"

"More or less," said Mrs Gregory. "I think I popped into Little Waitrose and got a couple of things before I went to the station."

"Did you walk to and from the station to Miss Bailey's house?"

"Yes, it's not far."

Patel was struck by Anne Gregory's calmness. Surely she must have realised she was a suspect. He couldn't help thinking that the questions had mostly been anticipated and the answers prepared in advance.

"Sergeant Patel tells me you decided to return to work after the death of your husband," said Taylor. "Were you planning to join another company?"

"No, I had thought I would set up on my own."

"How many clients are you planning to take on?"

"I hadn't a clear idea about that," said Mrs Gregory. "Inevitably it will take me time to create a profile and build up my list."

Taylor nodded and consulted a file that was lying on the table in front of her. Glancing sideways, Patel could see that it was his report from his second interview with the suspect.

"Did you have a similar meeting with Joan Templeton?" said Taylor.

"Yes I did," said Mrs Gregory. "However, we met in a coffee shop in Wimbledon town centre."

"Was that her idea or yours?"

"Mine. Her house is a long way from the station."

"Did you discuss anything other than your proposal to become her agent?" said Taylor.

Anne Gregory frowned.

"No, I don't think so," she said.

Patel was becoming impatient. DCI Taylor's questions were verifying information that he had already collected and not getting to the heart of the matter. Perhaps she was simply trying to lull the suspect into a false sense of security. This seemed unnecessary to him in the circumstances.

"Did you ever go to Miss Templeton's house?" said Taylor.

This was more interesting.

"I went there a couple of times when I was acting as her agent," said Mrs Gregory. "Mostly she came to the office if we needed to meet."

"How did you come to visit her house?"

"Joan was in the habit of inviting me for lunch when one of her books was published. It was a sort of thank you and a celebration of course. When my husband was alive I usually declined the offer, using him as an excuse, but on a few occasions I agreed to go over there. I felt I couldn't keep on saying no all the time."

"What about after your husband died?" said Taylor.

"I haven't been to Joan's house since then."

"Are you sure?"

"Absolutely."

"Was it the same with Pearl Bailey?"

"She preferred me to go and see her at home."

"Isn't that unusual, for a literary agent I mean?"

"Oh yes," said Mrs Gregory. "But Pearl was no ordinary client."

"In what way?"

"She made the agency a lot of money."

Patel was unconvinced that this was the real reason for the agent's visits to the house. It seemed more likely to him that it was a convenient cover for her real purpose, to pursue her sexual relationship with the author.

"Did you ever stay overnight on those occasions?" he asked.

"I did once," said Mrs Gregory. "We'd worked late and I missed the last train."

Patel had already checked, so he knew that the last train from Wimbledon to Thames Ditton departed at eleven thirty. It was entirely believable that they had worked until that time. Did that mean that his suspicions were wrong? More likely she'd said 'once' because this answer was not directly incriminating. Still, she could have said 'never' and they would have no solid reason to doubt her answer. Also, she had answered the question without hesitation, suggesting to him once again that it may have been prepared in advance.

"Have you approached any of your other former clients about having you as an agent?" said Taylor.

"Not so far," said the agent. "To be honest, I was a bit discouraged when Pearl turned me down. I wondered if the whole thing was such a good idea after all, especially with Joan gone."

The lawyer had been becoming increasingly restless and at this point he intervened.

"I fail to see the relevance of these questions to the investigation you are conducting," he said. "My client has been interviewed on two previous occasions and has told you everything she knows."

"I can assure you these questions are entirely relevant," said Taylor. "The truth is that we don't think your client has been totally honest with us. That's why we're here today."

"Well then, I suggest you get to the point," said the lawyer.

Patel waited to see how DCI Taylor would react to this request. She made a show of consulting the folder in front of her and then looked directly at Anne Gregory.

"Did you have dinner with Pearl Bailey on the evening of April the eighteenth, the night she died," she said.

Anne Gregory returned her gaze without flinching.

"I've been asked that question before and I told Sergeant Patel I wasn't there," she said. "I'll repeat my answer for your benefit: I wasn't at Pearl's house the night she died."

Taylor held her gaze.

"We have reason to believe you were at Pearl Bailey's house on that night," she said.

"You'll need to support that allegation with evidence," said the lawyer.

A ghost of a smile played across Taylor's face. She turned to Anne Gregory.

"You don't own a car, do you?" she said.

"I've already told you that."

"So when you visited Pearl Bailey you always travelled by train, am I right?"

Mrs Gregory frowned.

"Yes," she said. "I've told you that as well."

Taylor turned to Patel.

"Show Mrs Gregory the CCTV footage, will you, Sergeant?" she said.

Patel opened the laptop computer that was on the desk in front of him, booted it up and turned it so that the suspect and her lawyer could see the screen.

"This was recorded at Wimbledon Station on the night Miss Bailey was killed," said Patel. "At the bottom of the screen you can see the time and date. Just after seven we see you coming up from the platform. Wait a minute. I'll zoom in a bit. There, you can see there's no doubt about it."

Patel noted a minute twitch of Anne Gregory's face. She quickly recovered.

"I'd forgotten I was in Wimbledon that evening," she said brightly. "I went to the theatre."

"Oh really?" said Patel. "What was on?"

"*Of Mice and Men*," said Mrs Gregory without hesitating.

"Can you prove it?"

"Yes," said Mrs Gregory. "Fortunately I kept my ticket stub. I thought this might come up today, so I've brought it with me."

She placed the ticket stub on the table. Patel examined it closely. The date and time were for the evening of the murder. He stared at it in disbelief. He had become convinced that Anne Gregory was the killer but now it seemed she was innocent. Or was she? It was a little odd that she had changed her story. Wait a minute, could someone else have used the ticket? That would have provided Anne Gregory with the perfect alibi. She could have bought the ticket and made a gift of it to an unsuspecting friend, someone who knew nothing about her murderous intentions. Of course she would have had to ask for the ticket stub back, which might have seemed odd to the person who had used it, but she could no doubt have made up a story to explain her request.

Taylor cleared her throat.

"Did you go to the theatre with anyone?" she said.

"No, I went on my own."

"Did you go round to Pearl Bailey's house after the play finished?"

Why didn't I think of that? thought Patel.

"No, I went straight home," said Mrs Gregory.

If only we'd looked at the CCTV for later in the evening, thought Patel. They'd stopped looking when they'd identified Anne Gregory arriving in Wimbledon.

"I'm a little confused," said Taylor. "You told Sergeant Patel you spent that evening at home."

"I was mistaken," said Anne Gregory. "I checked my diary after he'd gone and realised what I'd told him wasn't correct."

"You could have let us know," said Taylor.

Anne Gregory shrugged.

"I suppose I could," she said. "I didn't think it was important at the time."

"I find that hard to accept," said Taylor. "This ticket gives you an alibi, whereas you didn't have one when we last spoke. I'd have thought that was very important."

"When you put it like that, I suppose it is," said Mrs Gregory. "To be perfectly honest I didn't think I needed an alibi. Anyway I've told you about it now, so that's all right isn't it?"

Taylor closed the file on Pearl Bailey's death and opened the one concerning Joan Templeton.

"All right," she said. "Next I want to ask you about the death of Joan Templeton. Did you cut the brake lines on her car?"

Anne Gregory frowned.

"Why on earth would I have wanted to kill Joan?" she said.

"Miss Templeton was Pearl Bailey's lover at Cambridge," said Taylor. "I thought you might have hooked up with her as well."

Anne Gregory laughed.

"Whatever gave you that idea?" she said, shaking her head. "I was married to a dear man for forty years and we had the sort of sex life most married couples have, I should imagine. I never, even for a moment, considered having sex with anyone else, man or woman, particularly not a woman. I'm just not that way inclined."

Taylor was looking uneasy, Patel thought.

"So am I to understand you weren't Pearl Bailey's lover?" she said.

"Of course not," said Mrs Gregory scornfully. "I'd like to think we were friends, certainly, but there was nothing more to it than that."

Taylor turned to Patel.

"Do you have any further questions?" she asked.

"Do you know anything about the braking systems of modern cars?" said Patel.

Anne Gregory scoffed.

"No I don't," she said. "I've told you, I don't even own a car."

"Did you have one previously?"

"When my husband was alive, yes," she said. "I got rid of it when he was too ill to drive anymore."

"Do you have a driver's licence?"

"No I don't."

"I think it's time we terminated this interview," said the lawyer. "Much as we'd like to sit here and discuss the workings of the internal combustion engine and other irrelevant matters we, and I imagine you, have better things to do."

"I think we've covered everything for the time being," said Taylor. "However, we may well need to speak to Mrs Gregory again. I'd strongly advise you not to leave London, madam."

*

When they left the interview room Taylor told Patel to go with her to her office. When they were inside she closed the door and sat down on one of the chairs in front of her desk and indicated that Patel should sit on another.

"It seems I was wrong," he said.

"Probably," said Taylor. "Still, we need to check what time the play finished and then check CCTV at the station for the period after that."

"We'll get onto it straight away," said Patel. "Hopefully we should have the results from the forensic examination of her house in a day or two."

Taylor sat back in her seat and sighed.

"Obviously if they found a match between the fibres that were found at the scene and a garment in her wardrobe it would put a very different complexion on things," she said. "I'm not very hopeful though. Owen and Drake should be back from the theatre soon. If someone there confirms that Mrs Gregory was in the audience it doesn't prove she didn't go round to Pearl Bailey's house after the play had finished, but it does make it more or less certain she didn't have dinner with her."

Patel's heart sank. He had to admit that his theories about Michael Groves and Anne Gregory were not supported by compelling evidence but there had been reasons to suspect them both. A moment's thought convinced him that neither of those lines of enquiry had been entirely unjustified.

"You said yourself we had to explore all possible leads, however tenuous," he said. "Did you really think she might have killed Joan Templeton?"

"Not really," said Taylor. "It would have been nice to clear up both cases in one go."

That was certainly true. Patel got up to leave but Taylor told him to sit down again.

"There's something else," she said. "You remember we put in a request for the weapon used in the murder of Rita Groves?"

Patel nodded.

"They didn't have it but they had kept copies of the fingerprints that were on it. Turns out the unidentified set belong to a bloke who was put away for killing another woman a few years later. The case has been referred to the Criminal Case Review Commission and there's a good chance Michael Groves will be exonerated. So, well done."

"Great."

Patel thought for a moment then frowned.

"What is it?" said Taylor.

"I was just thinking that Michael Groves' life was ruined by that murder," said Patel. "He may get his freedom but he won't get his life back. He's missed the boat."

"You're right, of course," said Taylor. "Still, it wasn't our case and there's no guarantee we'd have got it right if we had been around at the time."

"That's true," said Patel.

CHAPTER FIFTY-TWO

As she sat in Superintendent Cheeseman's office, Tracy Taylor felt like a naughty schoolgirl in the headmaster's study. She wondered if she should have put an exercise book down the back of her trousers, metaphorically speaking. Cheeseman was pacing up and down in a state of agitation.

"I'm very disappointed, Tracy," he said. "Very disappointed indeed. Are you sure this Gregory woman didn't do it?"

"The forensic people went over her bungalow with a fine toothcomb and didn't find anything incriminating," said Taylor. "The report's there on your desk. The CCTV confirms she arrived at the station about twenty minutes after the performance at Wimbledon Theatre ended. That means that unless she didn't go to the theatre, she couldn't have had dinner at Pearl Bailey's house on the night of the murder."

"Have you got any evidence she was at the performance?"

"We spoke to the staff at the theatre," said Taylor. "One of them thought she remembered checking her ticket but she couldn't be certain. It was a full house that night."

"Could she have sneaked out during the interval and gone to the house, or even left during the first half of the play?"

"We asked the staff if they saw anyone leave during the play but none of them had."

Cheeseman scratched his head.

"According to the pathologist she was killed sometime between nine thirty and eleven forty-five when the 999 call was logged," he said. "Have I got that right?"

"Yes."

"So she could have killed her during the period she was supposed to be at the theatre. As Colin pointed out, the killer may not have had dinner with the victim. All we actually know for sure is that they had a drink together."

"That's true," said Taylor, "but there isn't any forensic evidence to establish that Anne Gregory was in Pearl Bailey's house. On the other hand, there are some fibres from a wool skirt that didn't belong to the victim. That suggests someone else was there."

Cheeseman nodded ruefully.

"The problem is this," he said, "I'm getting a lot of grief from upstairs over this. Two reasonably well-known writers have died on my patch and we don't seem to have a clue who did it. Have you at least got some other leads to follow up on? I need to have something to tell them that's vaguely encouraging."

Taylor decided she had to come up with something that would satisfy Cheeseman.

"There's always been some doubt that Joan Templeton's death was murder," she said. "It's possible she cut the brake lines herself. I know it's a bizarre way to kill yourself but she had spent her life coming up with original ways to bump people off. Personally, I think she chose this method so that her life assurance policy would pay out. If it was obviously suicide her insurers wouldn't be obliged to do so. She was thinking of her niece, the main beneficiary of her estate."

She squirmed inwardly as she spoke. This was Patel's latest theory but she felt she needed something to restore her credibility in the eyes of her senior officer. Cheeseman stopped pacing and turned to face Taylor.

"That works for Templeton but I can't tell them we think Pearl Bailey bashed herself on the head, now can I?" he said.

"No of course not, sir," said Taylor. "We haven't completely ruled out the possibility that Helena Cooke killed her to inherit her money. A number of witnesses support her story that she was out that evening but she could have killed her when she got home and then called the police."

"The trouble is that you don't have any evidence to establish that Miss Cooke knew about the will," said Cheeseman. "I know you think she was having a sexual relationship with the victim but you've got no real evidence for that either."

"We're still looking into it."

"I suppose I can tell the Borough Commander that, but I doubt he'll be impressed," said Cheeseman. "What about the convicted killer, what's his name?"

"Michael Groves."

"Right, could he have killed them both?"

"We've got a report from his probation officer," said Taylor. "According to him, Groves hasn't left the Bristol area since his release from prison. Obviously he isn't with him twenty-four hours a day so he mostly relies on what his client tells him. However, we've made considerable efforts to find a witness who saw someone arriving at Miss Bailey's house on the night of the murder, or leaving after she was dead, and we've drawn a complete blank. We've trawled through hours of CCTV from the station and haven't picked him up on that either."

Cheeseman subsided into his chair and drummed his fingers on his desk.

"Well, you've been thorough," he said. "I have to give you that. However, I am concerned that the investigation has lacked focus. Fair enough, early on you concentrated on Alan Musgrove. It got you nowhere, but you gave it your best shot. Since then you've been following up several leads at the same time. Am I right in thinking that the suggestions about Anne Gregory and Michael Groves came from the new man, Patel?"

"Originally, yes," said Taylor.

"Seems to me the tail's been wagging the dog," said Cheeseman. "You as CIO should have taken the lead in deciding the direction of the inquiry."

Taylor could feel her jaw clenching and her face flushing with anger.

"I don't think that's entirely fair," she said. "I have led this enquiry from the front but I am always open to suggestions from junior officers. I will concede that I may have let Sergeant Patel have his head at times when perhaps I should have been reining him in. The truth is I wanted to see what he was made of."

"I told you not to give him too much responsibility," said Cheeseman. "He's a very inexperienced detective. Seems to me you've ignored what I said."

"We agreed I would pair him with an experienced constable and that's what I've done," said Taylor. "I even supervised him myself early on. It soon became evident to me that he's a very good detective. With more experience he'll be even better."

"That's all very well, but you've had him interviewing suspects with you when that role should have been taken by Inspector Brewer."

"When the suspect was someone Colin had been investigating I did have him with me," said Taylor. "The suspects I interviewed with Sergeant Patel were people he already knew well."

Cheeseman seemed to have run out of steam. He collapsed into his chair and rotated it from side to side.

"It's possible they'll send someone in from outside the borough to investigate us over this," he said. "Quite frankly that's the last thing I need right now."

"Hopefully it won't come to that," said Taylor, trying to sound reassuring. "Anything else?"

"Not at the moment," said Cheeseman. "Keep me up to speed on the investigation, won't you?"

"Of course."

Back in her office DCI Taylor tried to calm down. From the beginning Cheeseman had given the impression he disapproved of her appointment and had done all he could to undermine her. She had thought about what he had said when he ordered her to stop investigating Alan Musgrove and had concluded he hadn't been honest with her on that occasion. After all, he had made no secret of his support for DCI Cook. There was only one way to silence her critics: solve the crimes and get a conviction. The trouble was she couldn't see how this could be done.

CHAPTER FIFTY-THREE

Amber put fried eggs onto slices of toast and brought the plates over to the table.

"Have this before it gets cold," she said.

Sanjay put down the Sunday paper and tucked into his breakfast.

Afterwards, as they sat at the table with their coffee, Amber picked up a copy of the *South London Echo*.

"Look, there's a piece about your case on the front page of the local paper," she said. "'Local writers' killers remain at large', it says. They don't mention you but there's a statement from a Detective Chief Inspector Taylor."

"Oh yes, that's Tracy," said Sanjay, from behind the sports section.

Amber put down the paper.

"Tracy, eh?" she said. "Is she attractive?"

"I don't know," said Sanjay.

"What do you mean, you don't know?" said Amber.

"She's my boss," said Sanjay. "Whether she's attractive or not is neither here nor there."

"Is she a good person to work with then?"

"Yes, very good as it happens," said Sanjay. "She's been really supportive. I had my doubts about her at first but I've been proved wrong."

"You've changed your tune," said Amber. "The last time we discussed her you gave the impression she was a scary woman."

"I've got to know her better, that's all."

Amber returned to the article. After a few moments she put the paper down.

"Who do you think killed them?" she said.

"I honestly don't know," said Sanjay.

"You must have some idea."

"The only credible suspect for Joan Templeton's killing was her niece's husband," he said. "The trouble is we couldn't find any evidence to prove he did it. As for Pearl Bailey, we seem to have run out of suspects."

"What will happen now?"

Sanjay shrugged.

"Both cases remain open but unless we get some new evidence, we're not actively pursuing the Templeton case," he said. "We're still trying to establish if Pearl Bailey's lodger knew she was inheriting her money. Quite frankly we're getting nowhere."

Amber picked up the paper and turned over a couple of pages, only glancing at the contents. Then she stopped and read an article on the next page.

"There's something by your favourite reporter here," she said.

"Who's that?"

"Mary Ogundipe."

Sanjay scoffed.

"Oh her," he said. "What inaccurate nonsense is she writing this time?"

"It's about foxes chewing through the brake lines of cars," said Amber. "According to some university professor they like to chew rubber and some of them get a taste for drinking brake fluid. The headline's 'Police out-foxed by Basil Brush.'"

Sanjay put down his paper.

"Have there been any accidents as a result of it?" he said.

"She didn't mention anything like that," said Amber. "Wait a minute. A garage owner said he'd had to recover one car because the brakes had completely failed. According to the paper, some motorists have been calling for the foxes to be culled. Who'd have thought it?"

"That could be it," said Sanjay.

Amber pulled a face.

"What are you on about?" she said.

"Maybe a fox chewed through the brake lines on Joan Templeton's car."

"You're not serious."

"I'm deadly serious," said Sanjay. "We'll never be able to prove it though." Then his face brightened. "Maybe we could look for fox DNA on the brake lines. I'll look into it."

Amber giggled and reached across the table to take his hand.

"Maybe," she said. "And if they could, you'd know which fox to arrest."

Sanjay made a face at her.

"There is another possibility," he said, looking thoughtful. "How long ago did they discover that foxes were doing this kind of thing?"

"Let's have a look," said Amber. "It says here the first case came to light about a year ago. At first there were doubts but as other cases were reported the idea came to be accepted."

"Has anyone written about it before?"

"Yes, there was an article in *The Times*," said Amber. "What are you thinking?"

"Suppose someone read about all this and realised it was a way to commit the perfect murder?" said Sanjay. "What's the name of this professor you mentioned?"

"His name's Green," said Amber. "It says here he works at Imperial College London."

Sanjay gasped and clapped a hand to his forehead.

"How could I have been so stupid?" he said.

CHAPTER FIFTY-FOUR

After a frantic four days, during which new evidence had been collected and evaluated, Patel and Taylor faced Rosemary Rogers across the table in the interview room once again. When he'd first floated the idea that she was the killer to the other team members they had looked at Patel with faces full of doubt and reproach. Gradually, as the evidence had stacked up, their looks had changed to something approaching admiration. Even Brewer had shown signs of grudging respect, though he tried to hide them behind his gruff manner.

The doctor was wearing a shapeless pair of trousers with a polo-neck sweater. She sat very upright and looked a little pale, Patel thought. Beside her sat her lawyer, a woman in a tailored suit with a mass of chestnut hair.

DCI Taylor had told Patel that he could take the lead in the questioning and that she would only take over if she felt he wasn't making headway. He was naturally grateful for the opportunity and determined not to let her down. He took a deep breath and asked his first question.

"You know Professor Simon Green, don't you?" he said.

"He's a colleague of mine," said Dr Rogers.

"He's a friend too, isn't he?"

"Yes."

"The professor is an acknowledged expert on the urban fox, isn't he?"

"So I believe."

"Could you get to the point?" said the lawyer tartly. "I fail to see where this is going."

Patel ignored her.

"We've been talking to Professor Green and he's told us about a conversation he had with you towards the end of last year," he said. "It was about foxes chewing through the brake lines of cars and disabling their brakes."

"I really don't remember," said Dr Rogers.

"Oh I think you do," said Patel. "I think it was that conversation that gave you the idea of sabotaging Joan Templeton's car."

Rosemary Rogers blinked. It was almost brief enough to have been spontaneous but Patel felt encouraged.

"I don't know what you're talking about," she said.

"It was after your husband's funeral you decided to kill Miss Templeton," said Patel. "When you saw how distressed she was, you concluded she must have been his lover."

"It is true she was upset," said Dr Rogers, "but I really didn't think anything of it. As I told you before it was typical of Joan's behaviour."

No blink this time.

"Not according to her niece," said Patel. "Joan Templeton showed very little emotion at the funerals they've attended together. That doesn't seem to tally with what you've said."

Dr Rogers scoffed.

"Her opinion is irrelevant," she said. "She was just waiting for Joan to die so she could cash in."

These words were spat out with considerable venom. Patel felt gratified. *I'm starting to get to her*, he thought. He wanted to look round to see how DCI Taylor was reacting to the suspect's answers but decided it wasn't wise to take his eyes off Dr Rogers.

"Actually, Sarah Musgrove specifically said her aunt wasn't one to cry at funerals," he said. "She was surprised how composed she was when they buried her mother, Joan's sister."

"Perhaps they didn't get on."

Patel smiled and shook his head.

"On the contrary, they were very close," he said. "Joan Templeton was devastated when her sister died. Mind you, she did say she was pleased she was no longer in pain."

Dr Rogers was stony faced.

"I can only tell you what I've observed at funerals I've attended with Joan," she said. "I wasn't at her sister's funeral, I never met her. What I can say is that some deaths occur in circumstances in which they can be considered to be a blessed release."

She was entitled to her opinion and Patel had no way of disproving what she had said. He decided to change tack.

"Did you visit Joan Templeton on the day before she died?" he said.

"No, I didn't."

"Are you sure about that?" said Patel.

"Quite sure."

Patel held her unwavering gaze.

"You see we've spoken to a cab driver who picked up someone answering your description at Wimbledon Station and dropped her at Miss Templeton's address that Monday," he said.

"You'll have to do better than that," said the lawyer. "There must be a lot of people in London who bear a resemblance to my client."

"I'm sure you're right," said Patel. "We'll arrange an identity parade in due course."

"I'd like to confer with my client," said the lawyer.

"Very well," said Taylor. "We'll wait outside."

Once they were in the incident room Taylor smiled at Patel. "You're doing great," she said.

"We'll just have to hope the cabby picks her out," said Patel.

"It may not come to that," said Taylor. "It all depends on how the next part of the interview goes."

Patel turned to Owen who was working on a computer.

"Anything new from her phone?" he said.

"No texts or emails about visiting Miss Templeton," said Owen. "No phone calls between them either."

"Makes sense," said Taylor. "She wouldn't want to leave any electronic breadcrumbs for us to follow. Anyway, keep at it."

When they were back in the interview room the lawyer spoke first.

"I have advised my client not to answer any more questions about the death of Joan Templeton," she said. "I suggest we arrange to meet again after the identity parade you have proposed has taken place."

"That's fair enough," said Taylor. "However, we have some questions about the death of Pearl Bailey as well. Sergeant Patel?"

The lawyer looked none too pleased but she said nothing and resumed her seat.

"You've told us previously that you had dinner with Pearl Bailey shortly after the funeral of Martin Rogers," said Patel. "Is that correct?"

"Yes, as I told you before, she invited me after Martin's funeral service," said Dr Rogers. "A few close friends, including Joan, came back to the house. I wasn't particularly keen to accept but Liz was very insistent."

"But you weren't able to make it that night, were you?" said Patel.

Rosemary Rogers shifted in her seat.

"What makes you say that?" she said.

"We spoke to your secretary at Imperial College and she told us there was a faculty meeting that evening," said Patel. "It was arranged at short notice and the minutes confirm that you attended. I assume you rearranged your dinner with Pearl Bailey for another evening."

"Oh yes, I'd forgotten all about that," said Dr Rogers, looking flustered. "You must forgive me, I haven't been myself since my husband died."

"That's understandable," said Patel. "However, I think you will remember the night you did go to dinner with Pearl Bailey. It would be hard to forget."

"What do you mean by that?" said the lawyer.

"I mean that Dr Rogers had dinner with Pearl Bailey the night she died," said Patel. "We have evidence to show she was there."

Rosemary Rogers flushed a little.

"What evidence?" said the lawyer.

"Well, firstly we found some fragments of wool on an armchair in Pearl Bailey's sitting room that matches a sample taken from a skirt belonging to Dr Rogers."

"A lot of people wear woollen skirts," said the lawyer.

Patel smiled.

"This particular wool is rather unusual," he said. "Our experts are certain it came from this particular skirt."

"It's not surprising you've found evidence of my sitting in one of Liz's armchairs," said Dr Rogers. "I've been to her house many times and it may surprise you to know that I've generally been invited to sit down. However, I wasn't there the night she died. I've already told you, I went to a concert that evening."

"Oh yes, the concert," said Patel. "At first I thought the ticket gave you an alibi. Tearing off the stub was smart. A less meticulous person might have forgotten to do that. There's only one problem: you didn't go to the concert. We checked with the venue and your seat was empty that evening. I imagine you planned to go but it clashed with your rearranged dinner with Pearl Bailey."

"I wasn't in Wimbledon that evening."

Patel was impressed by how well the suspect was maintaining her composure. The only sign of anxiety he could detect was a slight quickening of her breathing.

"Oh I think you were," he said. "In fact I'm sure of it. We have CCTV images from Wimbledon Station which clearly show you coming up the steps from platform eight just after six thirty that evening."

He opened her file and spread out several eight-by-ten prints on the table.

"There you are," he said pointing at the face in the middle of the picture. "The date and time are printed on the bottom of the photograph."

Until this point Rosemary Rogers had sat up straight but now her shoulders fell and started to heave. Tears trickled down her cheeks. Between sobs she said, "I should've known you'd work out what happened. God knows I thought of calling the police after I hit Liz. I didn't mean to kill either of them."

"I advise you not to say anything more," said the lawyer, but Rosemary Rogers didn't appear to hear what she had said.

"Why don't you tell us exactly what happened?" said Taylor gently.

Rosemary Rogers sighed and wiped the tears from her cheeks with the back of her hand.

"I knew my husband had been unfaithful to me when he was alive but I didn't know who his lover was," she said. "Oh, I'd had suspicions about various women he worked with but I was never able to find anything to incriminate them."

"What made you think he was unfaithful?" said Patel.

"When you've been with someone for the best part of forty years you become very much in tune with the nuances of their behaviour," she said. "I could read Martin like a book. He may have thought that his efforts to throw me off the scent went unnoticed, but they didn't. Of course I was aware that I'm no oil painting and our sex life was far from satisfactory, at least as far as he was concerned. I could see that he was likely to be looking for what he wasn't getting with me elsewhere. I even told myself it didn't matter as long as he stayed with me. The trouble is, it did matter. It mattered very much.

"As you suggested, Sergeant, I began to suspect it was Joan Templeton after the funeral. She was beside herself. At first I told myself it wasn't credible. After all, Joan was a dowdy frump and none of us are getting any younger. But as time went by and I thought about it over and over again I became more convinced it was true. I knew she was in love with Martin when we were at Cambridge; we all did. I very much doubt he loved her but he knew she'd do anything for him. The more I thought about it, the more it made sense. All he had to do was take the train on to Wimbledon rather than get off at Earlsfield on his way home from work. Joan's house was a short cab ride from the station so it wouldn't have been difficult for him to visit her and be back home in time for a late supper. He'd always had a plausible excuse for 'working late' but I had always thought they were probably a pack of lies.

"I decided she must be punished. I wanted to give her a nasty shock, but I never intended to kill her. I must make that very clear. It was then that the conversation I'd had with Simon Green came back to me. I asked him to show me photographs of brake lines that had been chewed by foxes then I went home and practised on an old piece of plastic tubing until I thought I'd got it right.

"As long as I could tamper with the car without being spotted, I didn't think anyone would suspect me. I had to do some research on modern car braking systems but there's plenty on the Internet, so that wasn't a problem. I even bought a manual for the Toyota Camry and studied it until I was sure I knew exactly what to do."

"You can't seriously tell me you didn't think she might die," said Taylor.

"None of the drivers whose brakes had been disabled by foxes died," said Dr Rogers defiantly. "My main concern was that she'd work out there was a problem before she got in the car. There was already a small pool of brake fluid under it when I left the garage."

"All right, carry on," said Taylor.

"I knew that Joan kept her car in the garage at the end of her garden, so I was confident I could cut the brake lines without being seen. All I needed was the opportunity to do it. I turned up unannounced in the afternoon and she was, as I had expected, delighted to see me. She asked if I'd like tea and I said I would. While she was fussing around in the kitchen I said I'd like to look around the garden and she told me to go ahead. I knew Joan always kept her car keys on a hook by her microwave oven and so while she wasn't looking I popped them into my bag. I was prepared to break into the garage if I had to but in the event the side door was unlocked. I soon had the bonnet open and had located the brake lines. As I told you, Simon had shown me pictures of the way they look when foxes have been at them and I used a Stanley knife to produce cuts that looked similar. I disposed of the knife afterwards and I wore gloves, of course. Then I went back up the garden and had tea with Joan.

"When I read in the paper she'd been killed I was horrified. I realised how stupid I'd been but there was no going back. I followed the story in the press and on television, waiting for someone to suggest that foxes had done it, but there was nothing. I did think about suggesting it to you as an explanation, Sergeant, but I thought you might think it odd and obviously I didn't want to become a suspect. I told myself it was an accident and it was really Joan's fault for not knowing how to control her own car and I almost convinced myself."

Dr Rogers paused and blew her nose.

"What about the killing of Pearl Bailey?" said Patel.

"Liz had invited me to dinner, as I told you," she said. "As you've already discovered, I had to change the date. The concert ticket was a gift from a friend and the programme wasn't really to my taste so I didn't mind not going. I almost gave it to another friend but fortunately they weren't free that evening, so I kept it.

If I hadn't I wouldn't have been able to use it as my alibi. On that Saturday evening I took the train to Wimbledon and walked to her house.

"After dinner we went through to the sitting room. Liz poured us both a brandy and we sat on either side of the fireplace and chatted. We'd already had a lot of wine with the meal and Liz had drunk more than her fair share. Despite that she started on the brandy. I'd had enough alcohol and so I didn't touch my drink.

"After a bit she started talking about Joan and how she'd behaved at the funeral. Liz said I must have thought she'd been Martin's lover. I denied it of course. She laughed. I asked what was so funny and she said she was the one he'd been with. It had gone on for years, on and off. And then I realised she'd invited me to dinner to tell me about her and Martin. I still don't know exactly why she did it. I suppose she wanted to humiliate me. Perhaps she was jealous of what I've achieved. After all, writing smutty books doesn't compare with a distinguished academic career like mine. And then it hit me: I'd killed the wrong person.

"Well, I just lost it then. She'd got up to pour herself another brandy. I grabbed that hideous ornament and hit her with it. I've never done anything like that before. I was completely out of control."

She paused while her whole body was convulsed by anguished sobs. The police officers sat in silence while she regained control. Patel wanted to pass her the box of tissues that was on the table but for some reason he was unable to move.

"She fell and hit her head on the corner of the mantelpiece," she said at last. "She dropped the glass she was holding and collapsed. As she went down she knocked a photograph off the mantelpiece and when it hit the hearth, the glass broke.

"At first I thought I'd simply knocked her out. Then I saw she wasn't breathing. I panicked. I stood there gazing down at her in total disbelief. Then, when I'd calmed down a bit, I decided I should get rid of any evidence that I'd been at the house that evening. As far as I was aware nobody knew I was due for dinner that night. In any case I had the concert ticket to give myself an alibi. At first I wasn't sure how to go about it, but then I remembered Joan's novel *Deadly Reckoning*. I've read all her books; I suppose you could say I was a fan of her writing. Anyway, there's a passage in which a murderer cleans the murder scene to avoid detection. Typical Joan, she described the process in minute detail. I went through to the kitchen and found a pair of rubber gloves. I put all the dinner things in the dishwasher and turned it on. I hadn't touched the wine bottles. Pearl did the pouring during the meal, so I left them on the work surface in the kitchen. I hadn't touched my brandy glass either, so I left it where it was. I tried to think of every surface where I might have left a print and cleaned them. Fortunately there was a cloth on the dining table, which saved some time. Even so, it took what seemed like ages and I was afraid Liz's lodger would come home and catch me in the act. Anyway, she didn't appear so I left and went home. Oh and I took the statue thing with me. I've disposed of it somewhere you'll never find it."

The lawyer had turned very pale. She looked as if she was about to speak but nothing came out of her mouth.

"Thank you," said Taylor. "Rosemary Rogers, I'm charging you with the murders of Joan Templeton and Pearl Bailey."

Dr Rogers sighed and shook her head.

"I didn't mean to kill either of them," she said. "I really didn't."

"That's for a court to decide," said Taylor.

Dr Rogers looked at her wide-eyed.

"What happens now?" she said.

"I'm going to get Sergeant Patel to type up your confession and then we'll ask you to sign it," said Taylor. "You'll be remanded in custody to await trial."

*

When Patel had prepared the confession, he took it through to DCI Taylor's office for her approval. She read through it and gave it back to him.

"You've done well with this case," she said. "I think you have the makings of a good detective."

"Thank you," said Patel. He could feel himself blushing.

"Don't let it go to your head," she said. "You've still got a lot to learn."

CHAPTER FIFTY-FIVE

Helena Cooke and Damian Fisher were slumped on a settee in Pearl Bailey's sitting room with their feet on her favourite coffee table. Between them on the table was an ice bucket in which there was a half empty bottle of champagne. They were drinking from lead crystal flutes and smoking weed.

"I'm going to sell this place," said Helena. "I mean, when everything's sorted out. It's too big and frankly the furnishings just aren't my style. I think I'll buy a big apartment nearer the centre of town. Get a huge TV and expensive hi-fi, the whole works."

"Sounds good to me," said Damian. "We should drink a toast to your benefactor."

They raised their glasses and giggled.

"It's a huge relief not to have to do all that stuff with her anymore," said Helena.

"I don't know how you stuck it," said Damien, making a face.

"Well, my darling," she said, turning to face him. "When she was fiddling about down there I tried to imagine you were inside me. And I had to fake orgasms, of course."

"Did it work? Thinking of me I mean."

"Not really," said Helena with a snort of laughter. "There's a huge difference between her bony fingers and your cock."

"I'm glad to hear it," he said, putting an arm round her shoulder.

They sat and drank for a while and then he said, "Do you realise I actually thought you bumped her off?"

She threw off his arm, turned towards him and sat up straight.

"You didn't, did you?" she said.

"No, not really, you silly cow."

He burst out laughing. Helena snorted in disgust. She settled back into the cushions and drained her glass.

"I think she was still breathing when I found her," she said.

"Are you having me on?" he said, sitting up straight and turning to face her.

Helena shook her head.

"I mean, I wasn't sure about it," she said. "I did think about calling for an ambulance or something but then I thought: this is our big chance. I know we could have waited till she croaked but that could have taken ages and she might have gone off me and changed the will. Anyway while I was thinking about it she started turning blue. So I called the cops instead."

"Oh my God."

He was looking pale and Helena regretted having spoken. The last thing she wanted was for Damian to go to the police. She had already formed the opinion that he was a bit of a Boy Scout.

"If you told anyone I'd deny it," she said.

"Oh God, Helena, I wouldn't."

"I'm glad to hear it," she said with a cheeky smile. "As long as you're a good boy you can share all this with me."

She made an expansive gesture with her left arm.

"Don't worry," he said. "I know which side my bread's buttered."

He put his glass on the table and made himself comfortable.

"The police gave you a hard time, didn't they, my poor darling," he said, tickling her under the chin.

"It was pretty gross," she said. "You hear these stories about the police pinning stuff on people who didn't do it, just to get a result. I was shit-scared at the time. Anyway it worked out all right in the end."

"Your dad must have been pretty pissed off when they pulled him in."

"He was but he deserved it," she said tartly. "He's treated Mummy like shit."

"Another result then."

"Just you take note," she said, wagging her finger at him. "If you mess with me you're going to lose, right?"

"I wouldn't dream of it," he said and enfolded her in his arms. "In any case now that woman who bashed her on the head has been convicted, you've got nothing to worry about."

"We should drink a toast to her as well."

They refilled their glasses and drank from them with their arms linked.

"If what they said in the paper is true, we were lucky she killed your benefactor," said Damian. "She planned the other woman's murder but she hadn't actually meant to kill old Pearl."

"It doesn't matter now," said Helena. "My only worry was that she'd get off."

"What, you think they'd have come after you again if she had?"

"Oh yes, I think so."